THE
VOICE
OF THE
WILD

THE VOICE OF THE WILD

OF THE WILD

An Anthology
of
Animal Stories

EDITED AND WITH AN
INTRODUCTION BY
PATRICIA BEARD

VIKING

VIKING
Published by the Penguin Group
Viking Penguin, a division of Penguin Books USA Inc.,
375 Hudson Street, New York, New York 10014, U.S.A.
Penguin Books Ltd, 27 Wrights Lane,
London W8 5TZ, England
Penguin Books Australia Ltd, Ringwood,
Victoria, Australia
Penguin Books Canada Ltd, 10 Alcorn Avenue, Suite 300,
Toronto, Ontario, Canada M4V 3B2
Penguin Books (N.Z.) Ltd, 182–190 Wairau Road,
Auckland 10, New Zealand

Penguin Books Ltd, Registered Offices:
Harmondsworth, Middlesex, England

First published in 1992 by Viking Penguin,
a division of Penguin Books USA Inc.

10 9 8 7 6 5 4 3 2 1

Page 245 constitutes an extension of this copyright page.

LIBRARY OF CONGRESS CATALOGING IN PUBLICATION DATA
The Voice of the wild : an anthology of animal stories / edited by Patricia Beard.
   p.   cm.
   ISBN 0–670–84293–1
   1. Animals—Literary collections.   I. Beard, Patricia.
PN6071.A7V57   1992
823.008′036—dc20   92–17329

Printed in the United States of America
Set in Sabon
Designed by Kathryn Parise

FOR ALEX AND HILLARY

The question is not,
Can they reason? nor,
Can they talk? but
Can they suffer?

Jeremy Bentham,
1748–1832

CONTENTS

INTRODUCTION

I'd been looking for a bear in Montana. I'm not sure why; maybe I felt a bear would make the wilderness feel more real to me. Why does anyone look for a bear, or, if the territory is right, an elephant, a lion? It was Labor Day, and I wasn't going to be in Montana much longer; it seemed that the bear would have to hold until the next trip, whenever that might be. When you're in a place, you always think it will be easy to come back—every year, maybe. But mostly, you don't.

That morning, I was lying on a screened porch, with a book facedown on my chest. Just outside the screens, a flower bed was filled with old-fashioned flowers like hollyhocks; the flowers were big, as big as they were going to get that summer, and the bees were brushing up against them, buzzing. There weren't many man-made sounds in the valley—although the day before, we'd heard helicopters ferrying smoke-jumpers to the forest fires in the north—and the bee-buzz had put me to sleep; no point telling myself it was the sound of industry. I would have let the phone ring until it stopped, but it didn't stop, so I got up and answered it. The call was about a bear.

I'd come pretty close to seeing bears and elk; I'd heard a mountain man imitate an elk's bugle, found elk wallows, elk and bear droppings, bear prints, bear-stripped bushes. I'd heard the cracking of sticks in the woods that meant something big was passing by, but the only animals I'd actually seen in the two weeks I'd been in Montana were horses, dogs, and cattle spread out on the deep open grazing lands. Now a bear had come to me; it was outside the ranch guesthouse.

I set off right away, on foot. I crossed the flatbed bridge over the trout stream, hurried up the dirt road, and cut over onto a hilly meadow track, heading for the bear, which was, I'd been told, in a tree. It didn't occur to me that the bear might have climbed down and could be loping along in my direction, that we might meet on terms that were not to my advantage. I could have taken one of the ranch cars and driven up to the guesthouse; I would have gotten there faster. But perhaps I had a little fantasy that I would see the bear and stretch out my hand and it would pad up to me in its head-and rump-swinging way and lick my palm, and I would feel its tongue on my skin, and then it would walk past me into the woods. Then it would be, in some way, my bear. I would carry the knowledge of its wildness with me, and it would carry a memory—if bears remember—of my tameness. I didn't expect that to happen, but I've read stories.

The bear was still in the tree when I got there. The man who had called me was standing well away from the tree, and when I came up, he made a tamping gesture with his hand, to tell me to go slowly, and then he lifted his chin slightly and looked up.

I couldn't find the bear at first. The tree was a big pine,

and there was a lot of shade, so it was hard to tell what was tree trunk and what was black fur. But then the bear moved, not much, just securing its hold, and I could see that it was young, and still not very big—smaller than a large dog. It wasn't looking at us, but I thought it gave off a bristling sense that it was aware of us, scared and considering its options.

The bear didn't do much for a while, so I moved in and squinted through the lens of my camera, which brought the bear closer. I could see its eyes—it still wasn't looking at us—and its black snout and its claws, which were big and sharp, like the teeth of a dead beached shark I once saw. The hand-licking idea receded to where it belonged, which was nowhere. Picture taking seemed more practical, although the only thing these pictures were going to be good for, I already knew, was to show my children that I'd seen an animal they would hardly be able to distinguish from a clump of pine needles. I clicked the shutter anyway, and then something happened. The bear jerked its head back, opened its eyes wide—or maybe it narrowed them—and hissed. It was a dangerous sound; I knew this because my heart started to beat so fast my ears felt the way they do at certain altitudes, when they're just about to pop. I backed away.

The bear had evidently had enough of being treed. Maybe it sensed that I was afraid, not much of a threat, because it scrabbled down the trunk and disappeared behind the storage shed.

"It's gone," I said.

My friend agreed that it was gone, picked up the hose he'd been using to water some newly planted bushes in what wasn't exactly a garden, and dragged the hose around to the side of the house. I went up the steps to the porch that overlooked the valley, the stream, and the mountains, which I knew harbored other bears like this one, as well as bobcats, mountain lions, elk and smaller antelope, and other animals I would have liked to see, and put my face up to the sun for a while.

Then the bear reappeared, rounding the corner of the shed, head down, browsing the berries off the bushes. It was close enough that when I looked through the lens again, I could frame it and my friend, the plant waterer, in the same shot. The man saw the bear too and made a clicking gesture with his first finger and grinned at me, before settling his face into a portrait mode. I pressed the shutter and stopped breathing, waiting to see if the bear would hiss again, if the man would have to turn the hose on it and vault over the porch railing. I didn't think this bear was a porch climber, but everything I knew about bears I'd learned that morning, and it was almost nothing at all.

The bear didn't react; it just kept on munching berries, not too close to the man, but not too far away. The man finished his watering, turned off the spigot, coiled the hose, and the two of us took the path through the meadow back to his house.

It wasn't much, this meeting with the bear, but it left me with a fleeting sense of wildness—of what it felt like to be wild. The feeling was conveyed—from the bear to me—because we had crossed each other's paths and had to take each other into account. Civilization doesn't offer many tools for situations like that; actually, civilization probably takes the tools away. For a little while, the bear and I shared the same atmosphere, and unlike the bees who had put me to sleep, the bear knew it too.

But what else did the bear know? What does any wild animal know, things we understand, and things we've lost touch with, that lurk below the rim of consciousness? Maybe the reason wild animals attract us so is that we hope they will reconnect us with what we've forgotten we once knew.

Some of the writers whose stories, or parts of stories, are in this book were using animals to illuminate these transactions with destiny, the passages in our lives that we come to whether we want to or not. Obstacles. Booby traps. Opportunities. Among them are coming of age, sexual awakening, love and other bonds between creatures, the transfer of power from old to young and from loser to winner, hunting and being hunted, and death. These matters affect animals in a purer way than they do people, because we try so hard to tamper with the inevitable, to adjust things. A way to get back to the place we came from is through wild animals, used as metaphors in a story or simply observed doing what we do too—but doing it unselfconsciously.

Take death. If you're human, being alive is defined by the foreknowledge of its opposite, death. The death of a person symbolizes all the deaths we know and anticipate; the heart-wrenching moment is the acknowledgment of finality—last words, last gestures, the last understanding in the eyes. Once the process becomes purely physical, watching a person's death seems voyeuristic, and the observer—friend, lover, writer, reader—delicately looks away. But when an animal dies, you don't feel as though you have to avert your eyes; seeing life evaporate from an animal's body doesn't intrude on its privacy. Children are fascinated by the dead birds they find. Drivers may mourn a bit when they see the heaps of fur flung to the side of country roads, but they don't look away.

Hunters field dress animals they have shot when the bodies are still warm, although most serious hunters will tell you that their feeling of triumph in the hunt is always laced with sadness at the taking of an animal's life. We look, and we feel as though it's not so overwhelming after all, that maybe we could do this too, let go, when we have to.

Jack London imagined the way death seemed to a wolf cub in *White Fang.* "He had no conscious knowledge of death, but like every animal of the Wild, he possessed the instinct of death. . . . It was the very essence of the unknown; it was the sum of the terrors of the unknown; the one culminating and unthinkable catastrophe that could happen to him, about which he knew nothing and about which he feared every-thing." Maybe that's how it was for us too, before rituals and superstitions got in the way.

One transaction with destiny animals and humans don't share is the loss of innocence, the expulsion from the Garden. Animals are not expelled; they live in the Garden until they die. Sometimes a reader can imagine what it might be like to inhabit the Garden by reading a story in which a person, usually a young boy, is adopted by wild animals and lives with them for a while, like Mowgli in *The Jungle Book,* adopted by wolves. We know what happens to these wild boys: they go back to civilization—grow up, learn to speak, read and write, use money, and cry. Mowgli never cries until he learns he has to return to the human world. He is so shocked by the tears that he thinks he must be dying, but his teacher, Bagheera the panther, says, "No, Little Brother. Those are only tears such as men use. Now I know thou art a man, and a man's cub no longer. The jungle is shut indeed to thee henceforward."

Mowgli was exiled when he began to grow up, to do things only men can do, so he upset the balance of power in the jungle. But the classic reason for expulsion is another result of growing up, sexual awakening. Sex is, of course, the obsession that comes second only to death, and another field for us to skulk around and look at from the corners of our eyes. Sometimes, using animals in a story helps both reader and writer get where they're going. That's what happens in Annabel Thomas's "Coon Hunt" when a young woman who is reluctant to leave childhood and get married witnesses the violent death of a raccoon. She watches her boyfriend climb out on the limb of a tree and shake the coon into the jaws of the dogs, and the man, back on the ground, hold up the bloody shreds of the carcass. Make of this what you will—hunter and hunted, a metaphor for the rending of maidenhead. And then, as the man walks the woman home, she hears "Mama's voice, faint and thin, . . . calling her name from the yard. By the time she started up the path, the calling had stopped and she heard the kitchen door closing." This is certainly better than a bodice-ripper, no matter how accurate the details of flesh on flesh, and as good as other, more sensitive and discreet sex scenes, because instead of reading about what happened (on which there are just so many variations), we know how the young woman feels: violated, excited, and far from childhood and home.

Wild-animal stories aren't always used to get at something else; they can be about what they say they're about—the animal itself—but even then they link people and nature. I think of Isak Dinesen's bushbuck, Lulu, who was for a while tame and wore a collar and a bell. Dinesen writes in *Out of Africa,* "the free union between my house and the antelope was a rare, honourable thing. Lulu came in from the wild world to show that we were on good terms with it, and she made my house one with the African landscape, so that nobody could tell where the one stopped and the other began." A lovely passage follows, a thematic variation on the melody of Lulu. "When I have . . . lain and thought of Lulu, I have wondered if in her life in the woods she ever dreamed of the bell. Would there pass in her mind, like shadows upon water, pictures of people and dogs?"

I too wonder what animals feel for us, how they are like us, and how unlike. Sometimes even wild animals behave in ways that are so familiar, it's hard to believe that if they had any vocabulary at all, it wouldn't include certain words— "love," for example. This may be because of the animals we do know, the ones that live in our houses and barns and fields, dependent on us, forever children, animals we buy or raise to sustain us with food or love. José Ortega y Gasset, in *Meditations on Hunting,* calls domestic animals "an intermediate reality between the pure animal and man," and Antoine de Saint-Exupéry explains that intermediate reality in *The Little Prince* when the fox asks the boy to tame him.

"What does that mean—'tame'?" the boy said.

" 'It means to establish ties. . . . One only understands the things that one tames,' said the fox."

At the root of writing about wild animals is our knowledge that they are not tame, that we do not understand them, and that they embody things we do not understand in ourselves, things we have almost lost the power to reach.

So we attach the leash of words to animals, trying to make connections between them and us. But the irony of writing is that the places we're trying to find—the reason we write at all—existed before we had words and can't be explained with words; they can only be evoked. The great wild-animal stories are made of experience without explanation. They bypass logic on the way to instinct, and they make us feel.

I guess that's why I was looking for a bear.

Patricia Beard

THE
VOICE
OF THE
WILD

FROM
THE WHITE RHINO HOTEL

BY BARTLE BULL

They were walking north in the early morning, following the elephant tracks on the edge of the swamp country beyond Kilimanjaro. Ernst and Anton were together. Banda and Karioki studied the trail ahead. Hugo von Decken followed slowly with the cook and six men bearing supplies. Eager to feast on fresh meat, the Africans walked lightly under their canvas-wrapped burdens.

From time to time the hunters gathered without speaking and studied the ground. Anton tingled at the first sighting. He squatted and touched the corrugated impressions in the dust. Remarkably round, unlike any other sign.

"How big do you reckon she is?" Ernst said. Without allowing a reply, the German spoke again. "About seven feet at the shoulder. Twice the girth of the front foot. They're the big feet, because they support the head and the ivory. See how she sets her rear foot right inside the print of the front foot?"

Karioki knelt beside Anton. He spoke after Ernst moved on.

"There is more than one, Tlaga," he said quietly, before standing. "They are clever. The followers place their feet over the prints of the one who goes before. Perhaps four, five."

"When did they come by?" Ernst said when Anton caught up to him. Anton crouched again. He noticed the tiny undisturbed pattern of dew over the prints. He observed the small mounds of sand gathered by ants within them as nature began to reclaim the path. He stood and walked along the tracks. Fragments of acacia bark and broken branches lay along the route, the leaves already shrivelled. The amber sap that had leaked from the wounds of the branches felt glazed hard and dry.

"Yesterday evening, I'd say."

"Not bad, for an English drifter." Ernst nodded. "Remember to watch for saliva on twigs and acacia pods. That's where they chew. If the spittle's wet, you'll need your rifle, because you're right on top of them."

Anton examined some smaller prints to one side.

"These're all calves and females. Mature bulls only go with the girls when they're mating," Ernst said. "The ivory keeps growing till they die. The bulls with the best ivory are too old to have fun, usually loners, or else roaming around with a couple of other old-timers. But the young bulls go about in small bands, fencing with one another when they feel sexy, like the university boys in Heidelberg. Then they break off on their own to mate."

Karioki picked up a block of dung, the outside dry and laced with fragments of coarse fibre and splinters of bark and branches. He broke it open like an egg and showed it to

Anton. The interior was dark and moist. Seeds and acacia pods nestled in the rich fertilizer.

"Look inside, Tlaga—" Karioki said.

"She's an old cow," Ernst interrupted, as if the African had not spoken.

Karioki dropped the block of dung and turned aside. Remembering the feeling, Anton understood Karioki's resentment.

"Her food's barely broken up," Ernst said, "because her teeth are worn down, worse than my papa's. Means she can't get much nourishment. Unless a hunter gets 'em first, they all die when their sixth set of molars wears out, 'bout sixty years old."

"Excuse me," Anton said to Karioki, pointing to the dung. "How old is it?"

"Two hours," said Karioki to Anton.

"We'll camp up ahead on the edge of the swamp," Ernst said. "After the others find us, we'll walk in and lie up by the water."

They took their positions late in the afternoon. Nestled among the reeds and grass on the steep bank of the river that ran through the marsh, Anton and Hugo von Decken waited with their rifles. The German cradled his old Merkel. Anton lay on his stomach with Ernst's Sauer & Sohn. It was an over-and-under double-barrelled rifle, without the fine balance of the Merkel's side-by-side barrels. An unusual, slightly difficult weapon, rather like Ernst himself, Anton thought. How would it perform?

Whenever he lifted one of the double rifles, Anton was struck by its massive perfection. Densely heavy, yet each moving part exquisitely fitted, they were built to contain thousands of violent explosions without the slightest change or damage. Even the way they opened was a marvel. Anton gently broke the rifle open, pushing the top lever to the side with his thumb. He checked the two brass .450s that waited, their rims set perfectly into the recessed edge of each barrel. Despite the razor-fine tightness when the metal came together, the hinge worked easily as he closed it. He felt the cool, slightly oiled smoothness of the gunmetal and the worn comfort of the walnut stock. Compared to the rough weapons of his youth, it was a jewel.

Close before his eyes, the sharp-tipped blades of coarse swamp grass formed a dense green palisade. Each stand of grass contained a village of its own. A bone-white snail shell, empty and large as his fist, rested against the stem of a tall lily. He could smell the yellow blossom in the still air. While he watched, the spiralling scalloped shell became a magic staircase for tiny red ants that coursed up it like a moving ribbon. He saw their goal. A knot of eggs or larvae rested atop the shell, their grey smoothness sheltered in a gauzy film, scant protection from the rending pincers of their attackers. Anton squinted to follow the assault.

The entire shell rocked under his eyes. Two broad-spread twitching antennae emerged, followed by a narrow black snout, then two long three-hinged arms attached to a round head. A massive, hard-shelled orange-and-black body covered in pointed spines drew itself from the shell and began to climb the lily. As the beetle paused to chop neat bites from the stalk, Anton recognized it from his studies in the library at Gepard Farm: a weevil, a vegetarian, probably an iron beetle.

He looked up. Thirty yards across the river an elephant stood at the edge of the water, the sound of its advance drowned by the stream. Slowly it flapped its ears. Dust rose from its shoulders as the uneven ears slapped against them, loose sails rippling against a mast. Unhurried, apparently hearing no disturbing sound, the animal raised its trunk. It directed the curving tip first upstream, then down, casting for scent. Anton thought of the stag coming to water. But instead of the wild grace of the stag, he saw primeval majesty. He watched a line of followers shuffle down to the water, huge grey blocks moving in the evening light, their pace stately, unlike any other animal, as if on an unending dignified march.

The big females entered the water to their knees. They dipped their trunks, flushing them with a fine spray. Then they drank. The very young elephants moved in among them, leaning against the legs of the females, splashing and experimenting with thin, bugle-like trunks. Anton rested his rifle on the grass with the safety on and stared while one baby stumbled in the mud. It struggled to get up. Its pointed mouse-like face was dark and messy. A young female moved to help the calf, righting it with her trunk like a fallen stool. Uncertain how to drink, the baby tried to use its trunk. Water dribbled out before it reached its mouth. The mother insinuated her own trunk into the calf's mouth, giving water. She sprayed the calf with fresh water and rubbed it with the side of her trunk. After they drank, the young elephants began to play, splashing and tumbling like puppies. The older females showered water over their own shoulders, cleaning and cooling themselves, ignoring the childish commotion beneath them.

As the afternoon darkened, Anton sensed movement behind him. The ground vibrated under his body. He turned his head slowly and discerned von Decken five yards to his right. Calmly, obeying his own injunction against hurried movements, the old hunter held out one hand, palm down, and gestured to stay in place. It was too late to bolt.

Anton leaned on his right shoulder and looked up through the grass behind him. An immense grey wall was advancing towards him. A line of elephants extended as far as he could see. Forty, fifty animals. They eased forward, several abreast, incredibly silent, the beasts in front raising their trunks when they smelled the water. From the river the drinking elephants began to trumpet. Welcome, or war? wondered Anton.

He lay frozen, prepared either to shoot or to roll into the water. Trying to disappear into the ground, he felt the gold earring on its leather cord press into his chest. The first elephant paused twelve yards to his left, a towering black mass against the darkening sky. Anton moved only his eyes. He remembered Lenares telling him never to stare at an animal when he wished not to be noticed. Like a man or woman, the beast would sense it was being watched. Anton looked down while the elephant resumed its march. He heard each footstep when the animal passed him. Coming to the riverbank, the elephant stiffened its front legs and slid down to the water with its forelegs straight and hind legs kneeling.

Soon the river was dappled with elephants. The arrivals approached the earlier drinkers, knocking their tusks gently together, bumping shoulders, entwining their trunks and trumpeting. Two young females put the tips of their trunks into each other's mouths.

Finally it became too dark to see, and Hugo von Decken beckoned to Anton. They crawled back to find Banda and Karioki, not speaking until they were on the way to camp.

"That was the beginning of the world," Anton said. "I'm glad we didn't shoot."

"It was getting dark for these old eyes, and I don't like shooting females," von Decken said. "But tomorrow we get our ivory. And the boys want their meat."

At dawn the hunters were back. They walked upstream where the river eddied into shallow pools under the branches of wild fig trees. Banda found the spoor of several males. The hunters lay waiting for them on the bank under a canopy of dark green leaves. Von Decken drew ashes from a pouch and let them fall from his fingers. The air drew the ash behind them, away from the river.

"If I point to you, you shoot first," Ernst said to Anton. "Remember, go for a heart shot behind the shoulder. Those bony heads are too tricky for beginners. The brain's bigger than yours, of course, the size of a nice loaf of pumpernickel. But it's buried a foot deep, and you'll never find it."

Before Anton could reply, three bulls came to the water. From his position to the right Ernst pointed to Anton, then tapped his own teeth. Searching for the heaviest ivory, Anton studied the animals while they drank.

Two males began to tussle. They stiffened their ears and made sham charges. They touched trunks, stepped back and crashed together. Their tusks clacked when they met. It was violent, but not desperate. The heavier animal pressed the other farther and farther back. Each time, the smaller male backed off, then gathered itself to try once more. A thick dark fluid ran unevenly down each side of its face from small cracks midway between its ears and eyes. A glandular secretion, Ernst had warned Anton, generally indicating a period of sexual arousal, when bulls grow more dangerous to the hunter.

The larger animal caught the other in the side, lightly puncturing its hide with a tusk. Anton raised his .450. The smaller elephant screamed and turned. Anton slipped off the safety catch with his thumb. He squeezed the trigger. There was a violent crashing sound where Banda was kneeling in an opening in the reeds to Anton's left.

Anton saw an enormous male hippopotamus strike Banda with its open jaw. It tore at Banda but missed with long curved canines. The man fell under it. The animal dashed for the water. Instantly on his feet, Ernst swung his rifle. He was unable to fire with Anton in between. Astonishingly swift for its immense bulk and short legs, the hippopotamus lunged into the water with the noise and violence of a locomotive. Anton fired his second barrel. His shot took the hippo behind the ear as it plunged into deeper water.

Rushing to Banda, Anton suddenly remembered the elephants. He looked up. Two had climbed the far bank. The third and largest, hit hard, was walking slowly after the others along the edge of the streambed. Blood seeped down its side. It approached the steep bank and tentatively raised one leg to climb. It paused with one foot on the bank and gave an echoing groan. It shook its head and swayed its trunk from side to side. The elephant it had been sparring with reached down and touched its trunk with its own. The third elephant descended the bank. Lowering its head against the wounded animal's side, it pressed its forehead against the big bull until the bleeding elephant wrapped its trunk around a tree and hauled itself up onto the bank. The three animals moved off, the wounded elephant in the middle.

Anton, Karioki and von Decken knelt over Banda.

The man's lower body was pulverized. His shorts, stomach and pelvis were an inseparable mass of flesh, cloth and crushed bone. Banda's one arm lay across his eyes. His fist was clenched. His mouth moved. Unable to help, sickened, Anton watched von Decken put one arm under the man's head and lie down beside him. Their cheeks touched while von Decken listened for his friend's words.

"Today we have taught these foolish boys never to stop on a path of the hippo," Banda whispered. "I wait for you one more time, my old bwana, at the next fire."

Karioki and Anton turned away. Von Decken lay holding the dead man in his arms. The German's shirt and leather shorts darkened with blood.

Finally von Decken rose. Anton moved to help, but von Decken lifted the body in his own arms and carried it to the fig trees. His eyes were red. His cheeks were wet.

"Help me dig here where it's cool, Karioki," von Decken said. "Deep so the hyena will not come. Your Englishman and Ernst must finish the hunt. Send four boys after them."

Anton and Ernst waded across the shallows, watching for the hippopotamus in the deeper water. At the far side Anton paused and looked back, unable to let go of the horror. They climbed the bank and followed the wide trail of broken branches and crushed bushes. Ernst bent down and wet his fingers in the elephant's blood.

"Bubbles. You got him in the lung. Be careful. They'll know we're coming."

For an hour the hunters walked rapidly in silence. After a time the blood became plentiful. They found it smeared against branches and gathered in dusty bubbly puddles like scarlet porridge. Emerging from a cluster of thornbushes, they saw the elephant sixty yards ahead.

The three were pressed together, the wounded animal supported in the middle. The elephants paused, aware of the hunters. The smallest one took a step towards the two men, rocking forward as it hesitated. Its trunk rose in the air. Its ears spread to the sides and stiffened. Behind it, unsupported, the wounded bull fell onto its front knees. Anton fired, hitting the dying elephant in the forehead. It collapsed to the side without a sound. Its young companion charged. With surprising speed the animal crashed through trees and thornbushes, trumpeting shrilly, its ears spread wide, its trunk extended straight ahead. Ernst fired into the ground in its path. The young bull came on. Ernst fired his second barrel. The bullet struck the elephant between the eyes. The animal crashed down five yards in front of him. The third bull cried out once, then turned and disappeared into the bush.

In moments the camp men joined them. Ernst sat on the ground and smoked a cigarette while they cut off the tails and chopped out the tusks with axes. The skinners slit open the belly of the larger animal and cut out the heart and liver. Despite the death of Banda, the men grew excited while they worked, laughing and joking as they sliced belts of fat from under the skin and long strips of meat from the shoulder.

That night they camped under the fig trees. The Gepard Farm cook served Ernst a plate of dumplings and elephant meat. Karioki began to make a meal for Anton and himself, preparing the meat in his own way. The other Africans feasted by a second fire.

Karioki built his fire over a circle of flat stones from the riverbed. He laid strips of liver and heart over the glowing-hot stones and covered them with wild herbs and hot ashes. Anton chopped farm onions and Karioki threw them in with the potatoes that hissed in a pan to one side. He and Anton ate a heavy meal.

Only the old German did not eat. He walked back and forth to the river, declining Anton's help and gathering rocks that he placed over Banda's grave.

Later Anton lay in his blanket, thinking about Banda and the elephant. For the first time Anton was unable to find satisfaction in a hunt. He thought of the wounded bull leaning on his comrades, his friends patient despite the deadly pursuit. Not many men would have waited and helped as they did. He remembered how he had watched Lenares take his beating. Before Anton's mind lost hold, hunters and hunted became the same. Like the leopard, and the gamekeeper in Windsor Great Park. While you hunt one creature, another hunts you.

In the morning Anton rose to find von Decken still sitting by the grave. Anton brought him coffee in a tin cup. The old man stood stiffly and tried to smile. His age was in his face.

"It is done now. It's time my boy and I went back to our farm. I'll accept a present of the ivory, young man, since you won't want to carry it."

"Of course, Mr. von Decken. I meant to give it to you anyway."

"And you must accept two presents from me. Here's the first." Von Decken handed Anton his Merkel and three cardboard boxes of Utterdoerfer Nitro Express .450s, the final sixty of his precious pre-war cartridges.

"She should bring you luck and help you remember an old hunter," von Decken said hurriedly.

Not able to speak, Anton accepted the gift. He knew the old man would never hunt again. And he himself would not shoot another elephant.

The hunters washed in the river before breakfast. A short way downstream, the hippopotamus floated on the surface, its body wedged among the rocks. The skinners cut out the two large lower teeth while the cook made breakfast and Anton and Karioki got ready to walk north. Each of them carried a blanket and a grey German army rucksack, faded and patched. The packs contained coffee and tobacco, salted elephant meat, maize and sugar. Ernst took a small parcel from his father and added it to Anton's pack.

Anton ate slowly, reluctant to end his last meal with his friends. When he was finished he drew his knife and sharpened it on a boot. He carved his initials and a Union Jack on one of the hippo teeth. He and Karioki lifted their packs and said goodbye to each of the men. Ernst stepped up and gripped Anton's hand. "Good luck, my young Engländer. Keep your blade sharp."

Anton picked up his new rifle and approached von Decken.

"Thank you, sir, and please take this." He handed von Decken the carved ivory.

"I wish I were marching with you." Von Decken gripped Anton's shoulders in almost-strong hands. "Just keep Kili behind you and walk west-northwest. You're right on the border now. You will find your way."

RIME OF
THE ANCIENT
PORCUPINE

FROM
JAGUARS RIPPED
MY FLESH

BY TIM CAHILL

This is a tale of murder most foul, of a crime against nature
and man, of instant retribution. It is a tale for those who
would believe that there are more things invisible than visible
in the universe, and nonetheless true for the fact that it happened in the ancient times, which is to say, about 1939. It is
a tale of storm blast and wondrous cold, and ice as green as
emerald, a tale, in short, of a bad winter in the north country.
The ice then, we might conjecture, was here, the ice was there,
the ice was all around. It cracked and growled and roared
and howled, as Samuel Taylor Coleridge would have it, like
noises in a swound—which is a swoon—something unconscious, a frigid, brittle dream. However, this tale is no dream,
but a true and locally well-known story. In the bad winter
of 1939, the unholy deed was done. It happened no more
than three miles from my house, tucked away in a pocketed
groin of the Absaroka Mountains.

To understand the nature of the crime, however, it is first
necessary to know a bit about the porcupines of the northern

Rockies. They can be pestiferous animals. Sometimes called quill pigs, porcupines are actually large rodents. Vegetarians all, they enjoy the tender layer of tissue beneath the bark of living trees. When especially hungry, or perhaps in a destructive mood, porcupines may completely girdle and kill a tree. They have been known to splinter used ax handles and canoe paddles for the salt and oil they contain.

Porcupines also relish rubber. A friend of mine once parked his car at a mountain trail-head. When he returned after a week of backpacking, he found that the car wouldn't start. Some animal had gnawed through the rubber on his generator coil, shorting it out. My friend decided to wait until morning to walk the ten miles down the old logging road to the main highway and hitchhike ten more miles into town for a replacement. That night, camped by the car, he heard a satisfied scratching and a moist munching under the hood. It was, of course, a porcupine, and the beast regarded him balefully, his large nocturnal eyes glinting in the glare of the flashlight. My friend levered the porcupine off his engine block with a long branch he was saving for his fire. He might have hammered the animal to death with the same branch, but that is not done, not here in the northern Rockies.

It took a full day to get back with the part he needed. He replaced the coil, and since he was already a day late for work, he drove the car hard down the logging road. About three miles from the main highway, the temperature gauge pegged at high and steam began spurting out from under the hood. My friend was more than a little irritated to discover that in his absence the porcupine had returned and eaten a hole through the underside of his bottom radiator hose.

We have more than our share of porcupines out here at

the Poison Creek Ranch. About once every six months, one of my dogs, to its detriment, tries to eat a porcupine. The dogs kill skunks with great regularity, and they return to the house with their heads held high, proud and malodorous. But when they've been quilled by a porcupine, they skulk about outside the front door, afraid and ashamed to come in for the doctoring they need.

The porcupine does not run from a dog. He will, instead, present his backside. My dogs, like a man who continually burns his mouth on the first piece of pizza, do not learn from history. They suppose an animal's arsenal is invariably located about the head, since that is so in their own species. The porcupine does not throw his quills but drives his powerful tail into the dog's mouth, leaving dozens of barbed and needlelike quills in the dog's tongue, and in the roof and bottom of its mouth.

The quills, which are modified hairs, range in size from half an inch to three inches. Since they are barbed, the quills will, with time, work their way into the dog, eventually reaching the brain and killing it. For that reason, every quill must be quickly and carefully removed. I do this with needle-nose pliers I bought especially for the operation. You want to roll the dog onto its back, under a bright light, get its mouth open, and pull out the quills. The dogs are never enthusiastic about this operation, and one of them once blackened my eye with a front paw trying to push me away. These days, I put a quilled dog into a large burlap sack, which I tie around his neck. It takes half an hour of intense and sweaty struggle to stuff a pain-crazed eighty-pound dog in a gunny sack.

I could, I suppose, wait for a fresh snow, track the porcupines, and blast them into eternity with the 12-gauge, but, as I say, that is not done in the northern Rockies. Since the days of the mountain men here, porcupines have been sacrosanct. Like the albatross in the old poem, a porcupine is considered a pious beast of good fortune, and for very practical reasons. A man or woman lost in the mountains hereabouts can usually find and kill a porcupine. In winter, especially, they show up as dark lumps in the crotches of bare trees. They do not run from man and may be killed with a branch or even a stone. The flesh, especially that of the tail, is rich and fatty, and the calories it contains may sustain a man for days. Of course, rabbits may be easily trapped, but their flesh is lean, its calories quickly burned away. There are documented tales of men who have eaten several rabbits a day while lost, men who died of what is known as "rabbit starvation."

So porcupines are slow-moving, ambulatory sources of food for the lost and injured, and that is why the killing of such a beast in any but the most dire circumstances is considered a dangerous and wanton act capable of generating the worst of luck. And in the bad winter of 1939, in the dismal sheen of the snowy cliffs, no more than three miles from my house, a man committed that very crime; and like the albatross in the old poem, the porcupine was avenged and death fires danced at night.

The man had built a wooden frame house, and he set it up on blocks so that he would not have to dig a foundation. As the long white mountain winter set in, the man discovered a major flaw in the design. Various small animals took to living under the house for shelter and warmth. Every night there was a commotion of yips and squeaks and howls. Every night, the sickly sweet fragrance of skunk drifted up into his kitchen.

The fellow was having trouble sleeping and eating, and as the drifts piled up over his windows and darkened the rooms, as the terrible psychic weight of cabin fever descended upon him, he developed a fanatical hatred for the squabbling things that lived under his house.

And so it happened that this man found a huge porcupine one dreary winter day. He was sitting on the lowest branch of a bare and icy tree, and the man who built his house on blocks looked upon that particular porcupine as the disturber of his sleep and the despoiler of his appetite. Perhaps he chuckled as he dug out the kerosene and matches. Quickly, he doused the porcupine, struck a match, and tossed it onto the animal, which erupted into a colorless flame. In his agony of fire, the porcupine ran to where he lived, ran to the area under the house. The flaming porcupine, this dying animal, set the wooden house aflame. It burned to the ground in a matter of hours.

The tale is true and can be verified. In my mind's eye I see that man, standing there thigh-deep in a drift, shivering in an icy wind and looking mournfully at the last glowing, gloating embers smoldering away in the ashy puddle where his house used to be. It was a long and bitter trek to the nearest shelter, and I like to think that this man, who set a porcupine afire, walked like one that hath been stunned and is of sense forlorn. A sadder and a wiser man, I imagine, he rose the morrow morn.

FROM
THE PRINCE OF
TIDES

BY PAT CONROY

It was almost summer when the strangers arrived by boat
in Colleton and began their long, inexorable pursuit of the
white porpoise. My mother was baking bread and the suf-
fusion of that exquisite fragrance of the loaves and roses
turned our house into a vial of the most harmonious seasonal
incense. She took the bread fresh from the oven, then slath-
ered it with butter and honey. We took it steaming in our
hands down to the dock to eat, the buttery honey running
through our fingers. We attracted the ornery attention of
every yellow jacket in our yard, and it took nerve to let them
walk on our hands, gorging themselves on the drippings from
our bread. They turned our hands into gardens and orchards
and hives. My mother brought the lid of a mayonnaise jar
full of sugar water down to the dock to appease the yellow
jackets and let us eat in peace.

We had almost finished the bread when we saw the boat,
The Amberjack, bearing Florida registry, move through the
channels of the Colleton River. No gulls followed the boat,

so we were certain it was not a fishing vessel. It lacked the clean, luxurious lines of a yacht, yet there was a visible crew of six men whose sun-stained burnt-amber color announced them as veteran mariners. We would learn the same day that it was the first boat ever to enter South Carolina waters whose function was to keep fish alive.

The crew of *The Amberjack* were not secretive about their mission and their business in these waters was known all over Colleton late that afternoon. Captain Otto Blair told a reporter from the *Gazette* that the Miami Seaquarium had received a letter from a Colleton citizen, who wished to remain anonymous, that an albino porpoise frequented the waters around Colleton. Captain Blair and his crew planned to capture the porpoise, then transport it back to Miami, where it would be both a tourist attraction and a subject for scientific inquiry. The crew of *The Amberjack* had come to Colleton in the interest of science, as marine biologists, inspired by a report that the rarest creature in the seven seas was a daily sight to the people of the lowcountry.

They may have known all there was to know about porpoises and their habits, but they had badly misjudged the character of the people they would find in the lower part of South Carolina. The citizens of Colleton were about to give them lessons free of charge. A collective shiver of rage passed invisibly through Colleton; the town was watchful and alarmed. The plot to steal Carolina Snow was an aberrant, unspeakable act to us. By accident, they had brought the rare savor of solidarity to our shores. They would feel the full weight of our dissent.

To them the white porpoise was a curiosity of science; to us she was the disclosure of the unutterable beauty and generosity of God among us, the proof of magic, and the ecstasy of art.

The white porpoise was something worthy to fight for.

THE AMBERJACK, mimicking the habits of the shrimpers, moved out early the next morning, but it did not sight the porpoise that day and it set no nets. The men returned to the shrimp dock grim-lipped and eager for rumors about recent sightings of the Snow. They were met with silence.

After the third day, Luke and I met their boat and listened to the crew talk about the long fruitless days on the river, trying to sight the white porpoise. Already, they were feeling the eloquent heft of the town's censure and they seemed eager to talk to Luke and me, to extract any information about the porpoise they could from us.

Captain Blair brought Luke and me on board *The Amberjack* and showed us the holding tank on the main deck where specimens were kept alive until they could reach the aquariums in Miami. He showed us the half mile of nets that they would use to encircle the porpoise. A man's hand could pass easily through the meshing of their nets. The captain was a cordial middle-aged man and the sun had burned deep lines in his face, like tread marks. In a soft, barely discernible voice he told us how they trained a porpoise to eat dead fish after a capture. A porpoise would fast for two weeks or more before it would deign to feed on prey it would ignore in the wild. The greatest danger in the capture of a porpoise was that the animal would become entangled in the nets and drown. Hunting dolphins required a swift and skilled crew to ensure that drowning did not occur. He then showed us the foam rubber mattresses they laid the porpoises on once they got them on board.

"Why don't you just throw them in the pool, Captain?" I asked.

"We do usually, but sometimes we've got sharks in the pool and sometimes a porpoise will hurt himself thrashing around in a pool that small. Often it's better to just lie 'em down on these mattresses and keep splashing 'em with sea-water so their skin won't dry out. We move 'em from side to side to keep their circulation right and that's about all there is to it."

"How long can they live out of the water?" Luke asked.

"I don't rightly know, son," the captain answered. "The longest I ever kept one out of the water was five days, but he made it back to Miami just fine. They're hardy creatures. When's the last time you boys spotted Moby in these waters?"

"Moby?" Luke said. "Her name is Snow. Carolina Snow."

"That's what they've named her down at Miami, boys. Moby Porpoise. Some guy in the publicity department came up with that one."

"That's the dumbest name I've ever heard," Luke said.

"It'll bring the tourists running, son," Captain Blair answered.

"Speaking of tourists, a whole boatful spotted the Snow yesterday morning in Charleston Harbor as they were heading out for Fort Sumter," said Luke.

"Are you sure, son?" the captain asked, and one of the crewmen leapt to his feet to hear the rest of the conversation.

"I didn't see it," Luke said, "but I heard it on the radio."

The Amberjack left for Charleston Harbor the next day, cruising the Ashley and the Cooper rivers looking for signs of the white porpoise. For three days they searched the waters around Wappoo Creek and the Elliott Cut before they realized that my brother Luke was a liar. They had also taught my brother how to keep a porpoise alive if the need ever arose.

THE CALL TO ARMS between *The Amberjack* crew and the town did not begin in earnest until the evening in June when the crew tried to capture the white porpoise in full view of the town. They had sighted the Snow in Colleton Sound, in water much too deep to set their nets for a successful capture. All day, they had followed the porpoise, remaining a discreet distance behind her, stalking her with infinite patience until she began moving into the shallower rivers and creeks.

Just as the crew tracked the porpoise, the shrimpers of the town kept issuing reports on the position of *The Amberjack* on their short-wave radios. Whenever the boat changed course, the eyes of the shrimp fleet noted and remarked upon the shift of position, and the airwaves filled up with the voices of shrimpers passing messages from boat to boat, from boat to town. The shrimpers' wives, monitoring their own radios, then got on the telephone to spread the news. *The Amberjack* could not move through county waters without its exact bearings being reported to a regiment of secret listeners.

"*Amberjack* turning into Yemassee Creek," we heard one day through the static of the radio my mother kept above the kitchen sink. "Don't look like they found any Snow today."

"Miami Beach just left Yemassee Creek and appears to be settin' to poke around the Harper Dogleg up by Goat Island."

The town carefully listened to these frequent intelligence reports of the shrimpers. For a week the white porpoise did not appear, and when she did it was one of the shrimpers who alerted the town.

"This is Captain Willard Plunkett, and Miami Beach has got the Snow in sight. They are pursuing her up the Colleton River and the crew is preparing the nets on deck. It looks like Snow is heading for a visit to town."

Word passed through the town in the old quicksilvering of rumor, and the prefigured power of that rumor lured the whole town to the river's edge. People kept their eyes on the river and talked quietly. The sheriff pulled into the parking lot behind the bank and monitored the shrimpers' reports. The eyes of the town were fixed on the bend in the Colleton River where *The Amberjack* would make its appearance. That bend was a mile from the point where the river joined three of its sister rivers and bloomed into a sound.

For twenty minutes we waited for *The Amberjack* to make the turn, and when it did a collective groan rose up in the throats of us all. The boat was riding high above the marsh on an incoming tide. One of the crewmen stood on the fore-deck with a pair of binoculars trained on the water in front of the boat. He stood perfectly still, rapt and statuesque, his complete immersion a testament to the passion he brought to his task.

Luke, Savannah, and I watched from the bridge, along with several hundred of our neighbors who had gathered to witness the moment of capture of the town's living symbol of good luck. The town was only curious until we saw Carolina Snow make her own luxurious appearance as she rounded the last curve of the river and began her silken, fabulous promenade through the town. She silvered as the sunlight caught her pale fin buttering through the crest of a small wave. In her move-

ment through town she achieved a fragile sublimity, so un-
aware was she of her vulnerability. Burnished by perfect light,
she dazzled us again with her complete and ambient beauty.
Her dorsal fin broke the surface again like a white chevron
a hundred yards nearer the bridge, and to our surprise, the
town cheered spontaneously and the apotheosis of the white
porpoise was fully achieved. The ensign of Colleton's wrath
unfurled in the secret winds and our status as passive ob-
servers changed imperceptibly as a battle cry, unknown to
any of us, formed on our lips. All the mottoes and passwords
of engagement appeared like fiery graffiti on the armorial
bearings of the town's unconscious. The porpoise disappeared
again, then rose up, arcing toward the applause that greeted
her sounding. She was mysterious and lunar. Her color was
a delicate alchemy of lily and mother-of-pearl. The porpoise
passed argentine beneath the sun-struck waters. Then we
looked up and saw *The Amberjack* gaining ground on the
Snow and the crew getting the nets into a small boat they
were going to lower into the water.

The town needed a warrior and I was surprised to find him
standing beside me.

Traffic jammed the bridge as drivers simply parked their
cars and went to the bridge's railing to watch the capture of
the porpoise. A truck loaded down with tomatoes from one
of Reese Newbury's farms was stuck on the bridge and the
driver was leaning on his horn in vain, trying to get the other
drivers back into their cars.

I heard Luke whisper to himself, "No. It just ain't right,"
and he left my side and mounted the back of the truck and
began to toss crates of tomatoes down among the crowd. I
thought Luke had gone crazy, but suddenly I understood, and

Savannah and I bashed a crate of tomatoes open and began to pass them along the railing. The driver got out and screamed for Luke to stop, but Luke ignored him and continued passing the wooden crates down to the outstretched arms of his friends and neighbors. The driver's voice grew more and more frantic as people began taking tire tools from their trunks and splitting the crates wide open. The sheriff's car moved out of the parking lot and headed out toward the Charleston highway on the opposite side of town.

When *The Amberjack* neared the bridge, two hundred tomatoes hit the deck in a green fusillade that put the man with the binoculars to his knees. The tomatoes were hard and green and one of the other crewmen working on the nets was holding his nose near the aft of the boat, blood leaking through his fingers. The second salvo of tomatoes followed soon afterward and the crew scrambled, dazed and insensible, toward the safety of the hold and cabin. A tire tool cracked against a lifeboat and the crowd roared its approval. Boxes of tomatoes were passed down the line, the driver still screaming and not a single soul listening to his pleadings.

The Amberjack disappeared beneath the bridge and two hundred people crossed to the other side in a delirious, headlong rush. When the boat reappeared we showered it with tomatoes again, like archers on high ground pouring arrows on an ill-deployed infantry. Savannah was throwing hard and with accuracy, finding her own good rhythm, her own style. She was screaming with pure pleasure. Luke threw a whole crate of tomatoes and it smashed on the rear deck, sending ruined tomatoes skittering like marbles toward the battened-down hold.

The Amberjack pulled out of range of all but the strongest arms when the porpoise, in a thoughtless gesture of self-preservation, reversed her course and turned back toward the town, passing the boat trailing her on its starboard side. She returned to our applause and our advocacy. We watched her move beneath the waters below the bridge, grizzling the bright waves like some abstract dream of ivory. When the boat made its long, hesitant turn in the river, even more crates of tomatoes were passed through the mob. By this time, even the truck driver had surrendered to whatever mass hysteria had possessed the rest of us and he stood with his arm cocked, holding a tomato, anticipating with the rest of us *The Amberjack*'s imminent return. The boat started back for the bridge, then turned abruptly away from us and moved north on the Colleton River as Carolina Snow, the only white porpoise on our planet, moved back toward the Atlantic.

THE NEXT DAY the town council passed a resolution enfranchising Carolina Snow as a citizen of Colleton County and making it a felony for anyone to remove her from county waters. At the same time, the South Carolina state legislature passed a similar law rendering it a felony for anyone to remove genus *Phocaena* or genus *Tursiops* from the waters of Colleton County. In less than twenty-four hours, Colleton County became the only place in the world where it was a crime to capture a porpoise.

Captain Blair went straight to the sheriff's office when he reached the shrimp dock that night and demanded that Sheriff Lucas arrest everyone who had thrown a tomato at *The Amberjack*. Unfortunately, Captain Blair could not provide the sheriff with a single name of even one of the miscreants, and the sheriff, after making several phone calls, could produce four witnesses who would swear in a court of law that no one had been on the bridge when *The Amberjack* passed beneath it.

"Then how did I get a hundred pounds of tomatoes on the deck of my boat?" the captain had asked.

And in a laconic reply that was well received in each Colleton household, the sheriff had answered, "It's tomato season, Captain. Those damn things will grow anywhere."

But the men from Miami quickly recovered their will and developed a new plan for the capture of the porpoise. They kept out of sight of the town and did not enter the main channel of the Colleton River again. They began to haunt the outer territorial limits of the county, waiting for that perfect moment when the Snow would wander out of county waters and beyond the protection of those newly contracted laws. But *The Amberjack* was shadowed by boats from the South Carolina Game and Fish Commission and by a small flotilla of recreational boats commanded by the women and children of the town. Whenever *The Amberjack* picked up the trail of the porpoise, the small crafts would maneuver themselves between the porpoise and the pursuing vessel and slow their motors. *The Amberjack* would try to weave between the boats, but these women and children of Colleton had handled small boats all their lives. They would interfere with the Florida boat's progress until the white porpoise slipped away in the enfolding tides of Colleton Sound.

Each day Luke, Savannah, and I would take our boat and ride up the inland waterway to join the flotilla of resistance. Luke would move the boat in front of *The Amberjack*'s bow, ignoring the warning horn, and slow the Whaler by imperceptible degrees. No matter how skillfully Captain Blair maneuvered his boat, he could not pass Luke. Savannah and I had our fishing gear rigged and we trolled for Spanish mackerel as Luke navigated between *The Amberjack* and the white porpoise. Often, the crew would come out to the bow of the ship to threaten and taunt us.

"Hey, kids, get out of our goddamn way before we get pissed off," one crewman yelled.

"Just fishing, mister," Luke would shoot back.

"What're you fishing for?" The man sneered in exasperation.

"We hear there's a white porpoise in these waters," said Luke, slowing the motor with a delicate movement of his wrist.

"Is that right, smartass? Well, you're not doing such a good job catching it."

"We're doing as good as you are, mister," Luke answered pleasantly.

"If this were Florida, we'd run right over you."

"It ain't Florida, mister. Or haven't you noticed?" Luke said.

"Hicks," the man screamed.

Luke pulled back the throttle and we slowed almost to a crawl. We could hear the big engines of *The Amberjack* throttling down behind us as the bow of the boat loomed over us.

"He called us hicks," Luke said.

"Me, a hick?" Savannah said.

"That hurts my feelings," I said.

Up ahead, the white porpoise turned into Langford Creek, the alabaster shine in her fin disappearing behind a green flange of marsh. There were three boats waiting at the mouth of the creek ready to intercept *The Amberjack* if it managed to get past Luke.

AFTER THIRTY DAYS of delay and obstruction, *The Amberjack* left the southern boundaries of Colleton waters and returned to its home base of Miami without the white porpoise. Captain Blair gave a final embittered interview to the *Gazette,* listing the many obstacles the citizens of Colleton had erected to disrupt the mission of *The Amberjack.* Such deterrence, he said, could not be allowed to frustrate the integrity of scientific investigation. But on their last day, he and his crew had taken sniper fire from Freeman's Island and he, as captain, had made the irrevocable decision to discontinue the hunt. The shrimp fleet observed *The Amberjack* as it passed the last barrier islands, maneuvered through the breakers, then turned south, angling toward the open seas.

BUT *THE AMBERJACK* did not go to Miami. It traveled south for forty miles, then turned into the mouth of the Savannah River, putting in to the shrimp dock at Thunderbolt. There it remained for a week to resupply and to let the passions in Colleton County cool, still monitoring the short-wave radio, following the travels of the white porpoise by listening to the Colleton shrimpers give accurate reports of her soundings. After a week *The Amberjack* left the harbor in Savannah in the middle of the night and turned north out beyond the three-mile limit. They cruised confidently out of sight of the shore-bound shrimp trawlers. They were waiting for one signal to come over the radio.

They had been offshore for three days when they heard the words they had been waiting for.

"There's a submerged log I just netted in Zajac Creek, shrimpers. You boys be careful if you're over this way. Out."

"There's no shrimp in Zajac Creek anyhow, Captain," a voice of another shrimp boat captain answered. "You a long way from home, ain't you, Captain Henry? Out."

"I'll catch the shrimp wherever I can find them, Captain. Out," my father answered, watching Carolina Snow moving a school of fish toward a sandbar.

Zajac Creek was not in Colleton County and *The Amberjack* turned west and came at full throttle toward the creek, the crew preparing the nets as the shoreline of South Carolina filled the eyes of Captain Blair for the last time. A shrimper from Charleston witnessed the capture of the white porpoise at 1130 hours that morning, saw Carolina Snow panic and charge the encircling nets, saw when she entangled herself, and admired the swiftness and skill of the crew as they got their ropes around her, held her head above the water to keep her from drowning, and maneuvered her into one of the motorboats.

By the time the word reached Colleton, *The Amberjack* was well outside the three-mile limit again, set on a southerly course that would take them into Miami in fifty-eight hours. The bells of the church were rung in protest, an articulation of our impotence and fury. It was as if the river had been deconsecrated, purged of all the entitlements of magic.

"SUBMERGED LOG" was the code phrase my father had worked out with Captain Blair and the crew of *The Amber-*

jack. He had agreed to fish the boundary waters at the edge of the county until he sighted the white porpoise moving into the territorial waters of Gibbes County to the north. My father was the anonymous Colletonian who had written the Miami Seaquarium informing them of the presence of an albino porpoise in our county. Two weeks after the abduction of Snow and a week after her picture appeared in the *Colleton Gazette,* being lowered into her aquarium tank in her new Miami home, my father received a letter of gratitude from Captain Blair and a check for a thousand dollars as a reward for his assistance.

"I'm ashamed of what you did, Henry," my mother said, barely able to control her temper as my father waved the check in front of us.

"I earned a thousand big ones, Lila, and it was the easiest money I ever made in my life. I wish every porpoise I passed was an albino so I could spend all my time eating chocolate and buying banks."

"If anybody in this town had any guts, they'd go to Miami and set that animal free. You'd better not let anyone in town hear that you're responsible, Henry. Folks are still steaming mad about that porpoise."

"How could you sell our porpoise, Daddy?" Savannah asked.

"Look, sweetie, that porpoise is gonna be in fat city, chowing down on gourmet mackerel and jumping through hoops to make kids happy. Snow doesn't have to worry about a shark the rest of her life. She's retired in Miami. You got to look at it in a positive light."

"I think you've committed a sin that not even God can forgive, Daddy," Luke said darkly.

"You do?" My father sneered. "Hey, I never saw 'Property of Colleton' tattooed on her back. I just wrote the Seaquarium that Colleton had a natural phenomenon that could lure in the crowds and they rewarded me for being on my toes."

"They couldn't have found him if you hadn't radioed every time you spotted him in the river," I said.

"I was their liaison officer in the area. Look, it's not that great a shrimping season. This thousand bucks is going to put food on the table and clothes on your back. This could pay for a whole year of college for one of you kids."

"I wouldn't eat a bite of food you bought with that money," Luke said. "And I wouldn't wear a pair of Jockey shorts you bought with it either."

"I've been watching the Snow for more than five years now," my mother said. "You once punished Tom for killing a bald eagle, Henry. There's a lot more eagles in the world than white porpoises."

"I didn't kill the porpoise, Lila. I delivered it to a safe harbor where it will be free of all fear. I look upon myself as the hero of this affair."

"You sold Snow into captivity," my mother said.

"They're going to make her a circus porpoise," Savannah added.

"You betrayed yourself and your sources," Luke said. "If it was a businessman, I could understand. Some low-life creepy Jaycee with shiny hair. But a shrimper, Dad. A shrimper selling Snow for money."

"I sell shrimp for money, Luke," my father shouted.

"Not the same," Luke said. "You don't sell what you can't replace."

"I saw twenty porpoises in the river today."

"And I promise you, Daddy, not one of them was white. None of them was special," Luke said.

"Our family is the reason they captured the Snow," said Savannah. "It's like being the daughter of Judas Iscariot, only I bet I'd have liked Judas a lot better."

"You shouldn't have done what you did, Henry," my mother said. "It'll bring bad luck."

"I couldn't have had any worse luck than I've had," my father answered. "Anyway, it's done. There's nothing anyone can do about it now."

"I can do something about it," said Luke. . . .

AFTER TEN HOURS of hard driving and two stops for gas, the city of Miami rose out of the sea as we drove past the sign for the Hialeah racetrack. Coconut palms rattled in the warm breezes, and the scent of gardens overwhelmed by bougain-villea cologned the broad avenues. We had never been to Florida in our lives and suddenly we were cruising the streets of Miami looking for a place to set our tents beneath the lime and avocado trees. . . .

That night we slept on a bench at Key Biscayne, and the sun was high when we arose the next morning, gathered our belongings, and headed for a visit to the Seaquarium.

We paid our admission fees and walked through the turn-stiles. For the first half-hour we circumnavigated the park, following the parabola made by the large Cyclone fence and its ugly toupee of barbed wire. Beside a cluster of palms contiguous to the parking lot, Luke stopped and said, "I'll back the truck up to these trees and I'll cut a hole right through here."

"What if they catch us, Luke?" I asked.

"We're just high school kids from Colleton who came down to rescue Snow on a dare from our classmates. We act like total hicks and pretend the coolest thing we ever did was spit watermelon seeds at sheets hanging in our mama's back yard."

"The guard at the gate was wearing a gun, Luke," Savannah said.

"I know, honey, but no guard is going to shoot at us."

"How do you know?" she asked.

"Because Tolitha gave me a whole bottle of sleeping pills. You know, the ones she calls her little red devils."

"Do we just tell him to say 'ah' and pop a pill in his mouth?" I said, fearing that Luke's master plan would prove a bit leaky in its execution.

"I haven't figured that out yet, little brother," Luke said. "I just found me the place where I'm going to cut the hole."

"How we gonna get Snow out of the water?" I asked.

"Same way. Sleeping pills," he answered.

"That'll be easy," I said. "We'll just jump in the water, swim our asses off until we catch a porpoise that it took experts a month to catch when they had all the equipment in the world, and then slip a few sleeping pills between her lips. Great plan, Luke."

"More than a few pills, Tom. We've got to make damn sure that the Snow is completely tranquilized."

"This will be the first porpoise in history to die of a drug overdose," Savannah said.

"No, I figure the Snow weighs about four hundred pounds. Tolitha weighs a hundred pounds. She takes one pill every night. We'll give Snow four or five of the babies."

"Who ever heard of a porpoise taking sleeping pills, Luke?" Savannah said. "Tom's right."

"I haven't either," Luke admitted. "But I've heard of a porpoise eating fish. And if that fish just happens to be chock-full of sleeping pills, then it's my theory that porpoise will be ready for rock-a-bye-baby time."

I asked, "Do porpoises sleep, Luke?"

"I don't know," he answered. "We're going to find out a lot about porpoises on this little expedition, Tom."

"What if it doesn't work, Luke?" Savannah asked.

Luke shrugged his shoulders and said, "No harm in that, Savannah. At least we'll know we tried to do something. And ain't we had some fun so far? All those people in Colleton crying about losing their porpoise, and you, me, and Tom down here in Miami planning the jailbreak. We'll tell our kids about it. If we manage to get Snow out of here, there'll be parades and confetti and riding in convertibles. We'll brag about it until the day we die. But first, you got to see it. Neither of you see it yet. Now that's real important. Here, I'll help you. Close your eyes . . ."

Savannah and I closed our eyes and listened to our brother's voice. "Okay. Tom and I have the porpoise in the water. We move her over to the place where Savannah is waiting with the stretcher. We get ropes around the Snow and very gently we roll her out of the water and tie her to the stretcher. The guard is asleep because we drugged his Pepsi a couple of hours before. See it? Can you visualize it? We get the porpoise in the pickup and we're off. And here's the important thing. Listen to this. We're standing in the boat landing in Colleton and we take the Snow and we untie the ropes and we set her free in the river where she was born and where she belongs. Can you see it? Can you see it all, Tom and Savannah?"

His voice was hypnotic, transported, and we both opened our eyes at the same time and we nodded toward each other. Both of us could see it.

We continued our long walk around the perimeter of the park and saw *The Amberjack* tied up at its berth at the south end of the Seaquarium. There was no sign of the crew around, but we avoided any approach to the boat. Turning toward the porpoise house, we crossed a wooden bridge suspended high over a deep clear moat where huge sharks moved sluggishly in an endless circle. The sharks swam at twenty-yard intervals and there was very little room or inclination for them to pass one another. We watched a hammerhead and a young mako make their torpid passage beneath us as the crowd watched with breathless wonder. So monotonous was the movement of their great tails, so proscribed was their freedom for improvisation or movement, that they seemed purged of all their ferocious grandeur. Beneath the gazes of tourists, they looked as docile and harmless as black mollies.

The crowd was large and good-natured and we followed a processional of Bermuda shorts and rubber-soled thongs toward the amphitheater where the killer whale, Dreadnought, would perform at noon. . . .

We listened to the tourists talking about the white porpoise as they filed into the rows of seats that ringed a vast two-million-gallon tank aquarium. When we were all seated, a well-made blond boy with coppery shoulders walked out onto a wooden peninsula jutting out over the water and waved to the crowd. A woman announcer presented the history of Dreadnought, the killer whale who had been captured in a pod of twelve whales near Queen Charlotte Strait off Vancouver Island and flown to Miami by special flight. The Seaquarium had paid sixty thousand dollars for the purchase of Dreadnought and it had taken a year to train the killer whale. The whale could not be incorporated into the porpoise show because porpoise was a favorite food of *Orcinus orca*.

As she spoke, a gate opened invisibly underwater and the passage of something awesome rolled the opaque depths below.

The tanned boy peered into the water, seeing something rising up toward him. His platform was twenty feet above the surface and you could study the intensity of his concentration by counting the lines on his forehead as he leaned forward holding a Spanish mackerel by the tail. The boy made a circling gesture with his hand and in obedience the water was suddenly runnelled with waves spun outward from the center of the aquarium. Then the whale went to the bottom of the tank, maintaining his speed and momentum, and came out of that water like a building launched from below and took the proffered fish daintily, like a girl accepting a mint. Then the whale fell back down in a long arc. His shadow blocked the sun for a moment and when he hit the surface of the aquarium it was as if a tree had toppled into the sea from a high ridge.

Then a massive wave, in answer, broke over the railing and drenched the crowd with seawater from row one to row twenty-three. You watched Dreadnought do his act and bathed at the same time, the salt water running out of your hair, smelling of the essence of whale.

As he made the circuit around his pool again, urging himself toward his moment of piebald beauty in the Florida sun, lifting out toward the heavy-scented odors of citrus and bougainvillea, we could glimpse his white-bottomed streaking image in the water and the amazing iridescences on his black head; he was the color of a good pair of saddle shoes. His dorsal fin was set like a black pyramid on his back and moved through the water like a blade hissing through nylon. His lines were clean and supple; his teeth were set in his grim mouth, each one the size of a table lamp. I had never seen such contained and implied power. Dreadnought leapt again and rang a bell that was suspended over the water. He opened his mouth and let the blond boy brush the whale's teeth with a janitor's broom. For his finale, Dreadnought came blasting out of the water, his flukes gleaming and shedding gallons of seawater, and the whale grasped a rope with his teeth and ran our American flag to the top of a flagpole high above the aquarium. Whenever the whale reached the apogee of one of his agile leaps, the crowd cheered, then braced itself for his graceful, streamlined plunge back into the water, when again we would be covered by a prodigious wave. . . .

After the killer whale, the porpoises looked diminutive and inconsequential and their act, though far more spunky and accomplished than the whale's, seemed trifling after Dreadnought's pièce de résistance. Their tricks were dazzlers, all right; they just weren't whales. But they were sure a happy, supererogatory tribe as they left the water like artillery shells leaping twenty feet in the air, their bodies jade-colored and smooth. Their heads were creased with perpetual harlequin smiles that lent sincerity to their high-spirited performances. They played baseball games, bowled, danced on their tails the full length of their aquarium, threw balls through hoops, and took lit cigarettes out of their trainer's mouth in a vain attempt to get him to give up smoking.

We found Carolina Snow in her own small enclosed pool,

cut off from the companionship of the other porpoises. A large and curious crowd surrounded her enclosure and she swam from side to side, looking disoriented and faintly bored. She had not yet learned a single trick but was certainly earning her keep as an item of curiosity. The announcer described the capture of the white porpoise and made it sound like the most dangerous, exotic venture since the discovery of the Northwest Passage. At three o'clock we watched a keeper bring a bucket of fish to feed the Snow. He threw a blue runner at the opposite end of the pool from where Snow was swimming. She turned and in a movement of surprising delicacy accelerated across the pool and took the fish from the top of the water. We listened as the tourists tried to describe her color. We, her liberators, listened with pride as we heard strangers speak of her pale luminous beauty.

We watched the feeding and noticed that the man kept alternating where he threw the fish and that it was all part of an elaborate design for the training of the Snow. Once he got her in one rhythm of going from side to side in the pool, he reversed the procedure and brought her closer and closer until she lifted out of the water and took the last fish from his hand. The keeper was patient and skillful and the crowd applauded when Snow came out of the water. It was like watching a priest administering the Eucharist to a young girl in a Communion veil when he put the blue runner in Snow's open mouth.

"We got to get to a fish market, Tom," Luke whispered. "Savannah, you try to make contact with the night watchman before closing time. It don't close until eight."

"I've always wanted to play the wicked seductress," she said.

"You aren't seducing anyone. You're just going to make friends with him. Then put the son of a bitch to sleep."

IN COCONUT GROVE we bought half a dozen whitings and a bucket of Kentucky Fried Chicken. When we returned to the Seaquarium it was a half-hour before closing time and we found Savannah talking with the night watchman, who had just arrived at the security office for duty.

"Brothers," Savannah said, "I have met the nicest man."

"Is she bothering you, mister?" Luke said. "She's only free on a daily pass from the nut house."

"Bothering me? It's not often I get to talk to such a pretty girl. I'm the one who's usually here when everybody's gone home."

"Mr. Beavers is from New York City."

"You want some fried chicken?" Luke offered.

"Don't mind if I do," Mr. Beavers said, pulling out a drumstick.

"How about a Pepsi?"

"I'm strictly a coffee man. Hey, it's getting close to closing time. I got to run you kids out of here. This job gets lonely. That's its only drawback."

He sounded a loud foghorn that was followed immediately by a recorded announcement asking that all visitors leave the grounds of the Seaquarium at once and giving the opening time for the next day. Mr. Beavers went outside his office door and blew his own whistle, walking between the killer whale amphitheater and the porpoise house. Savannah refreshed his coffee from the pot he had already brewed on his desk, snapped open the contents of two sleeping pills, and stirred the coffee until the powder dissolved completely.

Luke and I followed Mr. Beavers around the park as he good-humoredly urged the tourists to go home and return the next day. He stopped at the holding tank where the Snow was moving restlessly from one side to the other.

"She's an aberration of nature," he said. "But a beautiful aberration."

As he turned, he spotted a teenager throwing a Popsicle wrapper on the ground. "My good young man," he said, "littering is a crime against the maker of this green earth."

As he walked toward the boy, Luke dropped a whiting into the water of Carolina Snow's aquarium. The Snow passed it twice before she downed it.

"How many pills did you put in that fish?" I whispered.

"Enough to kill you or me," he answered.

Mr. Beavers was sipping his coffee as we waved goodbye to him. I whispered to Savannah as we walked to the pickup. "Nice work, Mata Hari."

Luke came walking up behind us and said, "I'm hot. How 'bout let's go swimming in Key Biscayne."

"What time are we coming back for the Snow?" I asked.

"I figure about midnight," he said.

We watched the moon rise like a pale watermark against the eastern sky. We swam until the sun began to set in an Atlantic so different from the ocean that broke against our part of the eastern seaboard that it did not seem possible that they were related in any way. The Florida ocean was clear-eyed and aquamarine, and I had never been able to see my own feet as I walked chest-deep in the sea.

"This water don't seem right," Luke said, expressing exactly what I felt.

The sea has always been feminine to me but Florida had softened its hard edges and tamed the azury depths with clarity. The mystery of Florida deepened on the shore as we ate mangoes for the first time. The fruit tasted foreign but indigenous, like sunlight a tree had changed through patience. We were strangers to a sea you could trust, whose tides were imperceptible and gentle, whose cologne-colored waters were translucent and calm below the palm trees. The moon laid a filament of silver across the water for a hundred miles before it nested in the braids of Savannah's hair. Luke stood up and fished his watch out from his jeans pocket.

"If we get caught tonight, Tom and Savannah, just let me do the talking. I got you into this and it's my responsibility to get you out if we hit trouble. Now let's pray that Mr. Beavers is counting sheep."

Through the window of his small office we could see Mr. Beavers with his head on his desk, sleeping soundly. Luke backed the pickup into a grove of trees by the Cyclone fence and, working quickly, cut a large hole in the fence using his wire cutters. Entering the fence, we made our way through the shadows, passing over the moat of sharks, where we could hear the creatures moving through the water below us in their endless circuit, their horrible punishment for having been born sharks. We were running by the amphitheater when we heard the sound of the killer whale's implosion of breath.

"Wait a minute," Luke said, removing a fish from the bag he had brought for Snow in case she wanted a snack on the ride north.

"No, Luke," I said, alarmed. "We don't have time for no foolishness."

But Luke was running up the stairs into the amphitheater and Savannah and I had no choice but to follow him. In the moonlight we watched him as he climbed the platform and we saw the great fin break the water below him. Then Luke moved to the edge of the platform, and mimicking the gestures of the blond trainer we had witnessed earlier in the day, he made a circular movement with his arm and we saw Dreadnought dive deep into his tank and heard the punished waters slapping against the sides of the aquarium as the invisible whale gathered speed beneath my brother. Luke put the whiting in his right hand and leaned far out over the water.

The whale exploded out from below and took the whiting from Luke's hand without so much as grazing his fingers. Then the lordly fall from space carried the whale over on his side, exposing his brilliant white underbelly, and he washed twenty-three rows of bleachers as he entered the water again in a fabulous wave.

"Stupid, stupid, stupid," I whispered as Luke joined us again.

"Wonderful, wonderful, wonderful," Savannah said, exhilarated.

We ran to *The Amberjack* and went to the storage bin on deck where the crew kept the equipment we knew we would need. Luke pulled out the ropes and the stretcher. He threw the foam rubber mattresses to Savannah. She took them and raced back to the truck to lay them out neatly on the flatbed. Luke and I hurried to the porpoise house and Luke again used his wire cutters to enter the area where the Snow was kept.

We reached her just in time. She was almost motionless in shallow water and I think she would have drowned if we had waited another hour. When we entered the water, she was so drugged that she did not even move. We caught her beneath the head and stomach and moved her over to the side of the pool where we had placed the stretcher. She was so white my hand looked brown against her head. She made a tender, human sound as we floated her across the pool. Savannah returned and the three of us girded the stretcher beneath her in the water and bound her with the ropes in three places.

Again, we passed through the shadows of palms and citrus trees, Luke and I bearing the stretcher like medics in a war zone, keeping low and moving fast. We passed through the opening in the ruined fence and untied the Snow gently and rolled her onto the mattresses. Savannah and I splashed her with the Key Biscayne water we had gathered in buckets and in our beer cooler. Luke closed the tailgate, and running to the cab, he started the motor and eased out of the parking lot and moved down the causeway toward the lights of Miami. I think we were the nearest to getting caught in those first two minutes, because going down that nearly deserted highway, the three Wingo kids from South Carolina were screaming, screaming, screaming.

Soon we had left Miami forever and Luke had his foot pressed against the accelerator almost to the floorboard, and the warm air streamed through our hair as every mile brought us closer to the border of Georgia. Snow's breathing was ragged at first, like the tearing of paper, and once or twice when it seemed as though she had stopped breathing I blew air into her blowhole. She answered me with a breath of her own but the effect of the pills did not seem to wear off until we stopped for gas at Daytona Beach. Then she rallied and was perky for the rest of the trip.

After we got gas, Luke drove the truck out onto the beach and Savannah and I leapt out and filled up the buckets and cooler with fresh seawater, then hopped back in as Luke spun through the sand and made it to the highway again.

"We're doing it. We're doing it," he screamed out the back window to us. "We got five more hours and we'll be home free."

We doused the porpoise with salt water and massaged her from head to tail to keep her circulation going and spoke to her with those phrases of endearment kids normally reserve for dogs. She was supple and pliable and her flesh was satiny to the touch. We sang lullabies to her, recited children's poems and nursery rhymes, and whispered that we were taking her home and she would never have to eat dead fish again. When we crossed into Georgia, Savannah and I danced around the flatbed and Luke had to slow down because he thought we might dance ourselves right out of the truck.

It was right outside of Midway, Georgia, that a highway patrolman pulled Luke over for going about forty miles over the speed limit. Luke said through the back window, "Cover Snow's head with one of those mattresses. I'll handle this."

The sun had already risen and the patrolman was young and slim as a blade. He had that maddening arrogance of the rookie. But Luke bounded out of that truck just bubbling over about something.

"Officer," I heard him say as Savannah and I got Snow's head covered. "I'm so sorry. Honest I am. But I was so excited about catching this here shark and I just had to get it back so my daddy could see it while it was still alive."

The patrolman came over to the truck and whistled as he looked in.

"He's a big 'un," the patrolman said. "But that's no cause for you speeding like that, son."

"You don't understand, Officer," Luke said. "This here is a world record. I caught him with a rod and reel. It's a white shark. They're the real man-eaters. I caught this one near the jetty off Saint Simons Island."

"What'd you catch him with?"

"I caught him with a live shrimp, if you can believe such a thing. They caught a white shark in Florida last year and found a man's boot and shinbone in his stomach."

"I got to give you a ticket, son."

"I expect that, sir. I was speeding I was so excited. You ever catch a fish this big?"

"I'm from Marietta. I once caught a twelve-pound bass in Lake Lanier."

"Then you know exactly how I feel, sir. Look, let me show you his teeth. He's got teeth like razor blades. My poor brother and sister are half dead from trying to hold this rascal down. Let the officer have a look, Tom."

"I don't cotton to seeing no shark, son. Just you run along now and slow it down a bit. I guess you got a right to be excited. That bass I caught, that was the biggest one taken out of Lake Lanier that whole day. My cat ate it before I could show it to my daddy."

"Thank you so much, sir. You sure you don't want to see its teeth? He's got a powerful mouthful."

"I'd sure rather be driving than sitting on that dang thing," the patrolman said to me and Savannah as he walked back to his car.

MY MOTHER was hanging out wash when we came blitzing down the dirt road and Luke made a few triumphant doughnuts on the lawn and we slid to a stop. My mother ran to the truck and did a little softshoe of triumph around the lawn, her arms raised in the air. Luke backed up the truck to the sea wall and we rolled the porpoise back onto the stretcher. Mama kicked off her shoes and the four of us stepped into the high tide and moved out toward deeper water. We held Snow in our arms and walked her into deeper water, letting her get used to the river again. We let her float by herself but she seemed unbalanced and unsure of herself. Luke held her head above the water until I felt her powerful tail flip me off her and she began to swim slowly and unsteadily away from us. For fifteen minutes she looked like a dying animal and it was painful to watch her suffer. We stood on the dock praying for her, my mother leading us through a rosary without beads. The Snow floundered; she seemed to have trouble breathing; her sense of balance and timing were not functioning. Then it changed before our eyes. Instinct returned and she dove and the old sense of rhythm and grace returned in the easy fluency of that dive. She sounded after a long minute and was two hundred yards further out in the river.

"She's made it," Luke yelled, and we gathered together, holding on to each other. I was exhausted, sweaty, famished, but I had never felt so wonderful in my life.

Up she rose again and, turning, she passed us standing on the dock.

We cheered and screamed and wept. And we danced a new dance on our floating dock on the most beautiful island in the world on the finest, the very finest, day of Tom Wingo's life.

THE PIPAL
PANI TIGER

FROM
MAN–EATERS
OF KUMAON

BY JIM CORBETT

Beyond the fact that he was born in a ravine running deep into the foothills and was one of a family of three, I know nothing of his early history.

He was about a year old when, attracted by the calling of a chital hind early one November morning, I found his pug marks in the sandy bed of a little stream known locally as Pipal Pani. I thought at first that he had strayed from his mother's care, but, as week succeeded week and his single tracks showed on the game paths of the forest, I came to the conclusion that the near approach of the breeding season was an all-sufficient reason for his being alone. Jealously guarded one day, protected at the cost of the parent life if necessary, and set adrift the next is the lot of all jungle folk; nature's method of preventing inbreeding.

That winter he lived on peafowl, kakar, small pig, and an occasional chital hind, making his home in a prostrate giant of the forest felled for no apparent reason and hollowed out by time and porcupines. Here he brought most of his kills, basking, when the days were cold, on the smooth bole of the tree, where many a leopard had basked before him.

It was not until January was well advanced that I saw the cub at close quarters. I was out one evening without any definite object in view, when I saw a crow rise from the ground and wipe its beak as it lit on the branch of a tree. Crows, vultures, and magpies always interest me in the jungle, and many are the kills I have found both in India and in Africa with the help of these birds. On the present occasion the crow led me to the scene of an overnight tragedy. A chital had been killed and partly eaten and, attracted to the spot probably as I had been, a party of men passing along the road, distant some fifty yards, had cut up and removed the remains. All that was left of the chital were a few splinters of bone and a little congealed blood off which the crow had lately made his meal. The absence of thick cover and the proximity of the road convinced me that the animal responsible for the kill had not witnessed the removal and that it would return in due course; so I decided to sit up, and made myself as comfortable in a plum tree as the thorns permitted.

I make no apology to you, my reader, if you differ with me on the ethics of the much-debated subject of sitting up over kills. Some of my most pleasant shikar memories center round the hour or two before sunset that I have spent in a tree over a natural kill, ranging from the time when, armed with a muzzle-loader whipped round with brass wire to prevent the cracked barrel from bursting, I sat over a langur killed by a leopard, to a few days ago, when with the most modern rifle across my knees, I watched a tigress and her two full-grown cubs eat up the sambur stag they had killed, and counted myself no poorer for not having secured a trophy.

True, on the present occasion there is no kill below me, but, for the reasons given, that will not affect my chance of a shot; scent to interest the jungle folk there is in plenty in the blood-soaked ground, as witness the old gray-whiskered boar who has been quietly rooting along for the past ten minutes, and who suddenly stiffens to attention as he comes into the line of the blood-tainted wind. His snout held high, and worked as only a pig can work that member, tells him more than I was able to glean from the ground, which showed no tracks; his method of approach, a short excursion to the right and back into the wind, and then a short excursion to the left and again back into the wind, each manœuver bringing him a few yards nearer, indicates the chital was killed by a tiger. Making sure once and again that nothing worth eating has been left, he finally trots off and disappears from view.

Two chital, both with horns in velvet, now appear and from the fact that they are coming down-wind, and making straight for the blood-soaked spot, it is evident they were witnesses to the overnight tragedy. Alternately snuffing the ground, or standing rigid with every muscle tensed for instant flight, they satisfy their curiosity and return the way they came.

Curiosity is not a human monopoly: many an animal's life is cut short by indulging in it. A dog leaves the verandah to bark at a shadow, a deer leaves the herd to investigate a tuft of grass that no wind agitated, and the waiting leopard is provided with a meal.

The sun is nearing the winter line when a movement to the right front attracts attention. An animal has crossed an opening between two bushes at the far end of a wedge of scrub that terminates thirty yards from my tree. Presently the bushes at my end part, and out into the open, with never a look to right or left, steps the cub. Straight up to the spot where his kill had been he goes, his look of expectancy giving place to one of disappointment as he realizes that his chital, killed, possibly, after hours of patient stalking, is gone. The splinters of bone and congealed blood are rejected, and his interest centers on a tree stump lately used as a butcher's block, to which some shreds of flesh are adhering. I was not the only one who carried fire-arms in these jungles and, if the cub was to grow into a tiger, it was necessary he should be taught the danger of carelessly approaching kills in daylight. A scatter-gun and dust-shot would have served my purpose better, but the rifle will have to do this time; and, as he raises his head to smell the stump, my bullet crashes into the hard wood an inch from his nose. Only once in the years that followed did the cub forget that lesson.

The following winter I saw him several times. His ears did not look so big now and he had changed his baby hair for a coat of rich tawny red with well-defined stripes. The hollow tree had been given up to its rightful owners, a pair of leopards, new quarters found in a thick belt of scrub skirting the foothills, and young sambur added to his menu.

On my annual descent from the hills next winter, the familiar pug marks no longer showed on the game paths and at the drinking places, and for several weeks I thought the cub had abandoned his old haunts and gone further afield. Then one morning his absence was explained, for side by side with his tracks were the smaller and more elongated tracks of the mate he had gone to find. I only once saw the tigers, for the cub was a tiger now, together. I had been out before dawn to try to bag a serow that lived on the foothills, and returning along a fire track my attention was arrested by a vulture, perched on the dead limb of a sal tree.

The bird had his back towards me and was facing a short stretch of scrub with dense jungle beyond. Dew was still heavy on the ground, and without a sound I reached the tree and peered round. One antler of a dead sambur, for no living deer would lie in that position, projected above the low bushes. A convenient moss-covered rock afforded my rubber-shod feet silent and safe hold, and as I drew myself erect, the sambur came into full view. The hind quarters had been eaten away, and lying on either side of the kill were the pair, the tiger being on the far side with only his hind legs showing. Both tigers were asleep. Ten feet straight in front, to avoid a dead branch, and thirty feet to the left would give me a shot at the tiger's neck, but in planning the stalk I had forgotten the silent spectator. Where I stood I was invisible to him, but before the ten feet had been covered I came into view and, alarmed at my near proximity, he flapped off his perch, omitting as he did so to notice a thin creeper dependent from a branch above him against which he collided, and came ignominiously to ground. The tigress was up and away in an instant, clearing at a bound the kill and her mate, the tiger not being slow to follow; a possible shot, but too risky with thick jungle ahead where a wounded animal would have all the advantages. To those who have never tried it, I can recommend the stalking of leopards and tigers on their kills as a most pleasant form of sport. Great care should however be taken over the shot, for if the animal is not killed outright, or anchored, trouble is bound to follow.

A week later the tiger resumed his bachelor existence. A change had now come over his nature. Hitherto he had not objected to my visiting his kills but, after his mate left, at the first drag I followed up I was given very clearly to understand that no liberties would in future be permitted. The angry growl of a tiger at close quarters, than which there is no more terrifying sound in the jungles, has to be heard to be appreciated.

Early in March the tiger killed his first full-grown buffalo. I was near the foothills one evening when the agonized bellowing of a buffalo, mingled with the angry roar of a tiger, rang through the forest. I located the sound as coming from a ravine about six hundred yards away. The going was bad, mostly over loose rocks and through thorn bushes, and when I crawled up a steep bluff commanding a view of the ravine the buffalo's struggles were over, and the tiger was nowhere to be seen. For an hour I lay with finger on trigger without seeing anything of the tiger. At dawn next morning I again crawled up the bluff, to find the buffalo lying just as I had left her. The soft ground, torn up by hoof and claw, testified to the desperate nature of the struggle, and it was not until the buffalo had been hamstrung that the tiger had finally succeeded in pulling her down, in a fight which had lasted from ten to fifteen minutes. The tiger's tracks led across the ravine and, on following them up, I found a long smear of blood on a rock, and, a hundred yards further on, another smear on a fallen tree. The wound inflicted by the buffalo's horns was in the tiger's head and sufficiently severe to make the tiger lose all interest in the kill, for he never returned to it.

Three years later the tiger, disregarding the lesson received when a cub (his excuse may have been that it was the close season for tigers), incautiously returned to a kill, over which a zamindar and some of his tenants were sitting at night, and received a bullet in the shoulder which fractured the bone. No attempt was made to follow him up, and thirty-six hours later, his shoulder covered with a swarm of flies, he limped through the compound of the Inspection Bungalow, crossed a bridge flanked on the far side by a double row of tenanted houses, the occupants of which stood at their doors to watch him pass, entered the gate of a walled-in compound and took possession of a vacant godown. Twenty-four hours later, possibly alarmed by the number of people who had collected from neighboring villages to see him, he left the compound the way he had entered it, passed our gate, and made his way to the lower end of our village. A bullock belonging to one of our tenants had died the previous night and had been dragged into some bushes at the edge of the village; this the tiger found, and here he remained a few days, quenching his thirst at an irrigation furrow.

When we came down from the hills two months later the tiger was living on small animals (calves, sheep, goats, etc.) that he was able to catch on the outskirts of the village. By March his wound had healed, leaving his right foot turned inwards. Returning to the forest where he had been wounded, he levied heavy toll on the village cattle, taking, for safety's sake, but one meal off each and in this way killing five times as many as he would ordinarily have done. The zamindar who had wounded him and who had a herd of some four hundred head of cows and buffaloes was the chief sufferer.

In the succeeding years he gained as much in size as in reputation, and many were the attempts made by sportsmen, and others, to bag him.

One November evening, a villager, armed with a single-barrel muzzle-loading gun, set out to try to bag a pig, selecting for his ground machan an isolated bush growing in a twenty-yard-wide *rowkah* (dry watercourse) running down the center of some broken ground. This ground was rectangular, flanked on the long sides by cultivated land and on the short sides by a road, and by a ten-foot canal that formed the boundary between our cultivation and the forest. In front of the man was a four-foot-high bank with a cattle track running along the upper edge; behind him a patch of dense scrub. At 8 p.m. an animal appeared on the track and, taking what aim he could, he fired. On receiving the shot the animal fell off the bank, and passed within a few feet of the man, grunting as it entered the scrub behind. Casting aside his blanket, the man ran to his hut two hundred yards away. Neighbors soon collected and, on hearing the man's account, came to the conclusion that a pig had been hard hit. It would be a pity, they said, to leave the pig for hyenas and jackals to eat, so a lantern was lit and as a party of six bold spirits set out to retrieve the bag, one of my tenants (who declined to join the expedition, and who confessed to me later that he had no stomach for looking for wounded pig in dense scrub in the dark) suggested that the gun should be loaded and taken.

His suggestion was accepted and, as a liberal charge of powder was being rammed home, the wooden ramrod jammed and broke inside the barrel. A trivial accident which undoubtedly saved the lives of six men. The broken rod was eventually and after great trouble extracted, the gun loaded, and the party set off.

Arrived at the spot where the animal had entered the bushes, a careful search was made and, on blood being found, every effort to find the "pig" was made; it was not until the whole area had been combed out that the quest for that night was finally abandoned. Early next morning the search was resumed, with the addition of my informant of weak stomach, who was a better woodsman than his companions and who, examining the ground under a bush where there was a lot of blood, collected and brought some bloodstained hairs to me, which I recognized as tiger's hairs. A brother sportsman was with me for the day and together we went to have a look at the ground.

The reconstruction of jungle events from signs on the ground has always held great interest for me. True, one's deductions are sometimes wrong, but they are also sometimes right. In the present instance I was right in placing the wound in the inner forearm of the right foreleg, but was wrong in assuming the leg had been broken and that the tiger was a young animal and a stranger to the locality.

There was no blood beyond the point where the hairs had been found and, as tracking on the hard ground was impossible, I crossed the canal to where the cattle track ran through a bed of sand. Here from the pug marks I found that the wounded animal was not a young tiger, as I had assumed, but my old friend the Pipal Pani tiger, who, when taking a short cut through the village, had in the dark been mistaken for a pig.

Once before when badly wounded he had passed through the settlement without harming man or beast, but he was older now, and if driven by pain and hunger might do considerable damage. A disconcerting prospect, for the locality was thickly populated, and I was due to leave within the week, to keep an engagement that could not be put off.

For three days I searched every bit of the jungle between

the canal and the foothills, an area of about four square miles, without finding any trace of the tiger. On the fourth afternoon, as I was setting out to continue the search, I met an old woman and her son hurriedly leaving the jungle. From them I learnt that the tiger was calling near the foothills and that all the cattle in the jungle had stampeded. When out with a rifle I invariably go alone; it is safer in a mix-up, and one can get through the jungle more silently. However, I stretched a point on this occasion, and let the boy accompany me, since he was very keen on showing me where he had heard the tiger.

Arrived at the foothills, the boy pointed to a dense bit of cover, bounded on the far side by the fire track to which I have already referred, and on the near side by the Pipal Pani stream. Running parallel to and about a hundred yards from the stream was a shallow depression some twenty feet wide, more or less open on my side and fringed with bushes on the side nearer the stream. A well-used path crossed the depression at right angles. Twenty yards from the path, and on the open side of the depression, was a small tree. If the tiger came down the path he would in all likelihood stand for a shot on clearing the bushes. Here I decided to take my stand and, putting the boy into the tree with his feet on a level with my head and instructing him to signal with his toes if from his raised position he saw the tiger before I did, I put my back to the tree and called.

You who have spent as many years in the jungle as I have need no description of the call of a tigress in search of a mate, and to you less fortunate ones I can only say that the call, to acquire which necessitates close observation and the liberal use of throat salve, cannot be described in words.

To my great relief, for I had crawled through the jungle for three days with finger on trigger, I was immediately answered from a distance of about five hundred yards, and for half an hour thereafter—it may have been less and certainly appeared more—the call was tossed back and forth. On the one side the urgent summons of the king, and on the other, the subdued and coaxing answer of his handmaiden. Twice the boy signaled, but I had as yet seen nothing of the tiger, and it was not until the setting sun was flooding the forest with golden light that he suddenly appeared, coming down the path at a fast walk with never a pause as he cleared the bushes. When half-way across the depression, and just as I was raising the rifle, he turned to the right and came straight towards me.

This manœuver, unforeseen when selecting my stand, brought him nearer than I had intended he should come and, moreover, presented me with a head shot which at that short range I was not prepared to take. Resorting to an old device, learned long years ago and successfully used on similar occasions, the tiger was brought to a stand without being alarmed. With one paw poised, he slowly raised his head, exposing as he did so his chest and throat. After the impact of the heavy bullet, he struggled to his feet and tore blindly through the forest, coming down with a crash within a few yards of where, attracted by the calling of a chital hind one November morning, I had first seen his pug marks.

It was only then that I found he had been shot under a misapprehension, for the wound which I feared might make him dangerous proved on examination to be almost healed and caused by a pellet of lead having severed a small vein in his right forearm.

Pleasure at having secured a magnificent trophy—he measured 10′ 3″ over curves and his winter coat was in perfect condition—was not unmixed with regret, for never again would the jungle folk and I listen with held breath to his deep-throated call resounding through the foothills, and never again would his familiar pug marks show on the game paths that he and I had trodden for fifteen years.

OUT OF AFRICA

BY ISAK DINESEN

Lulu was a young antelope of the bushbuck tribe, which is perhaps the prettiest of all the African antelopes. They are a little bigger than the fallow-deer; they live in the woods, or in the bush, and are shy and fugitive, so that they are not seen as often as the antelopes of the plains. But the Ngong Hills, and the surrounding country, were good places for bushbuck, and if you had your camp in the hills, and were out hunting in the early morning, or at sunset, you would see them come out of the bush into the glades, and as the rays of the sun fell upon them their coats shone red as copper. The male has a pair of delicately turned horns.

Lulu became a member of my household in this way:

I drove one morning from the farm to Nairobi. My mill on the farm had burnt down a short time before, and I had had to drive into town many times to get the insurance settled and paid out; in this early morning I had my head filled with figures and estimates. As I came driving along the Ngong Road a little group of Kikuyu children shouted to me from the roadside, and I saw that they were holding a very small bushbuck up for me to see. I knew that they would have found the fawn in the bush, and that now they wanted to sell it to me, but I was late for an appointment in Nairobi, and I had no thought for this sort of thing, so I drove on.

When I was coming back in the evening and was driving past the same place, there was again a great shout from the side of the road and the small party was still there, a little tired and disappointed, for they may have tried to sell the fawn to other people passing by in the course of the day, but keen now to get the deal through before the sun was down, and they held up the fawn high to tempt me. But I had had a long day in town, and some adversity about the insurance, so that I did not care to stop or talk, and I just drove on past them. I did not even think of them when I was back in my house, and dined and went to bed.

The moment that I had fallen asleep I was woken up again by a great feeling of terror. The picture of the boys and the small buck, which had now collected and taken shape, stood out before me, clearly, as if it had been painted, and I sat up in bed as appalled as if someone had been trying to choke me. What, I thought, would become of the fawn in the hands of the captors who had stood with it in the heat of the long day, and had held it up by its joined legs? It was surely too young to eat on its own. I myself had driven past it twice on the same day, like the priest and the Levite in one, and had given no thought to it, and now, at this moment, where was it? I got up in a real panic and woke up all my houseboys. I told them that the fawn must be found and brought me in the morning, or they would all of them get their dismissal from my service. They were immediately up to the idea. Two of my boys had been in the car with me the same day, and had not shown the slightest interest in the children or the fawn; now they came forward, and gave the others a long list of details of the place and the hour and of the family of the boys. It was a moonlight night; my people all took off and spread in the landscape in a lively discussion of the situation; I heard them expatiating on the fact that they were all to be dismissed in case the bushbuck were not found.

Early next morning when Farah brought me in my tea, Juma came in with him and carried the fawn in his arms. It was a female, and we named her Lulu, which I was told was the Swaheli word for a pearl.

Lulu by that time was only as big as a cat, with large quiet purple eyes. She had such delicate legs that you feared they would not bear being folded up and unfolded again, as she lay down and rose up. Her ears were smooth as silk and exceedingly expressive. Her nose was as black as a truffle. Her diminutive hoofs gave her all the air of a young Chinese lady of the old school, with laced feet. It was a rare experience to hold such a perfect thing in your hands.

Lulu soon adapted herself to the house and its inhabitants and behaved as if she were at home. During the first weeks the polished floors in the rooms were a problem in her life, and when she got outside the carpets her legs went away from her to all four sides; it looked catastrophic but she did not let it worry her much and in the end she learnt to walk on the bare floors with a sound like a succession of little angry finger-taps. She was extraordinarily neat in all her habits. She was headstrong already as a child, but when I stopped her from doing the things she wanted to do, she behaved as if she said: Anything rather than a scene.

Kamante brought her up on a sucking-bottle, and he also shut her up at night, for we had to be careful of her as the leopards were up round the house after nightfall. So she held to him and followed him about. From time to time when he did not do what she wanted, she gave his thin legs a hard butt with her young head, and she was so pretty that you could not help, when you looked upon the two together, seeing them as a new paradoxical illustration to the tale of the Beauty and the Beast. On the strength of this great beauty and gracefulness, Lulu obtained for herself a commanding position in the house, and was treated with respect by all.

In Africa I never had dogs of any other breed than the Scotch Deerhound. There is no more noble or gracious kind of dog. They must have lived for many centuries with men to understand and fall in with our life and its conditions the way they do. You will also find them in old paintings and tapestries, and they have in themselves a tendency to change, by their looks and manners, their surroundings into tapestry; they bring with them a feudal atmosphere. . . .

Now my dogs understood Lulu's power and position in the house. The arrogance of the great hunters was like water with her. She pushed them away from the milk-bowl and from their favourite places in front of the fire. I had tied a small bell on a rein round Lulu's neck, and there came a time when the dogs, when they heard the jingle of it approaching through the rooms, would get up resignedly from their warm beds by the fireplace, and go and lie down in some other part of the room. Still nobody could be of a gentler demeanour than Lulu was when she came and lay down, in the manner of a perfect lady who demurely gathers her skirts about her and will be in no one's way. She drank the milk with a polite, pernickety mien, as if she had been pressed by an overkind hostess. She insisted on being scratched behind the ears, in a pretty forbearing way, like a young wife who pertly permits her husband a caress.

When Lulu grew up and stood in the flower of her young loveliness she was a slim delicately rounded doe, from her nose to her toes unbelievably beautiful. She looked like a minutely painted illustration to Heine's song of the wise and gentle gazelles by the flow of the river Ganges.

But Lulu was not really gentle, she had the so-called devil in her. She had, to the highest degree, the feminine trait of appearing to be exclusively on the defensive, concentrated on guarding the integrity of her being, when she was really, with every force in her, bent upon the offensive. Against whom? Against the whole world. Her moods grew beyond control or computation, and she would go for my horse, if he displeased her. I remembered old Hagenbeck in Hamburg, who had said that of all animal races, the carnivora included, the deer are the least to be relied on, and that you may trust a leopard, but if you trust a young stag, sooner or later he falls upon you in the rear.

Lulu was the pride of the house even when she behaved like a real shameless young coquette; but we did not make her happy. Sometimes she walked away from the house for hours, or for a whole afternoon. Sometimes when the spirit came upon her and her discontent with her surroundings reached a climax, she would perform, for the satisfaction of her own heart, on the lawn in front of the house, a war-dance, which looked like a brief zig-zagged prayer to Satan.

"Oh Lulu," I thought, "I know that you are marvellously strong and that you can leap higher than your own height.

You are furious with us now, you wish that we were all dead, and indeed we should be so if you could be bothered to kill us. But the trouble is not as you think now, that we have put up obstacles too high for you to jump, and how could we possibly do that, you great leaper? It is that we have put up no obstacles at all. The great strength is in you, Lulu, and the obstacles are within you as well, and the thing is, that the fullness of time has not yet come."

One evening Lulu did not come home and we looked out for her in vain for a week. This was a hard blow to us all. A clear note had gone out of the house and it seemed no better than other houses. I thought of the leopards by the river and one evening I talked about them to Kamante.

As usual he waited some time before he answered, to digest my lack of insight. It was not till a few days later that he approached me upon the matter. "You believe that Lulu is dead, Msabu," he said.

I did not like to say so straight out, but I told him I was wondering why she did not come back.

"Lulu," said Kamante, "is not dead. But she is married."

This was pleasant, surprising, news, and I asked him how he knew of it.

"Oh yes," he said, "she is married. She lives in the forest with her *bwana*"—her husband, or master. "But she has not forgotten the people; most mornings she is coming back to the house. I lay out crushed maize to her at the back of the kitchen, then just before the sun comes up, she walks round there from the woods and eats it. Her husband is with her, but he is afraid of the people because he has never known them. He stands below the big white tree by the other side of the lawn. But up to the houses he dare not come."

I told Kamante to come and fetch me when he next saw Lulu. A few days later before sunrise he came and called me out. . . .

A bird began to sing, and then I heard, a little way off in the forest, the tinkling of a bell. Yes, it was a joy, Lulu was back, and about in her old places! It came nearer, I could follow her movements by its rhythm; she was walking, stopping, walking on again. A turning round one of the boys' huts brought her upon us. It suddenly became an unusual and amusing thing to see a bushbuck so close to the house. She stood immovable now, she seemed to be prepared for the sight of Kamante, but not for that of me. But she did not make off, she looked at me without fear and without any remembrance of our skirmishes of the past or of her own ingratitude in running away without warning.

Lulu of the woods was a superior, independent being, a change of heart had come upon her, she was in possession. If I had happened to have known a young princess in exile, and while she was still a pretender to the throne, and had met her again in her full queenly estate after she had come into her rights, our meeting would have had the same character. Lulu showed no more meanness of heart than King Louis Philippe did, when he declared that the King of France did not remember the grudges of the Duke of Orleans. She was now the complete Lulu. The spirit of offensive had gone from her; for whom, and why, should she attack? She was standing quietly on her divine rights. She remembered me enough to feel that I was nothing to be afraid of. For a minute she gazed at me; her purple smoky eyes were absolutely without expression and did not wink, and I remembered that the Gods or Goddesses never wink, and felt that I was face to face with the ox-eyed Hera. She lightly nipped a leaf of grass as she passed me, made one pretty little leap, and walked on to the back of the kitchen, where Kamante had spread maize on the ground.

Kamante touched my arm with one finger and then pointed it towards the woods. As I followed the direction, I saw, under a tall Cape-chestnut tree, a male bushbuck, a small tawny silhouette at the outskirt of the forest, with a fine pair of horns, immovable like a tree-stem. Kamante observed him for some time, and then laughed.

"Look here now," he said. "Lulu has explained to her husband that there is nothing up by the houses to be afraid of, but all the same he dares not come. Every morning he thinks that to-day he will come all the way, but, when he sees the house and the people, he gets a cold stone in the stomach"—this is a common thing in the Native world, and often gets in the way of the work on the farm—"and then he stops by the tree."

For a long time Lulu came to the house in the early mornings. Her clear bell announced that the sun was up on the hills. I used to lie in bed, and wait for it. Sometimes she stayed away for a week or two, and we missed her and began to talk of the people who went to shoot in the hills. But then again my houseboys announced: "Lulu is here," as if it had been the married daughter of the house on a visit. A few times more I also saw the bushbuck's silhouette amongst the trees, but Kamante had been right, and he never collected enough courage to come all the way to the house.

One day, as I came back from Nairobi, Kamante was keeping watch for me outside the kitchen door, and stepped forward, much excited, to tell me that Lulu had been to the farm the same day and had had her Toto—her baby—with her. Some days after, I myself had the honour to meet her amongst the boys' huts, much on the alert and not to be trifled with, with a very small fawn at her heels, as delicately tardive in his movements as Lulu herself had been when we first knew her. This was just after the long rains, and, during those summer months, Lulu was to be found near the houses in the afternoon, as well as at daybreak. She would even be round there at midday, keeping in the shadow of the huts.

Lulu's fawn was not afraid of the dogs, and would let them sniff him all over, but he could not get used to the Natives or to me, and if we ever tried to get hold of him, the mother and the child were off.

Lulu herself would never, after her first long absence from the house, come so near to any of us that we could touch her. In other ways she was friendly, she understood that we wanted to look at her fawn, and she would take a piece of sugar-cane from an outstretched hand. She walked up to the open dining-room door, and gazed thoughtfully into the twilight of the rooms, but she never again crossed the threshold. She had by this time lost her bell, and came and went away in silence.

My houseboys suggested that I should let them catch Lulu's fawn, and keep him as we had once kept Lulu. But I thought it would make a boorish return to Lulu's elegant confidence in us.

It also seemed to me that the free union between my house and the antelope was a rare, honourable thing. Lulu came in from the wild world to show that we were on good terms with it, and she made my house one with the African landscape, so that nobody could tell where the one stopped and the other began. Lulu knew the place of the Giant Forest-hog's lair and had seen the Rhino copulate. In Africa there is a cuckoo which sings in the middle of the hot days in the midst of the forest, like the sonorous heartbeat of the world, I had never had the luck to see her, neither had anyone that I knew, for nobody could tell me how she looked. But Lulu had perhaps walked on a narrow green deerpath just under the branch on which the cuckoo was sitting. I was then reading a book about the old great Empress of China, and of how after the birth of her son, young Yahanola came on a visit to her old home; she set forth from the Forbidden City in her golden, green-hung palanquin. My house, I thought, was now like the house of the young Empress's father and mother.

The two antelopes, the big and the small, were round by my house all that summer; sometimes there was an interval of a fortnight, or three weeks, between their visits, but at other times we saw them every day. In the beginning of the next rainy season my houseboys told me that Lulu had come back with a new fawn. I did not see the fawn myself, for by this time they did not come up quite close to the house, but later I saw three bushbucks together in the forest.

The league between Lulu and her family and my house lasted for many years. The bushbucks were often in the neighbourhood of the house; they came out of the woods and went back again as if my grounds were a province of the wild country. They came mostly just before sunset, and first moved in amongst the trees like delicate dark silhouettes on the dark green, but when they stepped out to graze on the lawn in the light of the afternoon sun their coats shone like copper. One of them was Lulu, for she came up near to the house, and walked about sedately, pricking her ears when a car arrived, or when we opened a window; and the dogs would know her. She became darker in colour with age. Once I came driving up in front of my house with a friend and found three bushbucks on the terrace there, round the salt that was laid out for my cows.

It was a curious thing that apart from the first big bushbuck, Lulu's bwana, who had stood under the Cape-chestnut with his head up, no male bushbuck was amongst the antelopes that came to my house. It seemed that we had to do with a forest matriarchy.

The hunters and naturalists of the Colony took an interest in my bushbucks, and the Game Warden drove out to the farm to see them, and did see them there. A correspondent wrote about them in the *East African Standard*.

The years in which Lulu and her people came round to my house were the happiest of my life in Africa. For that reason, I came to look upon my acquaintance with the forest antelopes as upon a great boon, and a token of friendship from Africa. All the country was in it, good omens, old covenants, a song:

> Make haste, my beloved and be thou like to a roe or to a young hart upon the mountain of spices.

During my last years in Africa I saw less and less of Lulu and her family. Within the year before I went away I do not think that they ever came. Things had changed. South of my farm land had been given out to farmers and the forest had been cleared here, and houses built. Tractors were heaving up and down where the glades had been. Many of the new settlers were keen sportsmen and the rifles sang in the landscape. I believe that the game withdrew to the West and went into the woods of the Masai Reserve.

I do not know how long an antelope lives; probably Lulu has died a long time ago.

Often, very often, in the quiet hours of daybreak, I have dreamed that I have heard Lulu's clear bell, and in my sleep my heart has run full of joy, I have woken up expecting something very strange and sweet to happen, just now, in a moment.

When I have then lain and thought of Lulu, I have wondered if in her life in the woods she ever dreamed of the bell. Would there pass in her mind, like shadows upon water, pictures of people and dogs?

If I know a song of Africa—I thought—of the Giraffe, and the African new moon lying on her back, of the ploughs in the fields, and the sweaty faces of the coffee-pickers, does Africa know a song of me? Would the air over the plain quiver with a colour that I had had on, or the children invent a game in which my name was, or the full moon throw a shadow over the gravel of the drive that was like me, or would the eagles of Ngong look out for me? . . .

FROM
EYELIDS OF
MORNING

BY ALISTAIR GRAHAM

Most of the crocs were out of range of a hunter walking along the water's edge. So we had to go in after them. Our technique was for one of us to walk in front with a torch, followed closely by a rifleman. Behind him came one of the men to tow our kills along. This was necessary because if we left them on shore they were quickly stolen by the lions or hyenas that followed us when we were hunting at night.

The torch bearer would cast around for crocs, whose eyes shine red in torchlight. Finding a suitable one, we would try to approach without alarming the wary animal, which more often than not would silently submerge and disappear. Once down, a croc can last up to an hour without breathing. Although the light dazzled the crocs, many things worked against us to warn them of danger. It was essential to keep downwind, for their sense of smell is extremely good. Their hearing is keen too, and this was our greatest problem, for the ground underfoot was seldom easy to traverse soundlessly. Mostly it was a vile ooze studded with sharp chunks of lava and rocks ("sharp stones are under him: he spreadeth sharp pointed things upon the mire"). Every now and then someone would plunge into a soft patch, for it was a constant struggle to keep upright. Many were the crocs lost at the last moment as somebody subsided noisily into the lake. Scattered about were hippo footprints, deep holes in which the lava chunks clutched at you like gin traps. A shoe torn off deep beneath the mud was almost impossible to retrieve without alarming a croc floating a few feet away.

The extensive weed beds the crocs liked were worse than the open water, for the weed contained sharp spicules that lacerated your legs. And in it dwelt a fiendish beast in the form of a small water bug with a bite like a bee sting. It was strange how often their attacks coincided with the critical moment when the gunman was about to squeeze the trigger, causing him to give an involuntary, disastrous twitch.

Early evening before the wind got up was the worst time, for one had to be particularly quiet in the still air. But the major problem was lake flies. These tiny insects swarmed in thousands around the light, constantly flying into our eyes and under our clothing. Sometimes the swarms were so dense that they reflected enough light back from the torch to expose us to the crocs. Or they would collect in the pool of light reflected off the water where the croc was, bothering it as they did us, so that it would submerge to avoid them. When the wind got up hunting was easier, for it masked our noise and dispersed the lake flies. But then the waves jostled us, making shooting more difficult, and late at night, after one had fallen over or waded into deep water, it was bitterly cold. Often we would startle six-foot Nile perch that swam off with vigor enough to knock us off our feet. Their heads were hard as iron when they collided with your shins.

Floating crocs presented small targets, for only their eyes and the tops of their heads were above water. To guarantee a hit each time we found we had to get within fifteen yards. To shoot at greater distances meant occasional misses, and we found that in the long run we got better results by patiently getting really close.

Having fired at a croc, it would invariably disappear beneath the muddy water, whether it was wounded, dead, or alive. If hit it was often not far under, and a foot would break the surface as it slowly rolled over and over. Usually, though, the bullet caused a sudden wriggle of its tail that drove it rapidly several yards even if it was dead. Thus by the time we stumbled to the spot where the croc had been shot there was seldom any sign of it, nor any means of telling whether it was dead or alive. So we would search for it by treading about until our toes bumped into it, at which point the success or otherwise of the shot would become apparent. As the dead ones give reflex movements long after death, the process of recovery was always full of scaly surprises.

The water was usually two or three feet deep, so once we located the croc we had to raise it to the surface, still unsure if it was alive. A stunned croc tends to lie motionless until disturbed, whereupon it abruptly regains consciousness. Once after "treading up" an eight-footer we took for dead, Peter began to tie a rope around its neck. Without warning the beast reared up with a violent thrashing. Its head struck Peter square in the middle of his chest with a noise like a mallet driving in a tent peg. The heavy bone of a croc's skull is covered only by a paper-thin layer of skin, and apparently it felt like being hit by a car. Luckily it did not crack his sternum, but the bruise lasted for weeks.

Of all the distasteful tasks we expected the Turkana to

perform, night hunting was the most hated. To go into the water in the dark and deliberately provoke crocodiles was to them ridiculous. It was only by appealing to their pride that I got them to do it at all. When Peter was not there I had to rely on one of the men to wield the torch, which meant standing in front of me, i.e., between me and the croc, while I shot. It was all I could do to aim, so hard did they shiver; and our respective ideas of what constituted close range differed widely.

My biggest difficulty was persuading them to hold their ground whenever the situation looked menacing. Once, while hunting with Tukoi in very shallow water, a magnum croc surfaced about six feet away. We had not known it was there and the abruptness of its appearance was alarming. Although a large croc so close looks fearsome, it is easy to kill at that range, and whipping round, I raised the gun to fire. But Tukoi took off like a reedbuck, his feet in the shallow water sounding like the skittering of a duck as it flies off water. The light went with him, of course, and just then the croc lunged past for deeper water, actually brushing my legs as it did so. There is at such times an awful moment of apprehension as one waits in the dark to find out whether the animal is attacking or fleeing.

On another occasion I was hunting in a patch of swamp where a lot of *msuaki* bushes had been drowned by the lake. Going along the water's edge on dry land, we approached a croc near the shore. I fired, but it was a bad shot, and the croc, wounded, made straight for us. Just as I was about to fire again, having let the croc get really close, my torch bearer fled. I never discovered if the croc was simply confused by its wound or attacking me, but in this case I think the latter.

As the light disappeared I leapt aside and the croc stormed past me in the dark. Moments later a violent commotion began in the bush behind me, where the croc was thrashing around and roaring. I shouted, not very politely, for the torch, and then saw what had happened. The croc's momentum had driven it firmly beneath the twisted stem of a fallen *msuaki* bush, where it wriggled helplessly, pinned to the ground.

Holding the torch was bad enough, but what the Turkana flatly refused to do was "tread up" the dead bodies. We did not blame them and accepted that as our duty. It was a lot easier on the nerves with a pistol in one hand. But in this as in other matters the Wildman was an exception, and far from having to encourage him, we had to restrain him.

The Wildman's night shooting debut was typical. He had been told by the others what to do and followed quietly behind us as we approached a croc. I shot at it, and we started looking for the body. After several minutes of fruitless search I realized it was probably only wounded. The Wildman meanwhile had been searching with us, and suddenly with a triumphant whoop he reached down into the water and came up clutching an enraged and wriggling croc. Scorning the beast's snapping jaws and whipping tail he staggered towards us to show his find. I gestured to him to let go of it, a command he found rather puzzling, and very reluctantly he dropped it into the lake, where I could finish it off.

We got the others to explain to him about wounded crocs and he agreed to be more circumspect in the future, though it in no way dampened his spirits. It seemed that he looked upon night shooting simply as a very fine way to spend an evening.

We got a taste of what could happen with a wounded croc

midway through the survey, and the scare of that night was a sharp reminder to shoot accurately. Peter and I were hunting in Moite Bay, along a rocky shore with deep water only a few yards out. The slippery stones underfoot made the going extremely difficult. The air was still and cold, with everything around us black as Egypt's night. Behind loomed the mountain, brooding over the bay, the haunt of many large crocs. Altogether it was an eerie place that we seldom hunted. That night we saw a good croc about nine feet long, and approaching successfully, I fired. It seemed a perfectly good shot, and wading up we were surprised when the croc, still very much alive, started thrashing about on the surface, snapping its jaws viciously. I saw that the wound was too far forward, leaving the brain undamaged.

I tried to kill it with my pistol but succeeded only in exciting it further. It began to attack us every time it surfaced, though the wound had dazed it enough for us to dodge each time. Suddenly it disappeared, and thinking that one of my pistol shots had taken effect, we looked for the carcass. The ferocity it had just displayed made us somewhat reluctant, though.

I soon found it. Stumbling around, I bumped into a scaly flank, felt it whip around, and next moment its jaws closed on my leg. I let out a great howl and wrenched my leg clear. Luckily it could not bite with more than a fraction of its normal strength or I would have been unable to free myself so easily; a croc that size is quite capable of killing a man.

Making a last feeble attempt to find the croc, we easily convinced ourselves that it had gone, and went ashore, glad to leave the place. Examining my leg, we found that I had escaped literally from the dragon's mouth, with nothing worse than deep gashes. They bled a lot but eventually healed without trouble.

The Turkana were aghast at our story. Why, they demanded, did I leave the croc alive after it had bitten me? How could I be so incompetent? Was it not a blatant messenger from God bent on mischief? The fact that I had been bitten and then escaped might mean it was a case of mistaken identity—probably the croc was after them, only realizing its error on tasting the wrong leg. This incident upset them much more than it did us, and they never forgot to remind me of my blunder at the start of each new trip to Moite. Somewhere out there in Moite Bay a vengeful crocodile was waiting for someone with a bad conscience.

FROM
THE MOTTLED LIZARD

BY ELSPETH HUXLEY

We advanced slowly towards a hummock crowned with bush, an old degenerated termite heap. Kioko crawled up on hands and knees, then waved me towards him. He had seen something he thought I should shoot. With the rifle in one hand, trying not to get out of breath, I crept up the slope until I lay at Kioko's side. He did not need to point now. About fifty yards away, below us in the open, was a grantii buck, dead and stretched out on his side, and over him crouched a lioness, as I thought, chewing a flank, in a sphinx-like posture, with a twitching tail.

I edged the rifle very slowly to my shoulder and brought the sights together on the easy yellow target. I had never shot at big game before and was not, indeed, supposed to do so; at all costs I must not bungle the shot through over-excitement. I aimed with all the concentration of which I was capable, low down and just behind the shoulder.

The rifle went off with its sharp crack, I heard the smack of the bullet, and the creature gave a convulsive leap, rolled

over and lay there kicking. I stood up and fired into it again.
. . . But . . . it was not a lioness after all but a cheetah. This
robbed the event of its splendour, but all the same I had never
shot a cheetah and ran eagerly towards it where it lay limply
stretched out, muscles twitching and blood on its handsome
black and yellow coat. I never shot an animal without feeling
sorry afterwards and somehow poorer, yet there was a feeling
of pleasure at the cleanness of the shot, a small victory. But
if I had known it was a cheetah perhaps I would not have
fired, for cheetahs were quite harmless and I already had the
skin given me by Alan. Especially I should not have shot it
had I known it was a female cheetah. Kioko knelt down beside
it, ran his hand over its velvety flank and said:

"There are cubs. Look, it has milk."

This was dreadful, and destroyed all the pleasure of the
hunt. Now the helpless blind cubs would mew themselves to
death in some shelter under the rocks.

"Perhaps we can find them," I suggested.

"Eeeh! These *chuis* go a long way to hunt meat."

"Perhaps if we looked for the male, he would show us.
Perhaps he is close by."

"We can look," Kioko said, without any confidence. And
so for a while we searched among the grass and scrub, and
in a shallow gully, but I knew it was a hopeless quest. . . .

On the evening of the day I shot the cheetah, a houseboy
came to say that Kioko wanted to see me. He was standing
near the kitchen with a basket in his hands.

"I have something here to please you," he said. "A *toto*
herding goats has brought them and will sell them for five
shillings." He pulled aside some grass; inside lay two small,
bedraggled objects the size of kittens. I touched them and

they were warm, but lay quite still and silent, paying no attention when I stroked their fur.

"They are nearly dead," Kioko said, "but if you give them milk perhaps they will recover. The *toto* found them in the grass and would have killed them, but God helped us, he took them to his father, who brought them here." It was much more likely that Kioko, scenting a reward, had gone back to look for the cheetah cubs, but that did not matter. He got his five shillings, we found a baby's bottle, and the cubs were offered warm milk and brandy. They were so weak that they would not suck, but I managed to squeeze a little milk into their mouths. Their eyes were closed and they had black markings on their blunt, blind faces. A little strengthened by the milk, they made faint noises like mewings. They spent the night beside the kitchen stove, and when I hurried in first thing next morning, one of them was dead. But the other was mewing for food. This time it took the teat and held on so strongly I had to tug at the bottle to cut short the feed. It had made up its mind to live, and the danger then became that I might overfeed it. Its rough yellow coat grew glossy and its little tummy round as a balloon. The houseboys laughed at it, thinking us absurd to fuss over a small, wild creature that would be useless to everyone if it grew up, and meanwhile was wasting good, fresh milk; but they humoured us, and did not wish it harm.

The survivor was a male, and in two or three days his eyes began to come ungummed. After that he soon grew active and tried to wriggle out of his box. The question of a name was freely discussed. Nothing fitted him completely, and in the end I decided on Rupert. This had always seemed to me a romantic sort of name, perhaps because of Prince Rupert,

Rupert of Hentzau and Rupert Brooke. The Joyces had a box made for him in which he could travel to Thika. . . .

A great deal of everybody's time, and especially mine, was now taken up by Rupert. From the first he was a strong cub and had a good appetite. After a while he started to swallow bits of raw meat, and to explore the house in a tentative manner. He was just like a kitten—which, of course, he was, since cheetahs are related to cats, but possess also certain dog-like features, notably about the feet, which are shaped for galloping and do not have retractable claws. Rupert attached himself closely to me and, after a period in a box, he was allowed to sleep on my bed. I think he was naturally clean, and much easier to house-train than a puppy. But he was worse than a puppy for chewing things. He demolished not only shoes, Tilly's knitting and a mosquito-boot, but gnawed table legs and cushions and ate a valuable book on trees and shrubs that had been left on a chair. Like most children brought up in places with servants, I was extremely untidy and left things lying about. Rupert taught me several sharp lessons; I had to start putting things away, and Tilly remarked that every household ought to have a cheetah, if only to instil the rudiments of tidiness into the young.

When he was small Rupert passed the day in a pen on the lawn with various bones and toys, but when he grew larger he was allowed his freedom and spent a good deal of time chasing birds. To begin with he rollicked with the dachshunds, but when he grew bigger and rolled them over roughly they wisely refused any further dealings, and would lie motionless gazing at him with a look of obstinate entreaty if he invited them to play. Should he refuse to take no for an answer, they would snarl and give a warning snap. This was always enough to quell Rupert. He was not an aggressive type, but rather humble. The only thing he could not resist was an object in motion. Anything that ran had to be chased. When he grew larger, and his spots darkened and became plainer, native strangers would sometimes mistake him for a leopard and take to precipitate flight. Then he would be after them with a few tremendous bounds, and his speed was prodigious. He meant no harm, but to see a hunting animal hurling itself in your direction was, of course, alarming, especially to children. At such times there would be roars from anyone present of "Stand still! Stand still!" and if the stranger had the sense to obey orders, Rupert would halt dead in his tracks—he could stop the fastest rush almost miraculously—give the half-paralyzed *toto* or adult a look of disappointment, and trot away.

To watch Rupert move was always a delight. His spotted skin became supple and soft as chamois leather and the sinews beneath it like wires, there was no fat on his body, and one could see the muscles rippling just under the skin like ears of corn when a wind passes over them. For his size his haunches were immensely powerful and his legs were loosely jointed to his body. He had a tremendous stride, but when he galloped you could not see how his legs moved, he was just a yellow projectile hurtling through the air. Cheetahs are faster than race horses, faster than greyhounds, and, like these, they are designed for speed: streamlined, hard and beautiful. When he was half-grown Rupert had a yellow mane down the ridge of his spine from his broad, flat head to his long, tufted tail. As he grew this disappeared, leaving him short-haired and velvety all over. From quite an early age he had a loud purr, and would rub his hard little head against my knees just like a cat, rumbling with affection. I often wondered what natural advantages a purr could bring to cheetahs or lions: how it helped them to survive, or to live more efficiently; perhaps there were evolutionary luxuries, as it were, and this was one of them. Rupert purred a great deal, and had an affectionate nature. I do not remember his ever showing ill-temper towards a human being.

From an early age he made great friends with Mustard and Cress. When they had first arrived the two goats had roamed at will about the garden and explored the house, but they had proved so destructive that Tilly had reluctantly confined them to a paddock. Rupert did his best to make playmates of them, but they were much too dignified to run away from a half-grown cheetah, and Mustard gave him a prod with his horns whenever he made a spring, provoking Rupert into a little squeal of protest. After that Rupert was fascinated by the goats, and spent a lot of time in their company. Mustard unbent sufficiently to make short rushes with a lowered head and pretend to drive Rupert away, while Rupert skipped about just out of reach and then made tremendous bounds across the paddock after an imaginary prey, fetching up short by the wire, spinning round and leaping towards Mustard, who butted at him all over again. Cress was more aloof, gazing into space, when he approached, with the air of a scholar intent on some esoteric calculation.

Rupert's favourite occupation was to come out for a ride. At first, his sudden movements had upset the ponies and they never quite got used to him; for his part he paid them no attention, and never tried to make friends. But as soon as he heard the jingle of a bit and the click of hooves he would dash out of the house and make short rushes of anticipation on the lawn, chasing a wagtail or even a butterfly. Then he would lope along at my side for a while, M'zee showing by the prick of his ears that he knew the creature was there, and was not going to give him any encouragement. Once away from the plantation, Rupert would be off in a yellow flash into the grass and bush to see what he could find: usually a flock of goats, who did not behave so disdainfully as Mustard and Cress but took to their heels, bleating frantically and crowding together. The small goatherd would squeal and fly too, throwing his stick in Rupert's direction in a desperate effort to perform his duty, and make headlong for his home. Cries and shouts from the women would summon an older youth to round up the goats, shaking his stick at Rupert, who by that time was lying down in the grass watching the confusion he had created with, I always felt, a sardonic pleasure. I was afraid that one day he would pounce upon a straggler and demolish it, and these rides were nerve-racking experiences, but Rupert enjoyed them so much that I could not leave him behind.

This was also very hard to do. The only method was to shut him in a loose box, where he fretted and sulked. Like all pets, Rupert was a responsibility. I could not take him with me to report polo tournaments, and it was always an anxiety to leave him behind. On these occasions, Njombo looked after him. He trusted Njombo, whom I believed to be fond of him, and who would stroke and pat his head and make him purr. At the same time Njombo was naturally not as devoted to him as I was, and at night returned to his hut, some distance away, leaving Rupert alone in a loose box which anyone could enter. I got a padlock and impressed on Njombo the need to fasten the stable door in case any of the

Kikuyu tried to poison him, but I could not be sure this was done, and in any case a padlock could be easily broken.

Although he never actually harmed the goats, Rupert soon discovered the joys of chasing duikers and steinbuck. He was off like a rocket as soon as the buck bounded from his form, and generally sprang before it had gone twenty or thirty yards. He did not bite it in the back of the neck as a lion does, but knocked it sideways with a kind of bump and then sprang and ripped its throat open. The buck died instantly and cleanly, but my feelings were torn between sympathy for Rupert, who so much enjoyed the hunt it was his very nature to indulge in, and for the buck, who did not have much chance of escape, and looked so pathetic when they were bedraggled and bloody. Now and again, however, by jinking about among the shambas and doubling back in its tracks, a clever buck managed to elude Rupert, and then he had no desire to go on chasing it, and no hunter's cunning. A short, lightning rush and it was all over—either he brought the prey down or he missed it, and if he missed it he did not fret or search, but waited for the next opportunity. Of course, he was not hungry, and might have behaved differently if he had been. He hunted on sight alone, and I never saw him cast round for a scent.

My principal fear was that one day Rupert might be mistaken for a leopard and speared, or that he would be poisoned. The Kikuyu did not like wild animals of any kind, even when they knew them to be harmless like Rupert. Anything wild was, in their opinion, better dead, whether a bird or an elephant. And a cheetah skin, although nothing like so valuable as a leopard, would fetch a few shillings. It was unlikely that any of the Kikuyu living on our land would venture to harm him, but people in the reserve might well be less inhibited. I seldom let Rupert out of my sight, but when we went away always felt a niggling anxiety. I was devoted to him, even more perhaps than to M'zee, and determined to keep him with me for the rest of his life, or of mine: no one seemed to know the normal life-span of a cheetah.

MOWGLI'S BROTHERS

FROM
THE JUNGLE BOOK

BY RUDYARD KIPLING

It was seven o'clock of a very warm evening in the Seeonee hills when Father Wolf woke up from his day's rest, scratched himself, yawned, and spread out his paws one after the other to get rid of the sleepy feeling in the tips. Mother Wolf lay with her big gray nose dropped across her four tumbling, squealing cubs, and the moon shone into the mouth of the cave where they all lived. "Augrh!" said Father Wolf, "it is time to hunt again"; and he was going to spring downhill when a little shadow with a bushy tail crossed the threshold and whined: "Good luck go with you, O Chief of the Wolves; and good luck and strong white teeth go with the noble children, that they may never forget the hungry in this world."

It was the jackal—Tabaqui, the Dish-licker—and the wolves of India despise Tabaqui because he runs about making mischief, and telling tales, and eating rags and pieces of leather from the village rubbish-heaps. They are afraid of him too, because Tabaqui, more than any one else in the jungle, is apt to go mad, and then he forgets that he was ever afraid of any one, and runs through the forest biting everything in his way. Even the tiger hides when little Tabaqui goes mad, for madness is the most disgraceful thing that can overtake a wild creature. We call it hydrophobia, but they call it *dewanee*—the madness—and run.

"Enter, then, and look," said Father Wolf, stiffly; "but there is no food here."

"For a wolf, no," said Tabaqui; "but for so mean a person as myself a dry bone is a good feast. Who are we, the Gidur-log [the Jackal People], to pick and choose?" He scuttled to the back of the cave, where he found the bone of a buck with some meat on it, and sat cracking the end merrily.

"All thanks for this good meal," he said, licking his lips. "How beautiful are the noble children! How large are their eyes! And so young too! Indeed, indeed, I might have remembered that the children of kings are men from the beginning."

Now, Tabaqui knew as well as any one else that there is nothing so unlucky as to compliment children to their faces; and it pleased him to see Mother and Father Wolf look uncomfortable.

Tabaqui sat still, rejoicing in the mischief that he had made, and then he said spitefully:

"Shere Khan, the Big One, has shifted his hunting-grounds. He will hunt among these hills during the next moon, so he has told me."

Shere Khan was the tiger who lived near the Waingunga River, twenty miles away.

"He has no right!" Father Wolf began angrily. "By the Law of the Jungle he has no right to change his quarters without fair warning. He will frighten every head of game within ten miles; and I—I have to kill for two, these days."

"His mother did not call him Lungri [the Lame One] for nothing," said Mother Wolf, quietly. "He has been lame in one foot from his birth. That is why he has only killed cattle. Now the villagers of the Waingunga are angry with him, and he has come here to make *our* villagers angry. They will scour the jungle for him when he is far away, and we and our children must run when the grass is set alight. Indeed, we are very grateful to Shere Khan!"

"Shall I tell him of your gratitude?" said Tabaqui.

"Out!" snapped Father Wolf. "Out, and hunt with thy master. Thou hast done harm enough for one night."

"I go," said Tabaqui, quietly. "Ye can hear Shere Khan below in the thickets. I might have saved myself the message."

Father Wolf listened, and in the dark valley that ran down to a little river, he heard the dry, angry, snarly, singsong whine of a tiger who has caught nothing and does not care if all the jungle knows it.

"The fool!" said Father Wolf. "To begin a night's work with that noise! Does he think that our buck are like his fat Waingunga bullocks?"

"H'sh! It is neither bullock nor buck that he hunts to-night," said Mother Wolf; "it is Man." The whine had changed to a sort of humming purr that seemed to roll from every quarter of the compass. It was the noise that bewilders wood-cutters, and gipsies sleeping in the open, and makes them run sometimes into the very mouth of the tiger.

"Man!" said Father Wolf, showing all his white teeth. "Faugh! Are there not enough beetles and frogs in the tanks that he must eat Man—and on our ground too!"

The Law of the Jungle, which never orders anything without a reason, forbids every beast to eat Man except when he is killing to show his children how to kill, and then he must hunt outside the hunting-grounds of his pack or tribe. The real reason for this is that man-killing means, sooner or later, the arrival of white men on elephants, with guns, and hundreds of brown men with gongs and rockets and torches. Then everybody in the jungle suffers. The reason the beasts give among themselves is that Man is the weakest and most defenseless of all living things, and it is unsportsmanlike to touch him. They say too—and it is true—that man-eaters become mangy, and lose their teeth.

The purr grew louder, and ended in the full-throated "Aaarh!" of the tiger's charge.

Then there was a howl—an untigerish howl—from Shere Khan. "He has missed," said Mother Wolf. "What is it?"

Father Wolf ran out a few paces and heard Shere Khan muttering and mumbling savagely, as he tumbled about in the scrub.

"The fool has had no more sense than to jump at a wood-cutters' camp-fire, so he has burned his feet," said Father Wolf, with a grunt. "Tabaqui is with him."

"Something is coming uphill," said Mother Wolf, twitching one ear. "Get ready."

The bushes rustled a little in the thicket, and Father Wolf dropped with his haunches under him, ready for his leap. Then, if you had been watching, you would have seen the most wonderful thing in the world—the wolf checked in mid-spring. He made his bound before he saw what it was he was jumping at, and then he tried to stop himself. The result was that he shot up straight into the air for four or five feet, landing almost where he left the ground.

"Man!" he snapped. "A man's cub. Look!"

Directly in front of him, holding on by a low branch, stood a naked brown baby who could just walk—as soft and as dimpled a little thing as ever came to a wolf's cave at night. He looked up into Father Wolf's face and laughed.

"Is that a man's cub?" said Mother Wolf. "I have never seen one. Bring it here."

A wolf accustomed to moving his own cubs can, if necessary, mouth an egg without breaking it, and though Father Wolf's jaws closed right on the child's back not a tooth even scratched the skin, as he laid it down among the cubs.

"How little! How naked, and—how bold!" said Mother Wolf, softly. The baby was pushing his way between the cubs to get close to the warm hide. "Ahai! He is taking his meal with the others. And so this is a man's cub. Now, was there ever a wolf that could boast of a man's cub among her children?"

"I have heard now and again of such a thing, but never in our pack or in my time," said Father Wolf. "He is altogether without hair, and I could kill him with a touch of my foot. But see, he looks up and is not afraid."

The moonlight was blocked out of the mouth of the cave, for Shere Khan's great square head and shoulders were thrust into the entrance. Tabaqui, behind him, was squeaking: "My Lord, my Lord, it went in here!"

"Shere Khan does us great honor," said Father Wolf, but his eyes were very angry. "What does Shere Khan need?"

"My quarry. A man's cub went this way," said Shere Khan. "Its parents have run off. Give it to me."

Shere Khan had jumped at a wood-cutter's camp-fire, as Father Wolf had said, and was furious from the pain of his burned feet. But Father Wolf knew that the mouth of the cave was too narrow for a tiger to come in by. Even where he was, Shere Khan's shoulders and fore paws were cramped for want of room, as a man's would be if he tried to fight in a barrel.

"The Wolves are a free people," said Father Wolf. "They take orders from the Head of the Pack, and not from any striped cattle-killer. The man's cub is ours—to kill if we choose."

"Ye choose and ye do not choose! What talk is this of choosing? By the Bull that I killed, am I to stand nosing into your dog's den for my fair dues? It is I, Shere Khan, who speak!"

The tiger's roar filled the cave with thunder. Mother Wolf shook herself clear of the cubs and sprang forward, her eyes, like two green moons in the darkness, facing the blazing eyes of Shere Khan.

"And it is I, Raksha [the Demon], who answer. The man's cub is mine, Lungri—mine to me! He shall not be killed. He shall live to run with the Pack and to hunt with the Pack; and in the end, look you, hunter of little naked cubs—frog-eater—fish-killer, he shall hunt *thee!* Now get hence, or by the Sambhur that I killed (*I* eat no starved cattle), back thou goest to thy mother, burned beast of the jungle, lamer than ever thou camest into the world! Go!"

Father Wolf looked on amazed. He had almost forgotten the days when he won Mother Wolf in fair fight from five other wolves, when she ran in the Pack and was not called the Demon for compliment's sake. Shere Khan might have faced Father Wolf, but he could not stand up against Mother Wolf, for he knew that where he was she had all the advantage of the ground, and would fight to the death. So he backed out of the cave-mouth growling, and when he was clear he shouted:

"Each dog barks in his own yard! We will see what the Pack will say to this fostering of man-cubs. The cub is mine, and to my teeth he will come in the end, O bush-tailed thieves!"

Mother Wolf threw herself down panting among the cubs, and Father Wolf said to her gravely:

"Shere Khan speaks this much truth. The cub must be shown to the Pack. Wilt thou still keep him, Mother?"

"Keep him!" she gasped. "He came naked, by night, alone and very hungry; yet he was not afraid! Look, he has pushed one of my babes to one side already. And that lame butcher would have killed him, and would have run off to the Waingunga while the villagers here hunted through all our lairs in revenge! Keep him? Assuredly I will keep him. Lie still, little frog. O thou Mowgli—for Mowgli, the Frog, I will call thee—the time will come when thou wilt hunt Shere Khan as he has hunted thee!"

"But what will our Pack say?" said Father Wolf.

The Law of the Jungle lays down very clearly that any wolf may, when he marries, withdraw from the Pack he belongs to; but as soon as his cubs are old enough to stand on their feet he must bring them to the Pack Council, which is generally held once a month at full moon, in order that the other wolves may identify them. After that inspection the cubs are free to run where they please, and until they have killed their first buck no excuse is accepted if a grown wolf of the Pack kills one of them. The punishment is death where the murderer can be found; and if you think for a minute, you will see that this must be so.

Father Wolf waited till his cubs could run a little, and then on the night of the Pack Meeting took them and Mowgli and Mother Wolf to the Council Rock—a hilltop covered with stones and boulders where a hundred wolves could hide. Akela, the great gray Lone Wolf, who led all the Pack by strength and cunning, lay out at full length on his rock, and below him sat forty or more wolves of every size and color, from badger-colored veterans who could handle a buck alone, to young black three-year-olds who thought they could. The Lone Wolf had led them for a year now. He had fallen twice into a wolf-trap in his youth, and once he had been beaten and left for dead; so he knew the manners and customs of men.

There was very little talking at the Rock. The cubs tumbled over one another in the center of the circle where their mothers and fathers sat, and now and again a senior wolf would go quietly up to a cub, look at him carefully, and return to his place on noiseless feet. Sometimes a mother would push her cub far out into the moonlight, to be sure that he had not been overlooked. Akela from his rock would cry: "Ye know the Law—ye know the Law! Look well, O Wolves!" And the anxious mothers would take up the call: "Look— look well, O Wolves!"

At last—and Mother Wolf's neck-bristles lifted as the time came—Father Wolf pushed "Mowgli, the Frog," as they called him, into the center, where he sat laughing and playing with some pebbles that glistened in the moonlight.

Akela never raised his head from his paws, but went on with the monotonous cry, "Look well!" A muffled roar came up from behind the rocks—the voice of Shere Khan crying, "The cub is mine; give him to me. What have the Free People to do with a man's cub?"

Akela never even twitched his ears. All he said was, "Look well, O Wolves! What have the Free People to do with the orders of any save the Free People? Look well!"

There was a chorus of deep growls, and a young wolf in his fourth year flung back Shere Khan's question to Akela: "What have the Free People to do with a man's cub?"

Now, the Law of the Jungle lays down that if there is any dispute as to the right of a cub to be accepted by the Pack, he must be spoken for by at least two members of the Pack who are not his father and mother.

"Who speaks for this cub?" said Akela. "Among the Free People, who speaks?" There was no answer, and Mother Wolf got ready for what she knew would be her last fight, if things came to fighting.

Then the only other creature who is allowed at the Pack Council—Baloo, the sleepy brown bear who teaches the wolf cubs the Law of the Jungle; old Baloo—who can come and go where he pleases because he eats only nuts and roots and honey—rose up on his hind quarters and grunted.

"The man's cub—the man's cub?" he said. "*I* speak for the man's cub. There is no harm in a man's cub. I have no gift of words, but I speak the truth. Let him run with the Pack, and be entered with the others. I myself will teach him."

"We need yet another," said Akela. "Baloo has spoken, and he is our teacher for the young cubs. Who speaks besides Baloo?"

A black shadow dropped down into the circle. It was Bagheera, the Black Panther, inky black all over, but with the panther markings showing up in certain lights like the pattern of watered silk. Everybody knew Bagheera, and nobody cared to cross his path; for he was as cunning as Tabaqui, as bold as the wild buffalo, and as reckless as the wounded elephant.

But he had a voice as soft as wild honey dripping from a tree, and a skin softer than down.

"O Akela, and ye, the Free People," he purred, "I have no right in your assembly; but the Law of the Jungle says that if there is a doubt which is not a killing matter in regard to a new cub, the life of that cub may be bought at a price. And the Law does not say who may or may not pay that price. Am I right?"

"Good! good!" said the young wolves, who are always hungry. "Listen to Bagheera. The cub can be bought for a price. It is the Law."

"Knowing that I have no right to speak here, I ask your leave."

"Speak then," cried twenty voices.

"To kill a naked cub is shame. Besides, he may make better sport for you when he is grown. Baloo has spoken in his behalf. Now to Baloo's word I will add one bull, and a fat one, newly killed, not half a mile from here, if ye will accept the man's cub according to the Law. Is it difficult?"

There was a clamor of scores of voices, saying: "What matter? He will die in the winter rains. He will scorch in the sun. What harm can a naked frog do us? Let him run with the Pack. Where is the bull, Bagheera? Let him be accepted." And then came Akela's deep bay, crying: "Look well—look well, O Wolves!"

Mowgli was still playing with the pebbles, and he did not notice when the wolves came and looked at him one by one. At last they all went down the hill for the dead bull, and only Akela, Bagheera, Baloo, and Mowgli's own wolves were left. Shere Khan roared still in the night, for he was very angry that Mowgli had not been handed over to him.

"Ay, roar well," said Bagheera, under his whiskers; "for the time comes when this naked thing will make thee roar to another tune, or I know nothing of Man."

"It was well done," said Akela. "Men and their cubs are very wise. He may be a help in time."

"Truly, a help in time of need; for none can hope to lead the Pack forever," said Bagheera.

Akela said nothing. He was thinking of the time that comes to every leader of every pack when his strength goes from him and he gets feebler and feebler, till at last he is killed by the wolves and a new leader comes up—to be killed in his turn.

"Take him away," he said to Father Wolf, "and train him as befits one of the Free People."

And that is how Mowgli was entered into the Seeonee wolf-pack for the price of a bull and on Baloo's good word.

Now you must be content to skip ten or eleven whole years, and only guess at all the wonderful life that Mowgli led among the wolves, because if it were written out it would fill ever so many books. He grew up with the cubs, though they of course were grown wolves almost before he was a child, and Father Wolf taught him his business, and the meaning of things in the jungle, till every rustle in the grass, every breath of the warm night air, every note of the owls above his head, every scratch of a bat's claws as it roosted for a while in a tree, and every splash of every little fish jumping in a pool, meant just as much to him as the work of his office means to a business man. When he was not learning he sat out in the sun and slept, and ate, and went to sleep again; when he felt dirty or hot he swam in the forest pools; and when he wanted honey (Baloo told him that honey and nuts were just as pleasant to eat as raw meat) he climbed up for it, and that Bagheera showed him how to do.

Bagheera would lie out on a branch and call, "Come along, Little Brother," and at first Mowgli would cling like the sloth, but afterward he would fling himself through the branches almost as boldly as the gray ape. He took his place at the Council Rock, too, when the Pack met, and there he discovered that if he stared hard at any wolf, the wolf would be forced to drop his eyes, and so he used to stare for fun.

At other times he would pick the long thorns out of the pads of his friends, for wolves suffer terribly from thorns and burs in their coats. He would go down the hillside into the cultivated lands by night, and look very curiously at the villagers in their huts, but he had a mistrust of men because Bagheera showed him a square box with a drop-gate so cunningly hidden in the jungle that he nearly walked into it, and told him it was a trap.

He loved better than anything else to go with Bagheera into the dark warm heart of the forest, to sleep all through the drowsy day, and at night see how Bagheera did his killing. Bagheera killed right and left as he felt hungry, and so did Mowgli—with one exception. As soon as he was old enough to understand things, Bagheera told him that he must never touch cattle because he had been bought into the Pack at the price of a bull's life. "All the jungle is thine," said Bagheera, "and thou canst kill everything that thou art strong enough to kill; but for the sake of the bull that bought thee thou must never kill or eat any cattle young or old. That is the Law of the Jungle." Mowgli obeyed faithfully.

And he grew and grew strong as a boy must grow who does not know that he is learning any lessons, and who has nothing in the world to think of except things to eat.

Mother Wolf told him once or twice that Shere Khan was not a creature to be trusted, and that some day he must kill Shere Khan; but though a young wolf would have remembered that advice every hour, Mowgli forgot it because he was only a boy—though he would have called himself a wolf if he had been able to speak in any human tongue.

Shere Khan was always crossing his path in the jungle, for as Akela grew older and feebler the lame tiger had come to be great friends with the younger wolves of the Pack, who followed him for scraps, a thing Akela would never have allowed if he had dared to push his authority to the proper bounds. Then Shere Khan would flatter them and wonder that such fine young hunters were content to be led by a dying wolf and a man's cub. "They tell me," Shere Khan would say, "that at Council ye dare not look him between the eyes"; and the young wolves would growl and bristle.

Bagheera, who had eyes and ears everywhere, knew something of this, and once or twice he told Mowgli in so many words that Shere Khan would kill him some day; and Mowgli would laugh and answer: "I have the Pack and I have thee; and Baloo, though he is so lazy, might strike a blow or two for my sake. Why should I be afraid?"

It was one very warm day that a new notion came to Bagheera—born of something that he had heard. Perhaps Ikki, the Porcupine, had told him; but he said to Mowgli when they were deep in the jungle, as the boy lay with his head on Bagheera's beautiful black skin: "Little Brother, how often have I told thee that Shere Khan is thy enemy?"

"As many times as there are nuts on that palm," said Mowgli, who, naturally, could not count. "What of it? I am sleepy, Bagheera, and Shere Khan is all long tail and loud talk, like Mao, the Peacock."

"But this is no time for sleeping. Baloo knows it, I know it, the Pack know it, and even the foolish, foolish deer know. Tabaqui has told thee too."

"Ho! ho!" said Mowgli. "Tabaqui came to me not long ago with some rude talk that I was a naked man's cub, and not fit to dig pig-nuts; but I caught Tabaqui by the tail and swung him twice against a palm-tree to teach him better manners."

"That was foolishness; for though Tabaqui is a mischief-maker, he would have told thee of something that concerned thee closely. Open those eyes, Little Brother! Shere Khan dares not kill thee in the jungle for fear of those that love thee; but remember, Akela is very old, and soon the day comes when he cannot kill his buck, and then he will be leader no more. Many of the wolves that looked thee over when thou wast brought to the Council first are old too, and the young wolves believe, as Shere Khan has taught them, that a man-cub has no place with the Pack. In a little time thou wilt be a man."

"And what is a man that he should not run with his brothers?" said Mowgli. "I was born in the jungle; I have obeyed the Law of the Jungle; and there is no wolf of ours from whose paws I have not pulled a thorn. Surely they are my brothers!"

Bagheera stretched himself at full length and half shut his eyes. "Little Brother," said he, "feel under my jaw."

Mowgli put up his strong brown hand, and just under Bagheera's silky chin, where the giant rolling muscles were all hid by the glossy hair, he came upon a little bald spot.

"There is no one in the jungle that knows that I, Bagheera, carry that mark—the mark of the collar; and yet, Little Brother, I was born among men, and it was among men that my mother died—in the cages of the King's Palace at Oo-deypore. It was because of this that I paid the price for thee at the Council when thou wast a little naked cub. Yes, I too was born among men. I had never seen the jungle. They fed me behind bars from an iron pan till one night I felt that I was Bagheera, the Panther, and no man's plaything, and I broke the silly lock with one blow of my paw, and came away; and because I had learned the ways of men, I became more terrible in the jungle than Shere Khan. Is it not so?"

"Yes," said Mowgli; "all the jungle fear Bagheera—all except Mowgli."

"Oh, *thou* art a man's cub," said the Black Panther, very tenderly; "and even as I returned to my jungle, so thou must go back to men at last—to the men who are thy brothers—if thou art not killed in the Council."

"But why—but why should any wish to kill me?" said Mowgli.

"Look at me," said Bagheera; and Mowgli looked at him steadily between the eyes. The big panther turned his head away in half a minute.

"*That* is why," he said, shifting his paw on the leaves. "Not even I can look thee between the eyes, and I was born among men, and I love thee, Little Brother. The others they hate thee because their eyes cannot meet thine; because thou art wise; because thou hast pulled out thorns from their feet—because thou art a man."

"I did not know these things," said Mowgli, sullenly; and he frowned under his heavy black eyebrows.

"What is the Law of the Jungle? Strike first and then give tongue. By thy very carelessness they know that thou art a man. But be wise. It is in my heart that when Akela misses his next kill—and at each hunt it costs him more to pin the buck—the Pack will turn against him and against thee. They will hold a jungle Council at the Rock, and then—and then . . . I have it!" said Bagheera, leaping up. "Go thou down quickly to the men's huts in the valley, and take some of the Red Flower which they grow there, so that when the time comes thou mayest have even a stronger friend than I or Baloo or those of the Pack that love thee. Get the Red Flower."

By Red Flower Bagheera meant fire, only no creature in the jungle will call fire by its proper name. Every beast lives in deadly fear of it, and invents a hundred ways of describing it.

"The Red Flower?" said Mowgli. "That grows outside their huts in the twilight. I will get some."

"There speaks the man's cub," said Bagheera, proudly. "Remember that it grows in little pots. Get one swiftly, and keep it by thee for time of need."

"Good!" said Mowgli. "I go. But art thou sure, O my Bagheera"—he slipped his arm round the splendid neck, and looked deep into the big eyes—"art thou sure that all this is Shere Khan's doing?"

"By the Broken Lock that freed me, I am sure, Little Brother."

"Then, by the Bull that bought me, I will pay Shere Khan full tale for this, and it may be a little over," said Mowgli; and he bounded away.

"That is a man. That is all a man," said Bagheera to himself, lying down again. "Oh, Shere Khan, never was a blacker hunting than that frog-hunt of thine ten years ago!"

Mowgli was far and far through the forest, running hard, and his heart was hot in him. He came to the cave as the evening mist rose, and drew breath, and looked down the valley. The cubs were out, but Mother Wolf, at the back of the cave, knew by his breathing that something was troubling her frog.

"What is it, Son?" she said.

"Some bat's chatter of Shere Khan," he called back. "I hunt among the plowed fields tonight"; and he plunged downward through the bushes, to the stream at the bottom of the valley. There he checked, for he heard the yell of the Pack hunting, heard the bellow of a hunted Sambhur, and the snort as the buck turned at bay. Then there were wicked, bitter howls from the young wolves: "Akela! Akela! Let the Lone Wolf show his strength. Room for the leader of our Pack! Spring, Akela!"

The Lone Wolf must have sprung and missed his hold, for Mowgli heard the snap of his teeth and then a yelp as the Sambhur knocked him over with his fore foot.

He did not wait for anything more, but dashed on; and the yells grew fainter behind him as he ran into the croplands where the villagers lived.

"Bagheera spoke truth," he panted, as he nestled down in some cattle-fodder by the window of a hut. "To-morrow is one day for Akela and for me."

Then he pressed his face close to the window and watched the fire on the hearth. He saw the husbandman's wife get up and feed it in the night with black lumps; and when the morning came and the mists were all white and cold, he saw the man's child pick up a wicker pot plastered inside with earth, fill it with lumps of red-hot charcoal, put it under his blanket, and go out to tend the cows in the byre.

"Is that all?" said Mowgli. "If a cub can do it, there is

nothing to fear"; so he strode around the corner and met the boy, took the pot from his hand, and disappeared into the mist while the boy howled with fear.

"They are very like me," said Mowgli, blowing into the pot, as he had seen the woman do. "This thing will die if I do not give it things to eat"; and he dropped twigs and dried bark on the red stuff. Half-way up the hill he met Bagheera with the morning dew shining like moonstones on his coat.

"Akela has missed," said the panther. "They would have killed him last night, but they needed thee also. They were looking for thee on the hill."

"I was among the plowed lands. I am ready. Look!" Mowgli held up the fire-pot.

"Good! Now, I have seen men thrust a dry branch into that stuff, and presently the Red Flower blossomed at the end of it. Art thou not afraid?"

"No. Why should I fear? I remember now—if it is not a dream—how, before I was a wolf, I lay beside the Red Flower, and it was warm and pleasant."

All that day Mowgli sat in the cave tending his fire-pot and dipping dry branches into it to see how they looked. He found a branch that satisfied him, and in the evening when Tabaqui came to the cave and told him, rudely enough, that he was wanted at the Council Rock, he laughed till Tabaqui ran away. Then Mowgli went to the Council, still laughing.

Akela the Lone Wolf lay by the side of his rock as a sign that the leadership of the Pack was open, and Shere Khan with his following of scrap-fed wolves walked to and fro openly, being flattered. Bagheera lay close to Mowgli, and the fire-pot was between Mowgli's knees. When they were all gathered together, Shere Khan began to speak—a thing he would never have dared to do when Akela was in his prime.

"He has no right," whispered Bagheera. "Say so. He is a dog's son. He will be frightened."

Mowgli sprang to his feet. "Free People," he cried, "does Shere Khan lead the Pack? What has a tiger to do with our leadership?"

"Seeing that the leadership is yet open, and being asked to speak—" Shere Khan began.

"By whom?" said Mowgli. "Are we *all* jackals, to fawn on this cattle-butcher? The leadership of the Pack is with the Pack alone."

There were yells of "Silence, thou man's cub!" "Let him speak; he has kept our law!" And at last the seniors of the Pack thundered: "Let the Dead Wolf speak!"

When a leader of the Pack has missed his kill, he is called the Dead Wolf as long as he lives, which is not long, as a rule.

Akela raised his old head wearily:

"Free People, and ye too, jackals of Shere Khan, for twelve seasons I have led ye to and from the kill, and in all that time not one has been trapped or maimed. Now I have missed my kill. Ye know how that plot was made. Ye know how ye brought me up to an untried buck to make my weakness known. It was cleverly done. Your right is to kill me here on the Council Rock now. Therefore I ask, 'Who comes to make an end of the Lone Wolf?' For it is my right, by the Law of the Jungle, that ye come one by one."

There was a long hush, for no single wolf cared to fight Akela to the death. Then Shere Khan roared: "Bah! What have we to do with this toothless fool? He is doomed to die!

It is the man-cub who has lived too long. Free People, he was my meat from the first. Give him to me. I am weary of this man-wolf folly. He has troubled the jungle for ten seasons. Give me the man-cub, or I will hunt here always, and not give you one bone! He is a man—a man's child, and from the marrow of my bones I hate him!"

Then more than half the Pack yelled: "A man—a man! What has a man to do with us? Let him go to his own place."

"And turn all the people of the villages against us?" snarled Shere Khan. "No; give him to me. He is a man, and none of us can look him between the eyes."

Akela lifted his head again, and said: "He has eaten our food; he has slept with us; he has driven game for us; he has broken no word of the Law of the Jungle."

"Also, I paid for him with a bull when he was accepted. The worth of a bull is little, but Bagheera's honor is something that he will perhaps fight for," said Bagheera in his gentlest voice.

"A bull paid ten years ago!" the Pack snarled. "What do we care for bones ten years old?"

"Or for a pledge?" said Bagheera, his white teeth bared under his lip. "Well are ye called the Free People!"

"No man's cub can run with the people of the jungle!" roared Shere Khan. "Give him to me."

"He is our brother in all but blood," Akela went on; "and ye would kill him here. In truth, I have lived too long. Some of ye are eaters of cattle, and of others I have heard that, under Shere Khan's teaching, ye go by dark night and snatch children from the villager's doorstep. Therefore I know ye to be cowards, and it is to cowards I speak. It is certain that I must die, and my life is of no worth, or I would offer that in the man-cub's place. But for the sake of the Honor of the Pack—a little matter that, by being without a leader, ye have forgotten—I promise that if ye let the man-cub go to his own place, I will not, when my time comes to die, bare one tooth against ye. I will die without fighting. That will at least save the Pack three lives. More I cannot do; but, if ye will, I can save ye the shame that comes of killing a brother against whom there is no fault—a brother spoken for and bought into the Pack according to the Law of the Jungle."

"He is a man—a man—a man!" snarled the Pack; and most of the wolves began to gather round Shere Khan, whose tail was beginning to switch.

"Now the business is in thy hands," said Bagheera to Mowgli. "*We* can do no more except fight."

Mowgli stood upright—the fire-pot in his hands. Then he stretched out his arms, and yawned in the face of the Council; but he was furious with rage and sorrow, for, wolf-like, the wolves had never told him how they hated him.

"Listen, you!" he cried. "There is no need for this dog's jabber. Ye have told me so often to-night that I am a man (though indeed I would have been a wolf with you to my life's end) that I feel your words are true. So I do not call ye my brothers any more, but *sag* [dogs], as a man should. What ye will do, and what ye will not do, is not yours to say. That matter is with *me;* and that we may see the matter more plainly, I, the man, have brought here a little of the Red Flower which ye, dogs, fear."

He flung the fire-pot on the ground, and some of the red coals lit a tuft of dried moss that flared up as all the Council drew back in terror before the leaping flames.

Mowgli thrust his dead branch into the fire till the twigs

lit and crackled, and whirled it above his head among the cowering wolves.

"Thou art the master," said Bagheera, in an undertone. "Save Akela from the death. He was ever thy friend."

Akela, the grim old wolf who had never asked for mercy in his life, gave one piteous look at Mowgli as the boy stood all naked, his long black hair tossing over his shoulders in the light of the blazing branch that made the shadows jump and quiver.

"Good!" said Mowgli, staring around slowly, and thrusting out his lower lip. "I see that ye are dogs. I go from you to my own people—if they be my own people. The jungle is shut to me, and I must forget your talk and your companionship; but I will be more merciful than ye are. Because I was all but your brother in blood, I promise that when I am a man among men I will not betray ye to men as ye have betrayed me." He kicked the fire with his foot, and the sparks flew up. "There shall be no war between any of us and the Pack. But here is a debt to pay before I go." He strode forward to where Shere Khan sat blinking stupidly at the flames, and caught him by the tuft on his chin. Bagheera followed close, in case of accidents. "Up, dog!" Mowgli cried. "Up, when a man speaks, or I will set that coat ablaze!"

Shere Khan's ears lay flat back on his head, and he shut his eyes, for the blazing branch was very near.

"This cattle-killer said he would kill me in the Council because he had not killed me when I was a cub. Thus and thus, then, do we beat dogs when we are men! Stir a whisker, Lungri, and I ram the Red Flower down thy gullet!" He beat Shere Khan over the head with the branch, and the tiger whimpered and whined in an agony of fear.

"Pah! Singed jungle-cat—go now! But remember when next I come to the Council Rock, as a man should come, it will be with Shere Khan's hide on my head. For the rest, Akela goes free to live as he pleases. Ye will *not* kill him, because that is not my will. Nor do I think that ye will sit here any longer, lolling out your tongues as though ye were somebodies, instead of dogs whom I drive out—thus! Go!"

The fire was burning furiously at the end of the branch, and Mowgli struck right and left round the circle, and the wolves ran howling with the sparks burning their fur. At last there were only Akela, Bagheera, and perhaps ten wolves that had taken Mowgli's part. Then something began to hurt Mowgli inside him, as he had never been hurt in his life before, and he caught his breath and sobbed, and the tears ran down his face.

"What is it? What is it?" he said. "I do not wish to leave the jungle, and I do not know what this is. Am I dying, Bagheera?"

"No, Little Brother. Those are only tears such as men use," said Bagheera. "Now I know thou art a man, and a man's cub no longer. The jungle is shut indeed to thee henceforward. Let them fall, Mowgli; they are only tears." So Mowgli sat and cried as though his heart would break; and he had never cried in all his life before.

"Now," he said, "I will go to men. But first I must say farewell to my mother"; and he went to the cave where she lived with Father Wolf, and he cried on her coat, while the four cubs howled miserably.

"Ye will not forget me?" said Mowgli.

"Never while we can follow a trail," said the cubs. "Come to the foot of the hill when thou art a man, and we will talk to thee; and we will come into the crop-lands to play with thee by night."

"Come soon!" said Father Wolf. "Oh, wise little Frog, come again soon; for we be old, thy mother and I."

"Come soon," said Mother Wolf, "little naked son of mine; for, listen, child of man, I loved thee more than ever I loved my cubs."

"I will surely come," said Mowgli; "and when I come it will be to lay out Shere Khan's hide upon the Council Rock. Do not forget me! Tell them in the jungle never to forget me!"

The dawn was beginning to break when Mowgli went down the hillside alone to the crops to meet those mysterious things that are called men.

HUNTING-SONG OF THE
SEEONEE PACK

As the dawn was breaking the Sambhur belled
    Once, twice, and again!
And a doe leaped up—and a doe leaped up
From the pond in the wood where the wild deer sup.
This I, scouting alone, beheld,
    Once, twice, and again!

As the dawn was breaking the Sambhur belled
    Once, twice, and again!
And a wolf stole back—and a wolf stole back
To carry the word to the waiting Pack;
And we sought and we found and we bayed on his track,
    Once, twice, and again!

As the dawn was breaking the Wolf-pack yelled
    Once, twice, and again!

Feet in the jungle that leave no mark!
Eyes that can see in the dark—the dark!
Tongue—give tongue to it! Hark! O Hark!
    Once, twice, and again!

THE WALL OF THE WORLD

FROM
WHITE FANG

BY JACK LONDON

By the time his mother began leaving the cave on hunting expeditions, the cub had learned well the law that forbade his approaching the entrance. Not only had this law been forcibly and many times impressed on him by his mother's nose and paw, but in him the instinct of fear was developing. Never, in his brief cave-life, had he encountered anything of which to be afraid. Yet fear was in him. It had come down to him from a remote ancestry through a thousand thousand lives. It was a heritage he had received directly from One Eye and the she-wolf; but to them, in turn, it had been passed down through all the generations of wolves that had gone before. Fear!—that legacy of the Wild which no animal may escape nor exchange for pottage.

So the gray cub knew fear, though he knew not the stuff of which fear was made. Possibly he accepted it as one of the restrictions of life. For he had already learned that there were such restrictions. Hunger he had known; and when he could not appease his hunger he had felt restriction. The hard obstruction of the cave-wall, the sharp nudge of his mother's nose, the smashing stroke of her paw, the hunger unappeased of several famines, had borne in upon him that all was not freedom in the world, that to life there were limitations and restraints. These limitations and restraints were laws. To be obedient to them was to escape hurt and make for happiness.

He did not reason the question out in this man-fashion. He merely classified the things that hurt and the things that did not hurt. And after such classification he avoided the things that hurt, the restrictions and restraints, in order to enjoy the satisfactions and the remunerations of life.

Thus it was that in obedience to the law laid down by his mother, and in obedience to the law of that unknown and nameless thing, fear, he kept away from the mouth of the cave. It remained to him a white wall of light. When his mother was absent, he slept most of the time, while during the intervals that he was awake he kept very quiet, suppressing the whimpering cries that tickled in his throat and strove for noise.

Once, lying awake, he heard a strange sound in the white wall. He did not know that it was a wolverine, standing outside, all a-tremble with its own daring, and cautiously scenting out the contents of the cave. The cub knew only that the sniff was strange, a something unclassified, therefore unknown and terrible—for the unknown was one of the chief elements that went into the making of fear.

The hair bristled up on the gray cub's back, but it bristled silently. How was he to know that this thing that sniffed was a thing at which to bristle? It was not born of any knowledge of his, yet it was the visible expression of the fear that was in him, and for which, in his own life, there was no accounting. But fear was accompanied by another instinct—that of concealment. The cub was in a frenzy of terror, yet he lay without movement or sound, frozen, petrified into immobility, to all appearances dead. His mother, coming home, growled as she smelt the wolverine's track, and bounded into the cave and licked and nozzled him with undue vehemence of affection. And the cub felt that somehow he had escaped a great hurt.

But there were other forces at work in the cub, the greatest of which was growth. Instinct and law demanded of him obedience. But growth demanded disobedience. His mother and fear impelled him to keep away from the white wall. Growth is life, and life is forever destined to make for light. So there was no damming up the tide of life that was rising within him—rising with every mouthful of meat he swallowed, with every breath he drew. In the end, one day, fear and obedience were swept away by the rush of life, and the cub straddled and sprawled toward the entrance.

Unlike any other wall with which he had had experience, this wall seemed to recede from him as he approached. No hard surface collided with the tender little nose he thrust out tentatively before him. The substance of the wall seemed as permeable and yielding as light. And as condition, in his eyes, had the seeming of form, so he entered into what had been wall to him and bathed in the substance that composed it.

It was bewildering. He was sprawling through solidity. And ever the light grew brighter. Fear urged him to go back, but growth drove him on. Suddenly he found himself at the mouth of the cave. The wall, inside which he had thought himself, as suddenly leaped back before him to an immeasurable distance. The light had become painfully bright. He was dazzled

by it. Likewise he was made dizzy by this abrupt and tremendous extension of space. Automatically, his eyes were
adjusting themselves to the brightness, focussing themselves
to meet the increased distance of objects. At first, the wall
had leaped beyond his vision. He now saw it again; but it
had taken upon itself a remarkable remoteness. Also, its appearance had changed. It was now a variegated wall, composed of the trees that fringed the stream, the opposing
mountain that towered above the trees, and the sky that out-
towered the mountain.

A great fear came upon him. This was more of the terrible
unknown. He crouched down on the lip of the cave and gazed
out on the world. He was very much afraid. Because it was
unknown, it was hostile to him. Therefore the hair stood up
on end along his back and his lips wrinkled weakly in an
attempt at a ferocious and intimidating snarl. Out of his
puniness and fright he challenged and menaced the whole
wide world.

Nothing happened. He continued to gaze, and in his interest
he forgot to snarl. Also, he forgot to be afraid. For the time,
fear had been routed by growth, while growth had assumed
the guise of curiosity. He began to notice near objects—an
open portion of the stream that flashed in the sun, the blasted
pine tree that stood at the base of the slope, and the slope
itself, that ran right up to him and ceased two feet beneath
the lip of the cave on which he crouched.

Now the gray cub had lived all his days on a level floor.
He had never experienced the hurt of a fall. He did not know
what a fall was. So he stepped boldly out upon the air. His
hind-legs still rested on the cave-lip, so he fell forward head
downward. The earth struck him a harsh blow on the nose

that made him yelp. Then he began rolling down the slope, over and over. He was in a panic of terror. The unknown had caught him at last. It had gripped savagely hold of him and was about to wreak upon him some terrific hurt. Growth was now routed by fear, and he ki-yi'd like any frightened puppy.

The unknown bore him on he knew not to what frightful hurt, and he yelped and ki-yi'd unceasingly. This was a different proposition from crouching in frozen fear while the unknown lurked just alongside. Now the unknown had caught tight hold of him. Silence would do no good. Besides, it was not fear, but terror, that convulsed him.

But the slope grew more gradual, and its base was grass-covered. Here the cub lost momentum. When at last he came to a stop, he gave one last agonized yelp and then a long, whimpering wail. Also, and quite as a matter of course, as though in his life he had already made a thousand toilets, he proceeded to lick away the dry clay that soiled him.

After that he sat up and gazed about him, as might the first man of the earth who landed upon Mars. The cub had broken through the wall of the world, the unknown had let go its hold of him, and here he was without hurt. But the first man on Mars would have experienced less unfamiliarity than did he. Without any antecedent knowledge, without any warning whatever that such existed, he found himself an explorer in a totally new world.

Now that the terrible unknown had let go of him, he forgot that the unknown had any terrors. He was aware only of curiosity in all the things about him. He inspected the grass beneath him, the moss-berry plant just beyond, and the dead trunk of the blasted pine that stood on the edge of an open space among the trees. A squirrel, running around the base of the trunk, came full upon him, and gave him a great fright. He cowered down and snarled. But the squirrel was as badly scared. It ran up the tree, and from a point of safety chattered back savagely.

This helped the cub's courage, and though the woodpecker he next encountered gave him a start, he proceeded confidently on his way. Such was his confidence, that when a moose-bird impudently hopped up to him, he reached out at it with a playful paw. The result was a sharp peck on the end of his nose that made him cower down and ki-yi. The noise he made was too much for the moose-bird, who sought safety in flight.

But the cub was learning. His misty little mind had already made an unconscious classification. There were live things and things not alive. Also, he must watch out for the live things. The things not alive remained always in one place; but the live things moved about, and there was no telling what they might do. The thing to expect of them was the unexpected, and for this he must be prepared.

He travelled very clumsily. He ran into sticks and things. A twig that he thought a long way off would the next instant hit him on the nose or rake along his ribs. There were inequalities of surface. Sometimes he over-stepped and stubbed his nose. Quite as often he under-stepped and stubbed his feet. Then there were the pebbles and stones that turned under him when he trod upon them; and from them he came to know that the things not alive were not all in the same state of stable equilibrium as was his cave; also, that small things not alive were more liable than large things to fall down or turn over. But with every mishap he was learning. The longer he walked, the better he walked. He was adjusting himself. He was learning to calculate his own muscular movements, to know his physical limitations, to measure distances between objects, and between objects and himself.

His was the luck of the beginner. Born to be a hunter of meat (though he did not know it), he blundered upon meat just outside his own cave-door on his first foray into the world. It was by sheer blundering that he chanced upon the shrewdly hidden ptarmigan nest. He fell into it. He had essayed to walk along the trunk of a fallen pine. The rotten bark gave way under his feet, and with a despairing yelp he pitched down the rounded descent, smashed through the leafage and stalks of a small bush, and in the heart of the bush, on the ground, fetched up amongst seven ptarmigan chicks.

They made noises, and at first he was frightened at them. Then he perceived that they were very little, and he became bolder. They moved. He placed his paw on one, and its movements were accelerated. This was a source of enjoyment to him. He smelled it. He picked it up in his mouth. It struggled and tickled his tongue. At the same time he was made aware of a sensation of hunger. His jaws closed together. There was a crunching of fragile bones, warm blood ran in his mouth. The taste of it was good. This was meat, the same as his mother gave him, only it was alive between his teeth and therefore better. So he ate the ptarmigan. Nor did he stop till he had devoured the whole brood. Then he licked his chops in quite the same way his mother did, and began to crawl out of the bush.

He encountered a feathered whirlwind. He was confused and blinded by the rush of it and the beat of angry wings. He hid his head between his paws and yelped. The blows increased. The mother ptarmigan was in a fury. Then he became angry. He rose up, snarling, striking out with his paws. He sank his tiny teeth into one of the wings and pulled and tugged sturdily. The ptarmigan struggled against him, showering blows upon him with her free wing. It was his first battle. He was elated. He forgot all about the unknown. He no longer was afraid of anything. He was fighting, tearing at a live thing that was striking at him. Also, this live thing was meat. The lust to kill was on him. He had just destroyed little live things. He would now destroy a big live thing. He was too busy and happy to know that he was happy. He was thrilling and exulting in ways new to him and greater to him than any he had known before.

He held on to the wing and growled between his tight-clenched teeth. The ptarmigan dragged him out of the bush. When she turned and tried to drag him back into the bush's shelter, he pulled her away from it and on into the open. And all the time she was making outcry and striking with her wing, while feathers were flying like a snow-fall. The pitch to which he was aroused was tremendous. All the fighting blood of his breed was up in him and surging through him. This was living, though he did not know it. He was realizing his own meaning in the world; he was doing that for which he was made—killing meat and battling to kill it. He was justifying his existence, than which life can do no greater; for life achieves its summit when it does to the uttermost that which it was equipped to do.

After a time, the ptarmigan ceased her struggling. He still held her by the wing, and they lay on the ground and looked at each other. He tried to growl threateningly, ferociously. She pecked on his nose, which by now, what of previous adventures, was sore. He winced but held on. She pecked him again and again. From wincing he went to whimpering. He tried to back away from her, oblivious of the fact that by his hold on her he dragged her after him. A rain of pecks fell on his ill-used nose. The flood of fight ebbed down in him, and, releasing his prey, he turned tail and scampered off across the open in inglorious retreat.

He lay down to rest on the other side of the open, near the edge of the bushes, his tongue lolling out, his chest heaving and panting, his nose still hurting him and causing him to continue his whimper. But as he lay there, suddenly there came to him a feeling as of something terrible impending. The unknown with all its terrors rushed upon him, and he shrank back instinctively into the shelter of the bush. As he did so, a draught of air fanned him, and a large, winged body swept ominously and silently past. A hawk, driving down out of the blue, had barely missed him.

While he lay in the bush, recovering from this fright and peering fearfully out, the mother-ptarmigan on the other side of the open space fluttered out of the ravaged nest. It was because of her loss that she paid no attention to the winged bolt of the sky. But the cub saw, and it was a warning and a lesson to him—the swift downward swoop of the hawk, the short skim of its body just above the ground, the strike of its talons in the body of the ptarmigan, the ptarmigan's squawk of agony and fright, and the hawk's rush upward into the blue, carrying the ptarmigan away with it.

It was a long time before the cub left his shelter. He had learned much. Live things were meat. They were good to eat. Also, live things, when they were large enough, could give hurt. It was better to eat small live things like ptarmigan chicks, and to let alone large live things like ptarmigan hens. Nevertheless he felt a little prick of ambition, a sneaking desire to have another battle with that ptarmigan hen—only the hawk had carried her away. Maybe there were other ptarmigan hens. He would go and see.

He came down a shelving bank to the stream. He had never seen water before. The footing looked good. There were no inequalities of surface. He stepped boldly out on it; and went down, crying with fear, into the embrace of the unknown. It was cold, and he gasped, breathing quickly. The water rushed into his lungs instead of the air that had always accompanied his act of breathing. The suffocation he experienced was like the pang of death. To him it signified death. He had no conscious knowledge of death, but like every animal of the Wild, he possessed the instinct of death. To him it stood as the greatest of hurts. It was the very essence of the unknown; it was the sum of the terrors of the unknown, the one culminating and unthinkable catastrophe that could happen to him, about which he knew nothing and about which he feared everything.

He came to the surface, and the sweet air rushed into his open mouth. He did not go down again. Quite as though it had been a long-established custom of his, he struck out with all his legs and began to swim. The near bank was a yard away; but he had come up with his back to it, and the first thing his eyes rested upon was the opposite bank, toward which he immediately began to swim. The stream was a small one, but in the pool it widened out to a score of feet.

Midway in the passage, the current picked up the cub and swept him down-stream. He was caught in the miniature rapid at the bottom of the pool. Here was little chance for swimming. The quiet water had become suddenly angry. Sometimes he was under, sometimes on top. At all times he was in violent motion, now being turned over or around, and, again, being smashed against a rock. And with every rock he struck, he yelped. His progress was a series of yelps, from which might have been adduced the number of rocks he encountered.

Below the rapid was a second pool, and here, captured by the eddy, he was gently borne to the bank and as gently deposited on a bed of gravel. He crawled frantically clear of the water and lay down. He had learned some more about the world. Water was not alive. Yet it moved. Also, it looked as solid as the earth, but was without any solidity at all. His conclusion was that things were not always what they appeared to be. The cub's fear of the unknown was an inherited distrust, and it had now been strengthened by experience. Thenceforth, in the nature of things, he would possess an abiding distrust of appearances. He would have to learn the reality of a thing before he could put his faith into it.

One other adventure was destined for him that day. He had recollected that there was such a thing in the world as his mother. And then there came to him a feeling that he wanted her more than all the rest of the things in the world. Not only was his body tired with the adventures it had undergone, but his little brain was equally tired. In all the days he had lived it had not worked so hard as on this one day. Furthermore, he was sleepy. So he started out to look for the cave and his mother, feeling at the same time an overwhelming rush of loneliness and helplessness.

He was sprawling along between some bushes, when he heard a sharp, intimidating cry. There was a flash of yellow before his eyes. He saw a weasel leaping swiftly away from him. It was a small live thing, and he had no fear. Then, before him, at his feet, he saw an extremely small live thing, only several inches long—a young weasel, that, like himself, had disobediently gone out adventuring. It tried to retreat before him. He turned it over with his paw. It made a queer, grating noise. The next moment the flash of yellow reappeared before his eyes. He heard again the intimidating cry, and at the same instant received a severe blow on the side of the neck and felt the sharp teeth of the mother-weasel cut into his flesh.

While he yelped and ki-yi'd and scrambled backward, he saw the mother-weasel leap upon her young one and disappear with it into the neighboring thicket. The cut of her teeth in his neck still hurt, but his feelings were hurt more grievously, and he sat down and weakly whimpered. This mother-weasel was so small and so savage! He was yet to learn that for size and weight the weasel was the most ferocious, vindictive, and terrible of all the killers of the Wild. But a portion of this knowledge was quickly to be his.

He was still whimpering when the mother-weasel reappeared. She did not rush him, now that her young one was safe. She approached more cautiously, and the cub had full opportunity to observe her lean, snakelike body, and her head, erect, eager, and snakelike itself. Her sharp, menacing cry sent the hair bristling along his back, and he snarled warningly at her. She came closer and closer. There was a leap, swifter than his unpractised sight, and the lean, yellow body disappeared for a moment out of the field of his vision. The next moment she was at his throat, her teeth buried in his hair and flesh.

At first he snarled and tried to fight; but he was very young, and this was only his first day in the world, and his snarl became a whimper, his fight a struggle to escape. The weasel never relaxed her hold. She hung on, striving to press down with her teeth to the great vein where his life-blood bubbled. The weasel was a drinker of blood, and it was ever her preference to drink from the throat of life itself.

The gray cub would have died, and there would have been no story to write about him, had not the she-wolf come bounding through the bushes. The weasel let go the cub and flashed at the she-wolf's throat, missing, but getting a hold on the jaw instead. The she-wolf flirted her head like the snap of a whip, breaking the weasel's hold and flinging it high in the air. And, still in the air, the she-wolf's jaws closed on the lean, yellow body, and the weasel knew death between the crunching teeth.

The cub experienced another access of affection on the part of his mother. Her joy at finding him seemed greater even than his joy at being found. She nozzled him and caressed him and licked the cuts made in him by the weasel's teeth. Then, between them, mother and cub, they ate the blood-drinker, and after that went back to the cave and slept.

FROM
RING OF
BRIGHT WATER

BY GAVIN MAXWELL

Mij slept in my bed (by now, as I have said, he had abandoned the teddy-bear attitude and lay on his back under the
bedclothes with his whiskers tickling my ankles and his body
at the crook of my knees) and would wake with bizarre punc-
tuality at exactly twenty past eight in the morning. I have
sought any possible explanation for this, and some "feed-
back" situation in which it was actually I who made the first
unconscious movement, giving him his cue, cannot be altogether discounted; but whatever the reason, his waking time,
then and until the end of his life, summer or winter, remained
precisely twenty past eight. Having woken, he would come
up to the pillow and nuzzle my face and neck with small
attenuated squeaks of pleasure and affection. If I did not rouse
myself very soon he would set about getting me out of bed.
This he did with the business-like, slightly impatient efficiency
of a nurse dealing with a difficult child. He played the game
by certain defined and self-imposed rules; he would not, for
example, use his teeth even to pinch, and inside these limi-

131

tations it was hard to imagine how a human brain could, in the same body, have exceeded his ingenuity. He began by going under the bedclothes and moving rapidly up and down the bed with a high-hunching, caterpillar-like motion that gradually untucked the bedclothes from beneath the sides of the mattress; this achieved, he would redouble his efforts at the foot of the bed, where the sheets and blankets had a firmer hold. When everything had been loosened up to his satisfaction he would flow off the bed on to the floor—except when running on dry land the only appropriate word for an otter's movement is flowing; they pour themselves, as it were, in the direction of their objective—take the bedclothes between his teeth, and, with a series of violent tugs, begin to yank them down beside him. Eventually, for I do not wear pyjamas, I would be left quite naked on the undersheet, clutching the pillows rebelliously. But they, too, had to go; and it was here that he demonstrated the extraordinary strength concealed in his small body. He would work his way under them and execute a series of mighty hunches of his arched back, each of them lifting my head and whole shoulders clear of the bed, and at some point in the procedure he invariably contrived to dislodge the pillows while I was still in mid-air, much as a certain type of practical joker will remove a chair upon which someone is in the act of sitting down. Left thus comfortless and bereft both of covering and of dignity, there was little option but to dress, while Mij looked on with an all-that-shouldn't-really-have-been-necessary-you-know sort of expression. Otters usually get their own way in the end; they are not dogs, and they co-exist with humans rather than being owned by them.

His next objective was the eel-box in the burn, followed,

having breakfasted, by a tour of the water perimeter, the three-quarter circle formed by the burn and the sea; shooting like an under-water arrow after trout where the burn runs deep and slow between the trees; turning over stones for hidden eels where it spreads broad and shallow over sun-reflecting scales of mica; tobogganing down the long, loose sand slope by the sand-martin colony; diving through the waves on the sand beach and catching dabs; then, lured in with difficulty and subterfuge from starting on a second lap, home to the kitchen and ecstatic squirming among his towels.

This preamble to the day, when Mij had a full stomach and I had not, became, as he established favoured pools and fishing grounds which had every morning to be combed as for a lost possession, ever longer and longer, and after the first fortnight I took, not without misgiving, to going back indoors myself as soon as he had been fed. At first he would return after an hour or so, and when he had dried himself he would creep up under the loose cover of the sofa and form a round breathing hump at the centre of the seat. But as time went on he stayed longer about the burn, and I would not begin to worry until he had been gone for half the day.

There were great quantities of cattle at Camusfeàrna that year, for the owner of the estate was of an experimental turn of mind, and had decided to farm cattle on the lines of the Great Glen Cattle Ranch. The majority of these beasts were black, and, as at Monreith in the spring, Mij seemed to detect in them an affinity to his familiar water buffaloes of the Tigris marshes, for he would dance round them with excited chitterings until they stampeded. Thus massed they presented too formidable an appearance for him, and after a week or two he devised for himself a means of cattle-baiting at which he became a past master. With extreme stealth he would advance *ventre à terre* towards the rear end of some massive stirk whose black-tufted tail hung invitingly within his reach; then, as one who makes a vigorous and impatient tug at a bell-rope, he would grab the tuft between his teeth and give one tremendous jerk upon it with all his strength, leaping backward exactly in time to dodge the lashing hooves. At first I viewed this sport with the gravest alarm, for, owing to the structure of the skull, a comparatively light blow on the nose can kill an otter, but Mij was able to gauge the distance to an inch, and never a hoof so much as grazed him. As a useful by-product of his impish sense of humour, the cattle tended to keep farther from the house, thus incidentally reducing the number of scatological hazards to be skirted at the door. . . .

There is a patron saint of otters, St. Cuthbert—the cider drink, too, shares his patronage; clearly he was a man who bestowed his favours with the most enlightened discrimination . . .

Now it is apparent to me that whatever other saintly virtues St. Cuthbert possessed, he well merited canonization by reason of his forbearance alone. I know all about being dried by otters. I have been dried by them more times than I care to remember. Like everything else about otters, it takes place the wrong way round, so to speak. When one plays ball with a puppy, one throws the ball and the puppy fetches it back and then one throws it again; it is all comparatively restful and orderly. But when one plays ball with an otter the situation gets out of hand from the start; it is the otter who throws the ball—to a remarkable distance—and the human who fetches it. With the human who at the beginning is not trained to this the otter is fairly patient, but persistent and obstinate refusal meets with reprisals. The same upside-down situation obtains when being dried by otters. The otter emerges tempestuously from the sea or the river or the bath, as the case may be, carrying about half a gallon of water in its fur, and sets about drying you with a positively terrifying zeal and enthusiasm. Every inch of you requires, in the view of a conscientious otter, careful attention. The otter uses its back as the principal towel, and lies upon it while executing a series of vigorous, eel-like wriggles. In a surprisingly short space of time the otter is quite dry except for the last four inches of its tail, and the human being is soaking wet except for nothing. It is no use going to change one's clothes; in a few minutes the otter will come rampaging out of the water again intent upon its mission of drying people.

I have but little doubt what the good brother of Coldingham monastery really saw. St. Cuthbert had been praying at the water's edge, not, as the brother thought (it was, one must bear in mind, night, and the light was poor), up to his neck in the waves; and it was entirely the condition of the saint's clothing after he had been dried by the otters that led the observer to deduce some kind of sub-marine devotion. Clearly, too, it was an absolution rather than a simple benediction that the now shivering and bedraggled saint bestowed upon his tormentors. In the light of my interpretation St. Cuthbert's injunction to silence falls neatly into place, for he could not know of the brother's misapprehension, and not even a saint enjoys being laughed at in this kind of misfortune.

While otters undoubtedly have a special vocation for drying human beings, they will also dry other objects, most particularly beds, between the sheets, all the way from the pillows to the bed-foot. A bed dried by this process is unusable for a week, and an otter-dried sofa is only tolerable in the heat of summer. I perceive why St. Cuthbert required the ministrations of the eider ducks and the warm down of their breasts; the unfortunate man must have been constantly threatened with an occupational pneumonia.

This aspect of life with an otter had never really struck me before I brought Mij to Camusfeàrna; in London one could run the water out of the bath, and by using a monster towel could render him comparatively harmless before he reached the sitting-room, while at Monreith the loch was far enough from the house for him to be dry before reaching home. But at Camusfeàrna, with the sea a stone's throw on one side and the burn on the other, I have found no satisfactory solution beyond keeping the bedroom door closed, and turning, as it were, a blind posterior to wet sofas and chairs.

THE HEART OF THE GAME

BY THOMAS McGUANE

Hunting in your own back yard becomes with time, if you love hunting, less and less expeditionary. This year, when Montana's eager frost knocked my garden on its butt, the hoe seemed more like the rifle than it ever had before, the vegetables more like game.

My son and I went scouting before the season and saw some antelope in the high plains foothills of the Absaroka Range, wary, hanging on the skyline; a few bands and no great heads. We crept around, looking into basins, and at dusk met a tired cowboy on a tired horse followed by a tired blue-heeler dog. The plains seemed bigger than anything, bigger than the mountains that seemed to sit in the middle of them, bigger than the ocean. The clouds made huge shadows that traveled on the grass slowly through the day.

Hunting season trickles on forever; if you don't go in on a cow with anybody, there is the dark argument of the empty deep-freeze against headhunting ("You can't eat horns!"). But nevertheless, in my mind, I've laid out the months like playing cards, knowing some decent whitetails could be down in the river bottom and, fairly reliably, the long windy shots at antelope. The big buck mule deer—the ridge-runners—stay up in the scree and rock walls until the snow drives them out; but they stay high long after the elk have quit and broken down the hay corrals on the ranches and farmsteads, which, when you're hunting the rocks from a saddle horse, look pathetic and housebroken with their yellow lights against the coming of winter.

Where I live, the Yellowstone River runs straight north, then takes an eastward turn at Livingston, Montana. This flowing north is supposed to be remarkable; and the river doesn't do it long. It runs mostly over sand and stones once it comes out of the rock slots near the Wyoming line. But all along, there are deviations of one sort or another: canals, backwaters, sloughs; the red willows grow in the sometime-flooded bottom, and at the first elevation, the cottonwoods. I hunt here for the white-tail deer which, in recent years, have moved up these rivers in numbers never seen before.

THE FIRST MORNING, the sun came up hitting around me in arbitrary panels as the light moved through the jagged openings in the Absaroka Range. I was walking very slowly in the edge of the trees, the river invisible a few hundred yards to my right but sending a huge sigh through the willows. It was cold and the sloughs had crowns of ice thick enough to support me. As I crossed one great clear pane, trout raced around under my feet and a ten-foot bubble advanced slowly before my cautious steps. Then passing back into the trees, I found an active game trail, cut cross-lots to pick a better stand, sat in a good vantage place under a cottonwood with the ought-six across my knees. I thought, running my hands up into my sleeves, this is lovely but I'd rather be up in the hills; and I fell asleep.

I woke up a couple of hours later, the coffee and early-morning drill having done not one thing for my alertness. I had drooled on my rifle and it was time for my chores back at the ranch. My chores of late had consisted primarily of working on screenplays so that the bank didn't take the ranch. These days the primary ranch skill is making the payment; it comes before irrigation, feeding out, and calving. Some rancher friends find this so discouraging they get up and roll a number or have a slash of tanglefoot before they even think of the glories of the West. This is the New Rugged.

The next day, I reflected upon my lackadaisical hunting and left really too early in the morning. I drove around to Mission Creek in the dark and ended up sitting in the truck up some wash listening to a New Mexico radio station until my patience gave out and I started out cross-country in the dark, just able to make out the nose of the Absaroka Range as it faced across the river to the Crazy Mountains. It seemed maddeningly up and down slick banks, and a couple of times I had game clatter out in front of me in the dark. Then I turned up a long coulee that climbed endlessly south, and started in that direction, knowing the plateau on top should hold some antelope. After half an hour or so, I heard the mad laughing of coyotes, throwing their voices all around the inside of the coulee, trying to panic rabbits and making my hair stand on end despite my affection for them. The stars tracked overhead into the first pale light and it was nearly dawn before I came up on the bench. I could hear cattle below me and I moved along an edge of thorn trees to break my outline, then sat down at the point to wait for shooting light.

I could see antelope on the skyline before I had that light; and by the time I did, there was a good big buck angling across from me, looking at everything. I thought I could see well enough, and I got up into a sitting position and into the sling. I had made my moves quietly, but when I looked through the scope the antelope was two hundred yards out, using up the country in bounds. I tracked with him, let him bounce up into the reticle, and touched off a shot. He was down and still, but I sat watching until I was sure.

Nobody who loves to hunt feels absolutely hunky-dory when the quarry goes down. The remorse spins out almost before anything and the balancing act ends on one declination or another. I decided that unless I become a vegetarian, I'll get my meat by hunting for it. I feel absolutely unabashed by the arguments of other carnivores who get their meat in plastic with blue numbers on it. I've seen slaughterhouses, and anyway, as Sitting Bull said, when the buffalo are gone, we will hunt mice, for we are hunters and we want our freedom.

The antelope had piled up in the sage, dead before he hit the ground. He was an old enough buck that the tips of his pronged horns were angled in toward each other. I turned him downhill to bleed him out. The bullet had mushroomed in the front of the lungs, so the job was already halfway done. With antelope, proper field dressing is critical because they can end up sour if they've been run or haphazardly hog-dressed. And they sour from their own body heat more than from external heat.

The sun was up and the big buteo hawks were lifting on the thermals. There was enough breeze that the grass began to have directional grain like the prairie and the rim of the coulee wound up away from me toward the Absaroka. I felt peculiarly solitary, sitting on my heels next to the carcass in the sagebrush and greasewood, my rifle racked open on the ground. I made an incision around the metatarsal glands inside the back legs and carefully removed them and set them well aside; then I cleaned the blade of my hunting knife with handfuls of grass to keep from tainting the meat with those powerful glands. Next I detached the anus and testes from the outer walls and made a shallow puncture below the sternum, spread it with the thumb and forefinger of my left hand, and ran the knife upside down to the bone bridge between the hind legs. Inside, the diaphragm was like the taut lid of a drum and cut away cleanly, so that I could reach clear up to the back of the mouth and detach the windpipe. Once that was done I could draw the whole visceral package out onto the grass and separate out the heart, liver, and tongue before propping the carcass open with two whittled-up sage scantlings.

You could tell how cold the morning was, despite the exertion, just by watching the steam roar from the abdominal cavity. I stuck the knife in the ground and sat back against the slope, looking clear across to Convict Grade and the Crazy Mountains. I was blood from the elbows down and the antelope's eyes had skinned over. I thought, This is goddamned serious and you had better always remember that.

THERE WAS a big red enamel pot on the stove; and I ladled antelope chili into two bowls for my son and me. He said, "It better not be too hot."

"It isn't."

"What's your news?" he asked.

"Grandpa's dead."

"Which grandpa?" he asked. I told him it was Big Grandpa, my father. He kept on eating.

"He died last night."

He said, "I know what I want for Christmas."

"What's that?"

"I want Big Grandpa back."

It was nineteen fifty-something and I was small, under twelve say, and there were four of us: my father, two of his friends, and me. There was a good belton setter belonging to the one friend, a hearty bird hunter who taught dancing and fist-fought at any provocation. The other man was old and sick and had a green fatal look in his face. My father took me aside and said, "Jack and I are going to the head of this field"—and he pointed up a mile and a half of stalks to where it ended in the flat woods—"and we're going to take the dog and get what he can point. These are running birds. So you and Bill just block the field and you'll have some shooting."

"I'd like to hunt with the dog." I had a 20-gauge Winchester my grandfather had given me, which got hocked and lost years later when another of my family got into the bottle; and I could hit with it and wanted to hunt over the setter. With respect to blocking the field, I could smell a rat.

"You stay with Bill," said my father, "and try to cheer him up."

"What's the matter with Bill?"

"He's had one heart attack after another and he's going to die."

"When?"

"Pretty damn soon."

I blocked the field with Bill. My first thought was, I hope he doesn't die before they drive those birds onto us; but if he does, I'll have all the shooting.

There was a crazy cold autumn light on everything, magnified by the yellow silage all over the field. The dog found birds right away and they were shooting. Bill said he was sorry but he didn't feel so good. He had his hunting license safety-pinned to the back of his coat and fiddled with a handful of 12-gauge shells. "I've shot a shitpile of game," said Bill, "but I don't feel so good anymore." He took a knife out of his coat pocket. "I got this in the Marines," he said, "and I carried it for four years in the Pacific. The handle's drilled out and weighted so you can throw it. I want you to have it." I took it and thanked him, looking into his green face, and wondered why he had given it to me. "That's for blocking this field with me," he said. "Your dad and that dance teacher are going to shoot them all. When you're not feeling so good, they put you at the end of the field to block when there isn't shit-all going to fly by you. They'll get them all. They and the dog will."

We had an indestructible tree in the yard we had chopped on, nailed steps to, and initialed; and when I pitched that throwing knife at it, the knife broke in two. I picked it up and thought, *This thing is jinxed.* So I took it out into the crab-apple woods and put it in the can I had buried, along with a Roosevelt dime and an atomic-bomb ring I had sent away for. This was a small collection of things I buried over a period of years. I was sending them to God. All He had to do was open the can, but they were never collected. In any case, I have long known that if I could understand why I wanted to send a broken knife I believed to be jinxed to God, then I would be a long way toward what they call a personal philosophy as opposed to these hand-to-mouth metaphysics of who said what to who in some cornfield twenty-five years ago.

WE WERE in the bar at Chico Hot Springs near my home in Montana: me; a lout poet who had spent the day floating under the diving board while adolescent girls leapt overhead; and my brother John, who had glued himself to the pipe which poured warm water into the pool and announced over and over in a loud voice that every drop of water had been filtered through his bathing suit.

Now, covered with wrinkles, we were in the bar, talking to Alvin Close, an old government hunter. After half a century of predator control he called it "useless and half-assed."

Alvin Close killed the last major stock-killing wolf in Montana. He hunted the wolf so long he raised a litter of dogs to do it with. He hunted the wolf futilely with a pack that had fought the wolf a dozen times, until one day he gave up and let the dogs run the wolf out the back of a shallow canyon. He heard them yip their way into silence while he leaned up against a tree; and presently the wolf came tiptoeing down the front of the canyon into Alvin's lap. The wolf simply stopped because the game was up. Alvin raised the Winchester and shot it.

"How did you feel about that?" I asked.

"How do you think I felt?"

"I don't know."

"I felt like hell."

Alvin's evening was ruined and he went home. He was seventy-six years old and carried himself like an old-time army officer, setting his glass on the bar behind him without looking.

You stare through the plastic at the red smear of meat in the supermarket. What's this it says here? *Mighty Good? Tastee? Quality, Premium, and Government Inspected?* Soon enough, the blood is on your hands. It's inescapable.

Aldo Leopold was a hunter who I am sure abjured freeze-dried vegetables and extrusion burgers. His conscience was clean because his hunting was part of a larger husbandry in which the life of the country was enhanced by his own work. He knew that game populations are not bothered by hunting until they are already too precarious and that precarious game populations should not be hunted. Grizzlies should not be hunted, for instance. The enemy of game is clean farming and sinful chemicals; as well as the useless alteration of watersheds by promoter cretins and the insidious dizzards of land development, whose lobbyists teach us the venality of all governments.

A world in which a sacramental portion of food can be taken in an old way—hunting, fishing, farming, and gathering—has as much to do with societal sanity as a day's work for a day's pay.

For a long time, there was no tracking snow. I hunted on horseback for a couple of days in a complicated earthquake fault in the Gallatins. The fault made a maze of narrow canyons with flat floors. The sagebrush grew on woody trunks higher than my head and left sandy paths and game trails where the horse and I could travel.

There were Hungarian partridge that roared out in front of my horse, putting his head suddenly in my lap. And hawks tobogganed on the low air currents, astonished to find me there. One finger canyon ended in a vertical rock wall from which issued a spring of the kind elsewhere associated with the Virgin Mary, hung with ex-votos and the orthopedic supplications of satisfied miracle customers. Here, instead, were nine identical piles of bear shit, neatly adorned with undigested berries.

One canyon planed up and topped out on an endless grassy rise. There were deer there, does and a young buck. A thousand yards away and staring at me with semaphore ears.

They assembled at a stiff trot from the haphazard array of feeding and strung out in a precise line against the far hill in a dog trot. When I removed my hat, they went into their pogo-stick gait and that was that.

"WHAT DID a deer ever do to you?"

"Nothing."

"I'm serious. What do you have to go and kill them for?"

"I can't explain it talking like this."

"Why should they die for you? Would you die for deer?"

"If it came to that."

My boy and I went up the North Fork to look for grouse. We had my old pointer Molly, and Thomas's .22 pump. We flushed a number of birds climbing through the wild roses; but they roared away at knee level, leaving me little opportunity for my over-and-under, much less an opening for Thomas to ground-sluice one with his .22. We started out at the meteor hole above the last ranch and went all the way to the national forest. Thomas had his cap on the bridge of his nose and wobbled through the trees until we hit cross-fences. We went out into the last open pasture before he got winded. So we sat down and looked across the valley at the Gallatin Range, furiously white and serrated, a bleak edge of the world. We sat in the sun and watched the chickadees make their way through the russet brush.

"Are you having a good time?"

"Sure," he said and curled a small hand around the octagonal barrel of the Winchester. I was not sure what I had meant by my question.

THE REAR QUARTERS of the antelope came from the smoker so dense and finely grained it should have been sliced as prosciutto. We had edgy, crumbling cheddar from British Columbia, and everybody kept an eye on the food and tried to pace themselves. The snow whirled in the window light and puffed the smoke down the chimney around the cedar flames. I had a stretch of enumerating things: my family, hayfields, saddle horses, friends, thirty-ought-six, French and Russian novels. I had a baby girl, colts coming, and a new roof on the barn. I finished a big corral made of railroad ties and 2 × 6s. I was within eighteen months of my father's death, my sister's death, and the collapse of my marriage. Still, the washouts were repairing; and when a few things had been set aside, not excluding paranoia, some features were left standing, not excluding lovers, children, friends, and saddle horses. In time, it would be clear as a bell. I did want venison again that winter and couldn't help but feel some old ridge-runner had my number on him.

I didn't want to read and I didn't want to write or acknowledge the phone with its tendrils into the zombie enclaves. I didn't want the New Rugged; I wanted the Old Rugged and a pot to piss in. Otherwise, it's deteriorata, with mice undermining the wiring in my frame house, sparks jumping in the insulation, the dog turning queer, and a horned owl staring at the baby through the nursery window.

It was pitch black in the bedroom, and the windows radiated cold across the blankets. The top of my head felt this side of frost and the stars hung like ice crystals over the chimney. I scrambled out of bed and slipped into my long johns, put on a heavy shirt and my wool logger pants with the police suspenders. I carried the boots down to the kitchen so as not to wake the house and turned the percolator on. I put some cheese and chocolate in my coat, and when the coffee was done I filled a chili bowl and quaffed it against the winter.

When I hit the front steps I heard the hard squeaking of new snow under my boots, and the wind moved against my face like a machine for refinishing hardwood floors. I backed the truck up to the horse trailer, the lights wheeling against the ghostly trunks of the bare cottonwoods. I connected the trailer and pulled it forward to a flat spot for loading the horse.

I had figured that when I got to the corral I could tell one horse from another by starlight; but the horses were in the shadow of the barn and I went in feeling my way among their shapes trying to find my hunting horse, Rocky, and trying to get the front end of the big sorrel who kicks when surprised. Suddenly Rocky was looking in my face and I reached around his neck with the halter. A 1,200-pound bay quarter horse, his withers angled up like a fighting bull, he wondered where we were going but ambled after me on a slack lead rope as we headed out of the darkened corral.

I have an old trailer made by a Texas horse vet years ago. It has none of the amenities of newer trailers. I wish it had a dome light for loading in the dark; but it doesn't. You ought to check and see if the cat's sleeping in it before you load; and I didn't do that either. Instead, I climbed inside the trailer and the horse followed me. I tied the horse down to a D-ring and started back out, when he blew up. The two of us were confined in the small space and he was ripping and bucking between the walls with such noise and violence that I had a brief disassociated moment of suspension from fear. I jumped up on the manger with my arms around my head while the horse shattered the inside of the trailer and rocked it furiously on its axles. Then he blew the steel rings out of the halter and fell over backward in the snow. The cat darted out and was gone. I slipped down off the manger and looked for the horse; he had gotten up and was sidling down past the granary in the star shadows.

I put two blankets on him, saddled him, played with his feet, and calmed him. I loaded him without incident and headed out.

I went through the aspen line at daybreak, still climbing. The horse ascended steadily toward a high basin, creaking the saddle metronomically. It was getting colder as the sun came up, and the rifle scabbard held my left leg far enough from the horse that I was chilling on that side.

We touched the bottom of the basin and I could see the rock wall defined by a black stripe of evergreens on one side and the remains of an avalanche on the other. I thought how utterly desolate this country can look in winter and how one could hardly think of human travel in it at all, not white horsemen nor Indians dragging travois, just aerial raptors with their rending talons and heads like cameras slicing across the geometry of winter.

Then we stepped into a deep hole and the horse went to his chest in the powder, splashing the snow out before him as he floundered toward the other side. I got my feet out of the stirrups in case we went over. Then we were on wind-scoured rock and I hunted some lee for the two of us. I thought of my son's words after our last cold ride: "Dad, you know in 4-H? Well, I want to switch from Horsemanship to Aviation."

The spot was like this: a crest of snow crowned in a sculpted edge high enough to protect us. There was a tough little juniper to picket the horse to, and a good place to sit out of the cold and noise. Over my head, a long, curling plume of snow poured out, unchanging in shape against the pale blue sky. I ate some of the cheese and rewrapped it. I got the rifle down from the scabbard, loosened the cinch, and undid the flank cinch. I put the stirrup over the horn to remind me my saddle was loose, loaded two cartridges into the blind magazine, and slipped one in the chamber. Then I started toward the rock wall, staring at the patterned discolorations: old seeps, lichen, cracks, and the madhouse calligraphy of immemorial weather.

There were a lot of tracks where the snow had crusted out of the wind; all deer except for one well-used bobcat trail winding along the edges of a long rocky slot. I moved as carefully as I could, stretching my eyes as far out in front of my detectable movement as I could. I tried to work into the wind, but it turned erratically in the basin as the temperature of the new day changed.

The buck was studying me as soon as I came out on the open slope: he was a long way away and I stopped motionless to wait for him to feed again. He stared straight at me from five hundred yards. I waited until I could no longer feel my feet nor finally my legs. It was nearly an hour before he suddenly ducked his head and began to feed. Every time he fed I moved a few feet, but he was working away from me and I wasn't getting anywhere. Over the next half hour he made his way to a little rim and, in the half hour after that, moved the twenty feet that dropped him over the rim.

I went as fast as I could move quietly. I now had the rim to cover me and the buck should be less than one hundred yards from me when I looked over. It was all browse for a half mile, wild roses, buck brush, and young quakies where there was any runoff.

When I reached the rim, I took off my hat and set it in the snow with my gloves inside. I wanted to be looking in the right direction when I cleared the rim, rise a half step and be looking straight at the buck, not scanning for the buck with him running sixty, a degree or two out of my periphery. And I didn't want to gum it up with thinking or trajectory guessing. People are always trajectory guessing their way into gut shots and clean misses. So, before I took the last step, all there was to do was lower the rim with my feet, lower the buck into my vision, and isolate the path of the bullet.

As I took that step, I knew he was running. He wasn't in

the browse at all, but angling into invisibility at the rock wall, racing straight into the elevation, bounding toward zero gravity, taking his longest arc into the bullet and the finality and terror of all you have made of the world, the finality you know that you share even with your babies with their inherited and ambiguous dentition, the finality that any minute now you will meet as well.

He slid one hundred yards in a rush of snow. I dressed him and skidded him by one antler to the horse. I made a slit behind the last ribs, pulled him over the saddle and put the horn through the slit, lashed the feet to the cinch dees, and led the horse downhill. The horse had bells of clear ice around his hoofs, and when he slipped, I chipped them out from under his feet with the point of a bullet.

I hung the buck in the open woodshed with a lariat over a rafter. He turned slowly against the cooling air. I could see the intermittent blue light of the television against the bedroom ceiling from where I stood. I stopped the twirling of the buck, my hands deep in the sage-scented fur, and thought: This is either the beginning or the end of everything.

THE GRIZZLY BEAR

BY THOMAS McNAMEE

At the Cooke City Corral, you hear the same thing over and over. Three hairy, lethal-looking Hell's Angels types and their three pin-eyed speed-burnt molls uncoil out of three Harley-Davidson chopper trikes and demand besides burgers that the waitress enlighten them as to where all the bears is at. A pair of representatives of Yellowstone's most prominent constituency, American Retired Persons, bilious and cramped from hours of Cheez Doodle consumption at the helm of gargantuan Winnebagos, grumble that so many years ago you could walk right up to the bears out here and they'd practically eat right out of your hand. One little boy, who proclaims his future occupation to be explorer, has been driven all the way from Iowa to explore for bears and clearly holds it against his parents that he has seen not one. His father beards a Western-looking sort whom he takes to be a local —actually an insurance adjuster from San Bernardino who spends two weeks with his wife every June at the campground up the road and who therefore considers himself kind of an honorary semilocal—and this established authority on the state of the ecosystem solemnly informs his interlocutor that if the fedderl gummint had only kept their cottonpicking noses out of the problem and left it to the citizens there'd be plenty of bears, but as it is the Park Service has near-about killed them all, and those they haven't killed they're studying to death, and as a matter of fact there was a big old grizzly with one of their durn radio collars choking him, must have been half starved, going through his garbage just the other night, and like to scared the missus out of her wits.

One real live local—runs a restaurant and motel—finally got weary of the summer-long litany of disappointment and decided to take the matter in hand, private-enterprisewise. He figured that if the only bears turning up around Cooke City were doing so for garbage's sake, he might as well make a regular thing of it and see what happened.

Now, Cooke City, Montana, is not really a city. It consists of a single commercial strip about a quarter of a mile long, gas/motel/café/bar/souvenirs, and a few houses and trailers scattered here and there up the hill behind the strip. It was named City in expectation of a great mining boom that never quite materialized, and except for the eroding mining access roads and a few flecks of private land it is pretty much surrounded by howling wilderness, the Absaroka-Beartooth on three sides, with Yellowstone Park just to the west, beyond the still less prepossessing motel strip called Silver Gate. Cooke City comes alive only in the few months, roughly June to September in a favorable year, when the road from Billings and Red Lodge to the park's northeast entrance is open over

Beartooth Pass—ten thousand nine hundred thirty-three feet above sea level—and even then this is by far the least-used approach to Yellowstone Park. A number of businesses are boarded up, abandoned. Looking both ways before crossing the main drag may feel like something of an urban affectation. During the eight months or so when the pass is snowed under, the nearest civilization is Gardiner, Montana, fifty-six winding, slippery, blizzard-prone miles away through the park, and Gardiner's not much of a town either.

Since 1979, when the Park Service succeeded in getting the town dump closed by agreeing to haul the residents' trash the hundred and nine miles to Livingston—all on behalf of the bears who were feeding at the dump and so becoming a problem—Cooke City has had very little impact on the superlative grizzly habitat in which it is a tiny island. That is, it *had* little impact until that insightful entrepreneur started parking a dump truck under the stairs on the downhill side of his restaurant and shoveling his surplus french fries, T-bones, strawberry-rhubarb pie, and garlic bread into it every evening. The Hell's Angels and the Retired Persons and the little explorer are all delighted, of course, to find the truck full of scavenging bears, and the restaurant man congratulates himself for performing a valuable public service which also happens incidentally to facilitate the movement of visitors into his commercial premises. Everybody seems happy—excepting of course the fedderl gummint, which has been through all this before and seen how poorly it tends to turn out. The feds' problem is lack of legal ammunition. The Park Service, the Forest Service, and the Fish and Wildlife Service have all sat down and tried to hash it out, but there seems to be nothing in the Endangered Species Act or anywhere else about please do not feed the endangered species, and anyway the restaurant is private property and as such sacrosanct. The state of Montana has always considered Cooke City rather too remote to fool with much, but under pressure from the federals they reluctantly rack their lawbooks for . . . anything. They find a sanitation statute that may apply, but it's going to take time.

Meanwhile, the bears are getting bolder every night, less and less fretful of the gabbling, flashbulb-popping tourist hordes. The guy's motel and restaurant business is booming. Down the road a few dozen yards, Bill and Betty Sommers are out on the porch of Sommers Motel with highly dubious looks on their faces, watching little girls of six and their chirping mamas troop down the hill to see the bears. Besides their motel, the Sommerses run a backcountry guide service, and they have been in these parts a good long time, gaining ample knowledge of wildlife behavior along the way—to which the snowy-bearded mountain goat heads on their living room walls and the stupendous grizzly rug attest. Like most of their Cooke City neighbors, they know that their fellow citizen up the road is asking for big trouble. "Somebody," Bill Sommers muses quietly, "is going to get killed."

"Most likely a bear," adds Betty Sommers. Both the Sommerses were here in the days when the mountains harbored many grizzlies and there was a limited legal hunt, and they'd like nothing better than a truly recovered population.

Because a huntable population would be good for business?

"No, no," says Sommers. "We just like having them around."

"Just not in town, please," cracks his wife.

It has become a regular annual custom for the mother grizzly that as June comes on and carrion and prey grow scarcer, she moves north and east toward Cooke City. In her youth there had been the town dump to forage in, and in mating season the neighborhood remains an important social center. With cubs now, of course, she will avoid as much as possible any contact with other grizzlies—a stipulation against which she must weigh the temptation to use concentrated food sources. We may assume that as the bear and her cubs move into this area where grizzlies in fair numbers are already living in close proximity, she will be carefully investigating the traces of urine and other scents by which she can identify her fellow bears. It is likely that by scent alone she can tell the sex and the sexual status of the bears whose sign she is reading. She may also know how long ago the scent was left. With such information she can devise a route for herself and the cubs which will minimize the likelihood of conflict. As they approach Cooke City, however, the smell of garbage from somewhere nearby is deliriously intoxicating, and in its spell she lets her caution flag.

The scent leads right to the edge of town, to Soda Butte Creek, just across which, up the hill, there is the dump truck full of garbage and bears. She waits till midnight to approach, when the black bears have gone home to bed and the human gawkers are likely to be all asleep. Eventually the truck is free of grizzlies too, and the coast is clear. Still hanging back indecisively at the edge of the forest, she recognizes trotting out of the woods upcreek in the moonlight her own flesh and blood—none other than the calf-killing demon whose littermate was shot two springs ago. His easy stride and his blithe disregard for a sudden flash of truck lights from the road above suggest that he must be a regular at the chuckwagon jubilee. With a quiet woof of hard-earned restraint, the mother urges her cubs back into the gloom of the forest, and takes up another scent.

This one leads her east and south, across the state line into a valley of virgin timber interspersed with meadows where small herds of cows, grazing by Forest Service lease, have provided occasional prey and carrion for grizzly bears for half a century. The smell, unmistakably, is of beef, and plenty of it. Oddly, when she follows it to its source, the meat is up in a tree. You may have heard, and prefer to believe, that grizzly bears never climb trees, in which case you may wish to avert your eyes as this one proceeds unhesitatingly to do so. The meat, however, is hanging by a rope from a high limb, and try as she might she cannot reach it.

Returning disgruntled to earth, the mother bear discovers what her cubs have long since discerned: this place is a wonderland of good things to eat. There's a pile of cantaloupe peels over here, and over here a smelly dead ground squirrel, and over here some apples. Bacon is scattered everywhere. There is a length of steel culvert up on wheels, and at the far end of it, inside, there lies a huge and gorgeous chunk of beef, already swarming with delicious maggots.

She licks up a few, then sinks her teeth into the meat, and barely has she given it one good tug when CLANG! behind her, unimaginably, a steel-barred door has slammed shut.

She whirls. She pounds and pulls and butts and gnashes her teeth, and, *waaaw,* bawl the cubs, and, *aaargh,* she bellows, but the door holds tight. She crouches panting in the pipe and pushes her nose softly against the bars. The cubs come and stand on their hind legs and sniff back. As she claws in fury at the steel, the cubs begin excavating around the trap, trying to dig her out, or dig their own way in. All night, in panic and terror, the futile struggle continues.

At dawn, the mother bear lies exhausted in the culvert, smeared with her own excrement. The cubs pace hopelessly around the trap, wailing, hungry, scared.

A pickup jounces down the rutted track, and two men emerge. "Look, Larry!" one whispers. "We got another one!" This is Bart Schleyer, graduate student in wildlife biology.

"Bart, those bears are just waiting in line to get in your trap. They're getting to be worse than the girls up in Cooke." This is Larry Roop, research biologist for the Wyoming Department of Game and Fish.

As the men approach the culvert trap, the mother grizzly barks an impassioned dismissal at her little ones, and they hightail it dutifully for cover. "Cubs!" whispers Schleyer, smiling hard.

"All *right!*"

A female with cubs is an important capture. The trapping has been yielding many more males than females. That may be due to the fact of females' smaller home ranges, or because females are less bold and therefore less likely to approach the roads and developed areas where most of the traps are set, or simply because females are more cautious about getting into traps—but the sex ratio of trapped grizzlies has recently been so uneven that even allowing for trapping bias, the researchers have concluded that females are in severely short supply.

This bear shows very little gratitude for the biologists' concern. When they come near the trap, she lunges at them with all her might, smashing headlong into the bars. "Shhh,"

Schleyer tries to soothe her, "easy, easy, old mama. What do you say, Larry? Three twenty-five?"

"That sounds about right. I'm going to dose her on the light side anyway, so we can get her back to her cubs quick."

"Come on, come on, turn around," Schleyer says softly to the bear as Roop draws three and a quarter cubic centimeters of Sernylan into the syringe. Sernylan is the trade name for phencyclidine hydrochloride, or PCP, a veterinary anesthetic—and, in smaller doses, a rather violent hallucinogen, also known as Angel Dust. A dose equivalent on the basis of body weight would kill a human being several times over, but all it's going to do to the bear is put her swiftly to sleep. On top of the Sernylan, Roop draws in an equal amount of acepromazine, a tranquilizer, which will insure that she comes out of this strange experience in a relatively placid frame of mind. The syringe is fitted into a stainless-steel dart, and that in turn is loaded into an air pistol called a Cap-chur Gun. Schleyer prods the bear with a stick, and as she whirls in rage Roop aims at her haunch through the bars at the other end of the trap and fires. A little fluff of pink yarn in her fur marks the spot where the dart has sunk home. Again she whirls, but now rather than charge she sits down and curls around to see what this thing is pricking her derriere. She licks at it a couple of times, and seems not much concerned. Soon her head begins to droop, and then her legs give way. Her tongue begins to move slowly in and out as though she were lapping up water. Her eyes glaze over, and finally she lays down her head and sleeps.

Roop and Schleyer lift the heavy trap door open, grab the bear's back feet, and slide her gently to earth. Stretched out limp on the ground, she looks like nothing so much as a scruffy fur bag of assorted bear parts, but poke beneath that almost comically floppy caparison and you can feel an awesome musculature. Schleyer dabs at her lifelessly staring eyes with a tube of antibiotic ointment, and shields them from the sun with a scrap of towel. Roop pulls a premolar, a count of whose annual rings in the lab will tell her age, just like a tree's. A funny-looking pair of pliers, faced with reversed numbers made of little needles, is briefly clamped to the inside of her lip, and an indelible ink is painted over the tiny holes it has made—a tattoo. A bright yellow plastic tag bearing the same number is clipped through a hole Schleyer has punched in her ear. They take a blood sample with a syringe, and they pluck out a sample of her fur. (There has been some speculation that lighter-colored fur may be correlated with certain blood chemicals that are indicators of aggressiveness; they will send the fur sample to the scientist who is trying to find out.) The bear gets an injection of a diuretic, and after a few minutes—"Thar she blows!" cries Roop—a urine specimen is taken. They measure her from stem to stern, recording all on a schematic bear diagram:

Total length	150.2 cm. [58 in.]
Contour length	189.4 cm. [74 in.]
Girth	118.5 cm. [46 in.]
Height	102.9 cm. [40 in.]
Neck circumference	76 cm. [30 in.]
Head length	41 cm. [16 in.]
Head width	32 cm. [12 in.]
Fore foot pad width	140 mm. [5½ in.]
Fore foot pad length	65 mm. [2½ in.]
Length from heel to middle toe	125 mm. [5 in.]
Length from heel to middle claw tip	162 mm. [6 in.]

Hind foot pad width	130 mm. [5 in.]
Hind foot pad length	192 mm. [7½ in.]
Length from heel to middle toe	125 mm. [8 in.]
Length from heel to middle claw tip	205.7 mm. [8 in.]
Furred arch of hind foot	9 mm. [½ in.]

Roop and Schleyer lash a block and tackle to a stout pine limb, gather up the bear in a surplus cargo parachute, and hoist her aloft to be weighed. She is down to three hundred thirty-two pounds. This is probably her low point for the year, since as summer comes on, berries will be ripening and other bear foods more abundant in the subalpine and alpine zones. Finally they fit the bear with a radio collar—a tiny transmitter and battery embedded in waterproof plastic molded in turn to a heavy leather belt. The ends of the belt are joined together by a several-layered strip of cotton canvas, which is calculated to rot through so the collar will fall off at about the time the battery runs down. Schleyer records her description: "Dark underparts. Light grizzling on back. Light-colored stripe behind forelegs. Head quite light colored. Pelage thick and unrubbed." The sun is growing hot, and they drag the bear to a nice cool spot in the shade, and wait. (The researchers must stay with her till she comes out from under, because some other bear might happen along and try to take advantage of the situation—that is, eat her.)

While Roop and Schleyer wait for the mother grizzly to come around, the cubs reappear, timid but not especially afraid, and apparently not much bothered by their mother's condition. They both go to work kneading her teats to start the milk flowing, and soon they are nursing contentedly, producing a low, soft humming that sounds like a hive of bees.

Sernylan wears off from the top down, so the mother bear's first sign of life is a woozy shake of the head. "Describe recovery reactions," commands the study work sheet, so Schleyer is writing, "0905, tightening of muscles. 0910, some head movement." A few minutes later, she can rise on her front legs and turn to gaze in groggy mystification at her still useless hindparts and her humming progeny. "0920, head up, sprawled on stomach unable to get up. 0925, crawling. 0930, on feet but collapsed. 0938, staggered out of trap site into timber, followed by cubs."

OUR HEROINE is no longer her wild and private self alone. She is now also a source of data for the Yellowstone Interagency Grizzly Bear Study, one of the most comprehensive wildlife research projects ever undertaken, and as such she has gained a degree of power beyond even that mythic primacy with which grizzlies were invested in the days before the birth of modern firearms. She has the power now, as long as we continue to grant it to her, to reshape human values in the preeminent, most influential human culture in the world—the power to deflect American history from its collision course with her survival, and from the moral tragedy which that course represents. If we can come to know her and to love what we know and so to wish it to endure, we cannot but be the better for it, for her kind's survival will be an objective correlative of our kind's having come at last to the conviction that there is a higher good than the subjection of all nature to human will. For the grizzly bear will never yield to our will. This grizzly, like every other, will be herself, or perish. . . .

LARRY ROOP radio-locates the bear one last time, and spots her and [a] cub sunning themselves on the spill of excavated rubble below the den entrance. He flies past several times to see if the missing cub may be merely out of sight. He plots the den location on his map, and writes in his notes: "10/26. Possible mortality, cub. Check in spring."

IN DENDRITIC CLUSTERS along the oceansides, along the Great Lakes shores, along the great rivers, miles-wide brilliancies shine deep into space; scattered among them, thousands more, lesser versions of the same, spatter the continent; between them all, all night, pulse filaments of moving light. The whole vast constellation—cities, towns, glittering web of highways—hums, grinds, roars. And above the electrified nightscape hangs a dim and sour haze, the airborne waste of that combustion of long-dead plants which engenders all this motion and light.

The sun rises on an America transformed—transformed in the wink of history's eye, in one-ten-thousandth of one tick on the biological clock—by the hand of man. Humanity has surged into the megalopolis in such multitude that there is scant space or sustenance left for other creatures than those hardy few whose ancient way of life has fitted them, fortuitously, for man's close-quartered companionship—the likes of the robin, the roach, the occasional prowling raccoon. The rest is man and the man-made—rivers of asphalt, mountains of glass and steel, hybrid flowers in tidy rows, trees in holes in the sidewalk.

There is, to be sure, much good here; the privileges and pleasures of membership in the civilization of the late twentieth century hardly need cataloguing. But we must not forget that art and love and achievement and comfort and other of civilization's high glories all have their sources in nature, and from nature the modern city dweller is, as a rule, profoundly isolated. What do we see in our daily life? The television screen, the car just ahead, the perpetually perplexing faces of our fellow city dwellers; a squirrel, a tulip, a lawn? What do we smell? Exhaust, perfume, hot coffee? What do we hear? The radio, a jackhammer, the hiss of tires on pavement, a shout in the street; a barking dog, a chattering sparrow? Motion. Commotion. Noise.

Night falls on the small town in a shower of birdsong. Over the soybean field at the foot of the street the sun sets crimson above crimson maples. A south wind brings the scent of rain and a faint rumble of thunder. But John is underneath his truck, and Mary is watching the TV news. A kid or two may be out catching frogs, an old man may be out on his porch watching the nimbus-anvil rise from the horizon, but in the main the town today is as detached from the natural world, as turned in on itself and its consuming human affairs, as the city. That is the way we live now.

The clatter of quail wings is no longer heard in the high-plains wheat, gone with the coming of new pesticides; gone too are the butterflies that fed on now herbicide-killed weeds; gone are the rat snake's soft passage beneath and the eagle on the old oak snag above. An owl still roosts, this dawn, in the hayloft, and the geese still forage in the stubble; the wild mint still exhales sweet fragrance at the edge of a still clean spring; deer still glide among the shadows of the woodlot, and a fox still dens in the cow pasture hedge. Sometimes, just before dawn, coyotes still can be heard from the distant hills. But nature has been tamed on the farm: it is a resource, like a bank account, to be drawn on, fretted over, and, when convenient, ignored. The tractor is enclosed and air-conditioned now, and the shriek of a rabbit caught in the harrow goes unheard. The worst threat to the cows is that they will develop tolerance to their antibiotics.

And yet we may, from time to time, perhaps, in some lonely place, in one of those precious few patches of darkness in the megalopolitan constellation, stand on the snow in the middle of the night and feel stillness soaking into our grateful beings like rain into parched earth. And, then, we may sense, if only for a fugitive moment, how busy, how buffeted, how radically unpeaceful we have been all day . . . all week . . . all our lives.

It has been in our interest as members of a technologically advancing society to forget that we are animals, not far removed from an environment much unlike the one we live in now. We are biological strangers to this life. The world which we as animals evolved for was one in which man functioned as only one of several relatively dominant animals, dependent on wild foods, subject to the vagaries of weather and natural catastrophe, fellow of the wolf and the grizzly bear: alert in ways we nearly have lost, perceiving the world more with our senses than with our minds.

Presumably unlike the perceived world of their fellow beasts, however, that of our uncivilized ancestors was also, to a now inconceivable extent, a spirit-world. Where their senses left off, their human imagination took over. Darkness was full of brooding menace, silence alive with numinous voices, a starry sky the realm of divinity. It was a world they could not dream of mastering as we have mastered ours, and that humility bred awe, an awe which our own not unjustified civilized pride has obscured.

But not quite extinguished. It is not just as make-believe primitive man and fellow beast that we come into the wilderness, but also in quest of that lost sacred awe. We come as a king might come disguised among his peasantry, trying to feel unalien in a world that seems more real than our daily busy noisy own—which, in terms of biological familiarity, the wilderness truly is. False though our atavistic incursion into an image of the distant racial past may feel, we also feel our pulse really slow down, the muscles in our social face really relax. We hear the rustlings and stirrings of the living creatures around us, so immitigably unintelligible. We peer into the darkness, and wonder. We listen into the silence for voices too still and small to be heard within ourselves in the deafening life we usually lead. In half-pretended faith, we feel our way back toward a love of nature not unmingled with dread; we are at once alone and at one with all; and an ancient awe steals over us.

Still, the ultimate awestruck peace must always elude us—a fitting reminder, perhaps, of the weakness inherent in being as strong a force as we are even when we least mean to do harm. To the most hidden and tranquil of wilderness places, the remote subalpine mountainsides where grizzly bears prepare their winter dens and, in prehibernation lethargy, are now at their most vulnerable, we can come only in imagination; for if we were really to go there, the grizzly bears would leave. This is the paradox of modern citizens thronging into the wilderness: our very presence may degrade what we come for.

THE LAST BEARBERRIES and buffaloberries, wizened to raisins, have been plucked. The elk and deer and bighorn sheep have moved down to their winter range. Mouse and marmot and gopher and vole are all underground to stay. The roots and whitebark pine nut caches are locked in the hard-frozen soil. Even on the few windblown slopes where the meadows are free of snow, the last forbs and grasses have withered to straw.

The days are dark, the low clouds muttering as the last warm winds above clash against upwelling earthly chill. The ripple of a rill beneath the snow falls silent, frozen. The mother grizzly and her cub sleep such days away in snow beds near the den. They have nothing to do but wait. There is nothing to eat.

And then an auspicious mercy befalls them. The cub has been nursing a little, and has fallen deeply asleep. But a faint scent rouses the mother bear. As the cub still sleeps, she rises, moves downslope, stands up on her hind legs, and lifts her nose into a wisp of breeze. She returns to the cub and wakes him with a touch of her paw. They walk slowly into the trees.

An aging moose, his lungs and liver infested with worms, his teeth falling out from necrosis of the jaw, has wandered into the subalpine snows and died.

The bears eat until they can barely walk. They yawn and cannot stop yawning. Pacing dreamily back and forth on the porch of the den, they are already half insensate. You could probably walk right up and scratch them behind the ears.

And still they stagger to the moose carcass, half a dozen times a day for half a dozen days, grunting, belching, roly-poly and languorous as sultans. Their layers of fat grow thicker. Their coats are thick and oily-sleek.

At last their appetite fails them. When the blizzard comes, therefore, they are ready. They stretch, crawl in through the long dark tunnel, and snuggle up, the big bear curled around her curled-up cub.

Three days and nights of white tempest pass. The apron of spoil, their tracks, the den entrance, all signs of grizzly bear are gone.

The sun is a pale disc in the thinning silver overcast. All the windless afternoon, not a willow shoot quivers. All the windless night, the moon is a silver disc in a blackness pricked with stars. The aurora borealis shimmers over the far peaks. The stillness is complete.

FROM
AFRICAN GAME
TRAILS

BY THEODORE
ROOSEVELT

The Sotik country through which we had hunted was sorely stricken by drought. The grass was short and withered and most of the water-holes were drying up, while both the game and the flocks and herds of the nomad Masai gathered round the watercourses in which there were still occasional muddy pools, and grazed their neighborhood bare of pasturage. It was an unceasing pleasure to watch the ways of the game and to study their varying habits. Where there was a river from which to drink, or where there were many pools, the different kinds of buck, and the zebra, often showed comparatively little timidity about drinking, and came boldly down to the water's edge, sometimes in broad daylight, sometimes in darkness; although even under those conditions they were very cautious if there was cover at the drinking-place. But where the pools were few they never approached one without feeling panic dread of their great enemy the lion, who, they knew well, might be lurking around their drinking-place. At such a pool I once saw a herd of zebras come to water at nightfall. They stood motionless some distance off; then they slowly approached, and twice on false alarms wheeled and fled at speed; at last the leaders ventured to the brink of the pool and at once the whole herd came jostling and crowding in behind them, the water gurgling down their thirsty throats; and immediately afterward off they went at a gallop, stopping to graze some hundreds of yards away. The ceaseless dread of the lion felt by all but the heaviest game is amply justified by his ravages among them. They are always in peril from him at the drinking-places; yet in my experience I found that in the great majority of cases they were killed while feeding or resting far from water, the lion getting them far more often by stalking than by lying in wait. A lion will eat a zebra (beginning at the hind quarters, by the way, and sometimes having, and sometimes not having, previously disembowelled the animal) or one of the bigger buck at least once a week—perhaps once every five days. The dozen lions we had killed would probably, if left alive, have accounted for seven or eight hundred buck, pig, and zebra within the next year. Our hunting was a net advantage to the harmless game.

The zebras were the noisiest of the game. After them came the wildebeest, which often uttered their queer grunt; sometimes a herd would stand and grunt at me for some minutes as I passed, a few hundred yards distant. The topi uttered only a kind of sneeze, and the hartebeest a somewhat similar sound. The so-called Roberts' gazelle was merely the Grant's gazelle of the Athi, with the lyrate shape of the horns tending to be carried to an extreme of spread and backward bend. The tommy bucks carried good horns; the horns of the does were usually aborted, and were never more than four or five inches long. The most notable feature about the tommies was the incessant switching of their tails, as if jerked by electricity. In the Sotik the topis all seemed to have calves of about the same age, as if born from four to six months earlier; the young of the other game were of every age. The males of all the antelope fought much among themselves. The gazelle bucks of both species would face one another, their heads between the forelegs and the horns level with the ground, and each would punch his opponent until the hair flew.

Watching the game, one was struck by the intensity and the evanescence of their emotions. Civilized man now usually passes his life under conditions which eliminate the intensity of terror felt by his ancestors when death by violence was their normal end, and threatened them during every hour of the day and night. It is only in nightmares that the average dweller in civilized countries now undergoes the hideous horror which was the regular and frequent portion of his ages-vanished forefathers, and which is still an every-day incident in the lives of most wild creatures. But the dread is short-lived, and its horror vanishes with instantaneous rapidity. In these wilds the game dreaded the lion and the other flesh-eating beasts rather than man. We saw innumerable kills of all the buck, and of zebra, the neck being usually dislocated, and it being evident that none of the lion's victims, not even the truculent wildebeest or huge eland, had been able to make any fight against him. The game is ever on the alert against this greatest of foes, and every herd, almost every individual, is in imminent and deadly peril every few days or nights, and of course suffers in addition from countless false alarms. But no sooner is the danger over than the animals resume their feeding, or love making, or their fighting among themselves.

Two bucks will do battle the minute the herd has stopped running from the foe that has seized one of its number, and a buck will cover a doe in the brief interval between the first and the second alarm, from hunter or lion. Zebra will make much noise when one of their number has been killed; but their fright has vanished when once they begin their barking calls.

Death by violence, death by cold, death by starvation—these are the normal endings of the stately and beautiful creatures of the wilderness. The sentimentalists who prattle about the peaceful life of nature do not realize its utter mercilessness; although all they would have to do would be to look at the birds in the winter woods, or even at the insects on a cold morning or cold evening. Life is hard and cruel for all the lower creatures, and for man also in what the sentimentalists call a "state of nature." . . .

EVERYWHERE throughout the country we were crossing were signs that the lion was lord and that his reign was cruel. There were many lions, for the game on which they feed was extraordinarily abundant. They occasionally took the ostriches or stock of the settlers, or ravaged the herds and flocks of the natives, but not often; for their favorite food was yielded by the swarming herds of kongoni and zebras, on which they could prey at will. Later we found that in this region they rarely molested the buffalo, even where they lived in the same reedbeds; and this though elsewhere they habitually prey on the buffalo. But where zebras and hartebeests could be obtained without effort, it was evidently not worth their while to challenge such formidable quarry. Every "kill" I saw was a kongoni or a zebra; probably I came across fifty of each. One zebra kill, which was not more than eighteen hours old (after the lapse of that time the vultures and marabouts, not to speak of the hyenas and jackals, leave only the bare bones), showed just what had occurred. The bones were all in place, and the skin still on the lower legs and head. The animal was lying on its belly, the legs spread out, the neck vertebra crushed; evidently the lion had sprung clean on it, bearing it down by his weight while he bit through the back of the neck, and the zebra's legs had spread out as the body yielded under the lion. One fresh kongoni kill showed no marks on the haunches, but a broken neck and claw marks on the face and withers; in this case the lion's hind legs had remained on the ground, while with his fore paws he grasped the kongoni's head and shoulders, holding it until the teeth splintered the neck bone.

One or two of our efforts to get lions failed, of course; the ravines we beat did not contain them, or we failed to make them leave some particularly difficult hill or swamp—for lions lie close. But Sir Alfred knew just the right place to go to, and was bound to get us lions—and he did.

One day we started from the ranch house in good season for an all-day lion hunt. Besides Kermit and myself, there was a fellow-guest, Medlicott, and not only our host, but our hostess and her daughter; and we were joined by Percival at lunch, which we took under a great fig-tree at the foot of a high, rocky hill. Percival had with him a little mongrel bull-dog, and a Masai "boy," a fine, bold-looking savage, with a handsome head-dress and the usual formidable spear; master, man, and dog evidently all looked upon any form of en-counter with lions simply in the light of a spree.

After lunch we began to beat down a long donga, or dry watercourse—a creek, as we should call it in the Western plains country. The watercourse, with low, steep banks, wound in curves, and here and there were patches of brush, which might contain anything in the shape of lion, cheetah, hyena, or wild dog. Soon we came upon lion spoor in the sandy bed; first the footprints of a big male, then those of a lioness. We walked cautiously along each side of the donga, the horses following close behind so that if the lion were missed we could gallop after him and round him up on the plain. The dogs—for besides the little bull, we had a large brindled mongrel named Ben, whose courage belied his looks—began to show signs of scenting the lion; and we beat out each patch of brush, the natives shouting and throwing in stones, while we stood with the rifles where we could best command any probable exit. After a couple of false alarms the dogs drew toward one patch, their hair bristling, and showing such eager excitement that it was evident something big was inside; and in a moment one of the boys called, "simba" (lion), and pointed with his finger. It was just across the little ravine, there about four yards wide and as many feet deep; and I shifted my position, peering eagerly into the bushes for some moments before I caught a glimpse of tawny hide; as it moved, there was a call to me to "shoot," for at that distance, if the lion charged, there would be scant time to stop it; and I fired into what I saw. There was a commotion in the bushes, and Kermit fired; and immediately afterward there broke out on the other side, not the hoped-for big lion, but two cubs the size of mastiffs. Each was badly wounded and we finished them off; even if unwounded, they were too big to take alive.

This was a great disappointment, and as it was well on in the afternoon, and we had beaten the country most apt to harbor our game, it seemed unlikely that we would have another chance. Percival was on foot and a long way from his house, so he started for it; and the rest of us also began to jog homeward. But Sir Alfred, although he said nothing, intended to have another try. After going a mile or two he started off to the left at a brisk canter; and we, the other riders, followed, leaving behind our gun-bearers, saises, and porters. A couple of miles away was another donga, another shallow watercourse with occasional big brush patches along the winding bed; and toward this we cantered. Almost as soon as we reached it our leader found the spoor of two big lions; and with every sense acock, we dismounted and approached the first patch of tall bushes. We shouted and threw in stones, but nothing came out; and another small patch showed the same result. Then we mounted our horses again, and rode toward another patch a quarter of a mile off. I was mounted on Tranquillity, the stout and quiet sorrel.

This patch of tall, thick brush stood on the hither bank— that is, on our side of the watercourse. We rode up to it and shouted loudly. The response was immediate, in the shape of loud gruntings, and crashings through the thick brush. We were off our horses in an instant, I throwing the reins over the head of mine; and without delay the good old fellow began placidly grazing, quite unmoved by the ominous sounds immediately in front.

I sprang to one side; and for a second or two we waited, uncertain whether we should see the lions charging out ten yards distant or running away. Fortunately, they adopted the latter course. Right in front of me, thirty yards off, there appeared, from behind the bushes which had first screened him from my eyes, the tawny, galloping form of a big maneless lion. Crack! the Winchester spoke; and as the soft-nosed bullet ploughed forward through his flank the lion swerved so that I missed him with the second shot; but my third bullet went through the spine and forward into his chest. Down he came, sixty yards off, his hind quarters dragging, his head up, his ears back, his jaws open and lips drawn up in a prodigious snarl, as he endeavored to turn to face us. His back was broken; but of this we could not at the moment be sure, and if it had merely been grazed, he might have recovered, and then, even though dying, his charge might have done mischief. So Kermit, Sir Alfred, and I fired almost together, into his chest. His head sank, and he died.

This lion had come out on the left of the bushes; the other, to the right of them, had not been hit, and we saw him galloping off across the plain, six or eight hundred yards away. A couple more shots missed, and we mounted our horses to try to ride him down. The plain sloped gently upward for three-quarters of a mile to a low crest or divide, and long before we got near him he disappeared over this. Sir Alfred and Kermit were tearing along in front and to the right, with Miss Pease close behind; while Tranquillity carried me, as fast as he could, on the left, with Medlicott near me. On topping the divide Sir Alfred and Kermit missed the lion, which had swung to the left, and they raced ahead too far to the right. Medlicott and I, however, saw the lion, loping along close behind some kongoni; and this enabled me to get up to him as quickly as the lighter men on the faster horses. The going was now slightly downhill, and the sorrel took me along very well, while Medlicott, whose horse was slow, bore to the right and joined the other two men. We gained rapidly, and, finding out this, the lion suddenly halted and came to bay in a slight hollow, where the grass was rather long. The plain seemed flat, and we could see the lion well from horseback; but, especially when he lay down, it was most difficult to make him out on foot, and impossible to do so when kneeling.

We were about a hundred and fifty yards from the lion, Sir Alfred, Kermit, Medlicott, and Miss Pease off to one side, and slightly above him on the slope, while I was on the level, about equidistant from him and them. Kermit and I tried shooting from the horses; but at such a distance this was not effective. Then Kermit got off, but his horse would not let him shoot; and when I got off I could not make out the animal through the grass with sufficient distinctness to enable me to take aim. Old Ben the dog had arrived, and, barking loudly, was strolling about near the lion, which paid him not the slightest attention. At this moment my black sais, Simba, came running up to me and took hold of the bridle; he had seen the chase from the line of march and had cut across to join me. There was no other sais or gun-bearer anywhere near, and his action was plucky, for he was the only man afoot, with the lion at bay. Lady Pease had also ridden up and was an interested spectator only some fifty yards behind me.

Now, an elderly man with a varied past which includes rheumatism does not vault lightly into the saddle; as his sons for instance, can; and I had already made up my mind that in the event of the lion's charging it would be wise for me to trust to straight powder rather than to try to scramble into the saddle and get under way in time. The arrival of my two companions settled matters. I was not sure of the speed of

Lady Pease's horse; and Simba was on foot and it was of course out of the question for me to leave him. So I said, "Good, Simba, now we'll see this thing through," and gentle-mannered Simba smiled a shy appreciation of my tone, though he could not understand the words. I was still unable to see the lion when I knelt, but he was now standing up, looking first at one group of horses and then at the other, his tail lashing to and fro, his head held low, and his lips dropped over his mouth in peculiar fashion, while his harsh and savage growling rolled thunderously over the plain. Seeing Simba and me on foot, he turned toward us, his tail lashing quicker and quicker. Resting my elbow on Simba's bent shoulder, I took steady aim and pressed the trigger; the bullet went in between the neck and shoulder, and the lion fell over on his side, one foreleg in the air. He recovered in a moment and stood up, evidently very sick, and once more faced me, growling hoarsely. I think he was on the eve of charging. I fired again at once, and this bullet broke his back just behind the shoulders; and with the next I killed him outright, after we had gathered round him.

These were two good-sized maneless lions; and very proud of them I was. I think Sir Alfred was at least as proud, es-pecially because we had performed the feat alone, without any professional hunters being present. "We were all ama-teurs, only gentleman riders up," said Sir Alfred. It was late before we got the lions skinned. Then we set off toward the ranch, two porters carrying each lion skin, strapped to a pole; and two others carrying the cub skins. Night fell long before we were near the ranch; but the brilliant tropic moon lighted the trail. The stalwart savages who carried the bloody lion skins swung along at a faster walk as the sun went down and the moon rose higher; and they began to chant in unison, one uttering a single word or sentence, and the others joining in a deep-toned, musical chorus. The men on a safari, and indeed African natives generally, are always excited over the death of a lion, and the hunting tribes then chant their rough hunting songs, or victory songs, until the monotonous, rhythmical repetitions make them grow almost frenzied. The ride home through the moonlight, the vast barren landscape shining like silver on either hand, was one to be remembered; and above all, the sight of our trophies and of their wild bearers.

FROM
THE LITTLE PRINCE

BY ANTOINE DE
SAINT-EXUPÉRY

I̲t was then that the fox appeared.

"Good morning," said the fox.

"Good morning," the little prince responded politely, although when he turned around he saw nothing.

"I am right here," the voice said, "under the apple tree."

"Who are you?" asked the little prince, and added, "You are very pretty to look at."

"I am a fox," the fox said.

"Come and play with me," proposed the little prince. "I am so unhappy."

"I cannot play with you," the fox said. "I am not tamed."

"Ah! Please excuse me," said the little prince.

But, after some thought, he added:

"What does that mean—'tame'?"

"You do not live here," said the fox. "What is it that you are looking for?"

"I am looking for men," said the little prince. "What does that mean—'tame'?"

"Men," said the fox. "They have guns, and they hunt. It is very disturbing. They also raise chickens. These are their only interests. Are you looking for chickens?"

"No," said the little prince. "I am looking for friends. What does that mean—'tame'?"

"It is an act too often neglected," said the fox. "It means to establish ties."

" 'To establish ties'?"

"Just that," said the fox. "To me, you are still nothing more than a little boy who is just like a hundred thousand other little boys. And I have no need of you. And you, on your part, have no need of me. To you, I am nothing more than a fox like a hundred thousand other foxes. But if you tame me, then we shall need each other. To me, you will be unique in all the world. To you, I shall be unique in all the world . . ."

"I am beginning to understand," said the little prince. "There is a flower . . . I think that she has tamed me . . ."

"It is possible," said the fox. "On the Earth one sees all sorts of things."

"Oh, but this is not on the Earth!" said the little prince.

The fox seemed perplexed, and very curious.

"On another planet?"

"Yes."

"Are there hunters on that planet?"

"No."

"Ah, that is interesting! Are there chickens?"

"No."

"Nothing is perfect," sighed the fox.

But he came back to his idea.

"My life is very monotonous," he said. "I hunt chickens;

men hunt me. All the chickens are just alike, and all the men are just alike. And, in consequence, I am a little bored. But if you tame me, it will be as if the sun came to shine on my life. I shall know the sound of a step that will be different from all the others. Other steps send me hurrying back underneath the ground. Yours will call me, like music, out of my burrow. And then look: you see the grain-fields down yonder? I do not eat bread. Wheat is of no use to me. The wheat fields have nothing to say to me. And that is sad. But you have hair that is the color of gold. Think how wonderful that will be when you have tamed me! The grain, which is also golden, will bring me back the thought of you. And I shall love to listen to the wind in the wheat . . ."

The fox gazed at the little prince, for a long time.

"Please—tame me!" he said.

"I want to, very much," the little prince replied. "But I have not much time. I have friends to discover, and a great many things to understand."

"One only understands the things that one tames," said the fox. "Men have no more time to understand anything. They buy things all ready made at the shops. But there is no shop anywhere where one can buy friendship, and so men have no friends any more. If you want a friend, tame me . . ."

"What must I do, to tame you?" asked the little prince.

"You must be very patient," replied the fox. "First you will sit down at a little distance from me—like that—in the grass. I shall look at you out of the corner of my eye, and you will say nothing. Words are the source of misunderstandings. But you will sit a little closer to me, every day . . ."

The next day the little prince came back.

"It would have been better to come back at the same

hour," said the fox. "If, for example, you come at four o'clock in the afternoon, then at three o'clock I shall begin to be happy. I shall feel happier and happier as the hour advances. At four o'clock, I shall already be worrying and jumping about. I shall show you how happy I am! But if you come at just any time, I shall never know at what hour my heart is to be ready to greet you . . . One must observe the proper rites . . ."

"What is a rite?" asked the little prince.

"Those also are actions too often neglected," said the fox. "They are what make one day different from other days, one hour from other hours. There is a rite, for example, among my hunters. Every Thursday they dance with the village girls. So Thursday is a wonderful day for me! I can take a walk as far as the vineyards. But if the hunters danced at just any time, every day would be like every other day, and I should never have any vacation at all."

So THE LITTLE PRINCE tamed the fox. And when the hour of his departure drew near—

"Ah," said the fox, "I shall cry."

"It is your own fault," said the little prince. "I never wished you any sort of harm; but you wanted me to tame you . . ."

"Yes, that is so," said the fox.

"But now you are going to cry!" said the little prince.

"Yes, that is so," said the fox.

"Then it has done you no good at all!"

"It has done me good," said the fox, "because of the color of the wheat fields." And then he added:

"Go and look again at the roses. You will understand now

that yours is unique in all the world. Then come back to say goodbye to me, and I will make you a present of a secret."

THE LITTLE PRINCE went away, to look again at the roses.

"You are not at all like my rose," he said. "As yet you are nothing. No one has tamed you, and you have tamed no one. You are like my fox when I first knew him. He was only a fox like a hundred thousand other foxes. But I have made him my friend, and now he is unique in all the world."

And the roses were very much embarrassed.

"You are beautiful, but you are empty," he went on. "One could not die for you. To be sure, an ordinary passerby would think that my rose looked just like you—the rose that belongs to me. But in herself alone she is more important than all the hundreds of you other roses: because it is she that I have watered; because it is she that I have put under the glass globe; because it is she that I have sheltered behind the screen; because it is for her that I have killed the caterpillars (except the two or three that we saved to become butterflies); because it is she that I have listened to, when she grumbled, or boasted, or even sometimes when she said nothing. Because she is *my* rose."

AND HE WENT BACK to meet the fox.

"Goodbye," he said.

"Goodbye," said the fox. "And now here is my secret, a very simple secret: It is only with the heart that one can see rightly; what is essential is invisible to the eye."

"What is essential is invisible to the eye," the little prince repeated, so that he would be sure to remember.

"It is the time you have wasted for your rose that makes your rose so important."

"It is the time I have wasted for my rose—" said the little prince, so that he would be sure to remember.

"Men have forgotten this truth," said the fox. "But you must not forget it. You become responsible, forever, for what you have tamed. You are responsible for your rose . . ."

"I am responsible for my rose," the little prince repeated, so that he would be sure to remember.

"What is essential is invisible to the eye," the little prince repeated, so that he would be sure to remember.

"It is the time you have wasted for your rose that makes your rose so important."

"It is the time I have wasted for my rose—" said the little prince, so that he would be sure to remember.

"Men have forgotten this truth," said the fox. "But you must not forget it. You become responsible, forever, for what you have tamed. You are responsible for your rose . . ."

"I am responsible for my rose," the little prince repeated, so that he would be sure to remember.

men hunt me. All the chickens are just alike, and all the men are just alike. And, in consequence, I am a little bored. But if you tame me, it will be as if the sun came to shine on my life. I shall know the sound of a step that will be different from all the others. Other steps send me hurrying back underneath the ground. Yours will call me, like music, out of my burrow. And then look: you see the grain-fields down yonder? I do not eat bread. Wheat is of no use to me. The wheat fields have nothing to say to me. And that is sad. But you have hair that is the color of gold. Think how wonderful that will be when you have tamed me! The grain, which is also golden, will bring me back the thought of you. And I shall love to listen to the wind in the wheat . . ."

The fox gazed at the little prince, for a long time.

"Please—tame me!" he said.

"I want to, very much," the little prince replied. "But I have not much time. I have friends to discover, and a great many things to understand."

"One only understands the things that one tames," said the fox. "Men have no more time to understand anything. They buy things all ready made at the shops. But there is no shop anywhere where one can buy friendship, and so men have no friends any more. If you want a friend, tame me . . ."

"What must I do, to tame you?" asked the little prince.

"You must be very patient," replied the fox. "First you will sit down at a little distance from me—like that—in the grass. I shall look at you out of the corner of my eye, and you will say nothing. Words are the source of misunderstandings. But you will sit a little closer to me, every day . . ."

The next day the little prince came back.

"It would have been better to come back at the same

hour," said the fox. "If, for example, you come at four o'clock in the afternoon, then at three o'clock I shall begin to be happy. I shall feel happier and happier as the hour advances. At four o'clock, I shall already be worrying and jumping about. I shall show you how happy I am! But if you come at just any time, I shall never know at what hour my heart is to be ready to greet you . . . One must observe the proper rites . . ."

"What is a rite?" asked the little prince.

"Those also are actions too often neglected," said the fox. "They are what make one day different from other days, one hour from other hours. There is a rite, for example, among my hunters. Every Thursday they dance with the village girls. So Thursday is a wonderful day for me! I can take a walk as far as the vineyards. But if the hunters danced at just any time, every day would be like every other day, and I should never have any vacation at all."

So THE LITTLE PRINCE tamed the fox. And when the hour of his departure drew near—

"Ah," said the fox, "I shall cry."

"It is your own fault," said the little prince. "I never wished you any sort of harm; but you wanted me to tame you . . ."

"Yes, that is so," said the fox.

"But now you are going to cry!" said the little prince.

"Yes, that is so," said the fox.

"Then it has done you no good at all!"

"It has done me good," said the fox, "because of the color of the wheat fields." And then he added:

"Go and look again at the roses. You will understand now

that yours is unique in all the world. Then come back to say goodbye to me, and I will make you a present of a secret."

THE LITTLE PRINCE went away, to look again at the roses.

"You are not at all like my rose," he said. "As yet you are nothing. No one has tamed you, and you have tamed no one. You are like my fox when I first knew him. He was only a fox like a hundred thousand other foxes. But I have made him my friend, and now he is unique in all the world."

And the roses were very much embarrassed.

"You are beautiful, but you are empty," he went on. "One could not die for you. To be sure, an ordinary passerby would think that my rose looked just like you—the rose that belongs to me. But in herself alone she is more important than all the hundreds of you other roses: because it is she that I have watered; because it is she that I have put under the glass globe; because it is she that I have sheltered behind the screen; because it is for her that I have killed the caterpillars (except the two or three that we saved to become butterflies); because it is she that I have listened to, when she grumbled, or boasted, or even sometimes when she said nothing. Because she is *my* rose."

AND HE WENT BACK to meet the fox.

"Goodbye," he said.

"Goodbye," said the fox. "And now here is my secret, a very simple secret: It is only with the heart that one can see rightly; what is essential is invisible to the eye."

THE PRESERVER OF SNOWYRUFF

FROM
THE BIOGRAPHY OF
A SILVER FOX

BY ERNEST THOMPSON
SETON

The folk of the upper Shawban were all astir. A great Fox-hunt had been organized. The men who had lost lambs were going because they wanted that Fox killed; the boys were there for sport, and all were there because this was a prime Silver Fox. "I think I know just what to do with the coin if he comes my way," said one. "I'd be glad to lift the mortgage off our farm with a day's sport," said another. "That black fox robe means a new team to me," said a third; and so they talked.

The Jukes were not there. They had not lost any lambs, and there was bad feeling between them and the Bentons, who organized the hunt. Abner Jukes was elsewhere engaged—was on another hunt indeed—and his Hekla of course was not with the enemy.

A Yankee farmer fox-hunt is a barbarous affair. Every man carries a gun of some kind. The object is to kill the Fox with least damage to the fur. There may be twenty boys and only three or four Hounds. Such, indeed, was the company that went forth that March morning on the upper Shawban.

Foxes may make a new den every year, but sometimes return to the old one if it has proved a place of quiet and of pleasant memories. Thanks to their eternal vigilance, no foe had found them yet in the aspen-dale. So again the month of March found Snowyruff and Domino clearing out the old den and preparing for the new event.

Because this was their home, they were careful to invite no hostile notice. They came and went with care. They hunted only in far places. Snowyruff was prowling among the dales of the upper river when the Hounds came on her trail, and giving good tongue, they led away. The farm-boys do not attempt to follow. They scatter to points of view. Their plan is to keep in touch with the Hounds by the baying, then race across country to commanding places, or narrow passes, that the Fox is headed for, and shoot him as he runs by. For the Fox usually goes in a circle around his home region.

The far-reaching hunting-cry of the Hounds was the signal for the boys to scramble to the highest lookout, there to form their opinion of the line of hunt, and each post himself at what he thinks the likeliest place for a shot.

The nearing bay left Snowyruff no doubt of what was doing, and she loped down the sheltered valley of Benton's Creek. Crossing and recrossing by the many log bridges, a plan which would surely delay the Hounds, at first she sped away so fast that the trail had time to cool somewhat. On a dry day it would have been lost, but this, unfortunately, was a day of deep snow, warm winds, and heavy thaw. The creek was a whizzing torrent, the snow was slush, and the Fox went floundering at every bound. The Hounds had a red-hot scent, and their longer legs gave them the advantage.

The speed of her opening run was slackening, and the start she had added to at first was dwindling now. So far she had eluded the gunners, but it was clear that she could not hold out much longer; the snow got softer as the sun came blazing down, and by degrees her tail sank low. This truly is the Fox's danger, and the measure of his strength. A strong, brave Fox bears his tail aloft in the chase. If his courage fails, the brush droops: in wet snow-time it gets wet and heavy, then droops still more. It drags at last, soaks up wet and slush, and becomes a load that helps to hasten the end. Thus the strong heart lives the longest; the faint heart falls by the way. Snowy-ruff had never lacked courage, but the snow was very wet and deep, and, in only a few days more, a new brood of little Foxes was expected. What wonder that, as her strength was spent, her heart should fail? She was again crossing the freshet creek by a slender tree when her foot slipped, and she plunged into the flood. She swam out quickly, of course, but now, weighted with water, her case was indeed a hard one. There seemed no hope; it was little more than a despairing cry she gave as she topped the next ridge, but it brought an answer —the short, sharp bark of the Dog-fox—and the Domino, strong and brave, came like a black hawk skimming across the snow. She had no means of telling him her plight, but she had no need. He sensed it, and did what only the rarest, noblest partners do—took up her burden, followed her trail, and went back to meet the Hounds. This did not mean that he meant to sacrifice himself, but that he felt confidence in his powers that he could cut off the Hounds and lead them far away, while she might go quietly home.

THE STRONG HEART TRIED

Back for half a mile he went and the pack was coming very near—only three hundred yards away and running fast—only two hundred now, and he lingered, then he began to trot away from them on the trail of his mate. But he lingered still, for what?—to make sure, by a view! and whether he wished them to see him, or he merely wished to see them, is not clear, but the effect was the same. At one hundred and fifty yards they viewed each other. The pack burst into the clamor that spreads the news, they quit the trail and flashed after the Fox in sight, and he as quickly disappeared. But at the place they got his scent and here to their credit be it told—they knew that now they were leaving the trail of a tender mother, to take up the trail of a strong Dog-fox; yet there is in their nature an instinctive feeling that this is the right thing to do. The Domino went slowly, for he wished to make certain of them; he showed himself again, and now that the chase was surely his he led them far from the way his mate had taken. He crossed the open snow; there were glasses among the hunters and they were wildly excited when the news went forth that they had started the Silver Fox. The boys knew the country; they were posted at every pass. But there is a some-thing that cherishes the wild things—a something that for lack of a better name we call their *Angel,* and this silent one with the far-reaching voice was there to keep him. Only once was he in peril—watching the Dogs too closely he did not heed the warning of the wind, and a moment later came a loud report and a burning sting of shot. One pellet reached his flank and left a wound, not deep but galling. He had seen no hunters, but now the dark Fox knew just what to reckon with.

Now were all his powers alert—now every message read, and the Keeper surely warms to those who hear.

There was every reason that the Domino should go through one or another of the passes, and yet for once in his life his only desire was to keep the hilltops. After three miles, he turned abruptly across the open and followed the railway for twice as far. A mile past the switch he went, and was far ahead; then he walked on the rails back to the switch and took the track that forked. After a long trail there he fearlessly turned toward his home, tired, sore with the shot-wound, but bearing his tail aloft, as becomes the victor of a hard fight.

He cut across the country of the upper Shawban and, hungry now, was making for a cache in the woods, when he heard sounds that made his heart jump, and, rounding a hill, caught sight of a pack of Hounds, another, a fresh pack, at least thirty in number, with a dozen mounted men; and the wild clamor they made was unmistakable proof that they had found his trail and were after him. There was a time when he might have welcomed such a chase, but, oh, how unfair it was now!

He was wearied and hungry, he was footsore with a chase of hours, he was galled with a stinging wound, he needed rest. But this, at least, was a real hunt; there were no guns, and a "chase," not a "robe," was what they sought. Yet who can blame the Silver Fox if he made way with his speed indeed, but without the joy of the swift runner that knows that the race is his?

He did not know these hills well; they were far from his usual beat. The hills that he knew were miles away, and among them were the gunners ready at every point, and only too glad to profit by the new relay of hounds. This proved the poorest race he had ever made as a test of cunning, but the hardest he ever entered as a test of strength and speed. It was round and round the hills for hours, loping steadily on; but the blazing sun had reduced all the snow in the woods to slush. Every ditch was full of ice-cold water; every brook was a freshet. There were pools on all the solid ice, and that great full tail, the strong-heart flag, which on another day might still have been flaunted high, was splashed with wet and mud, and drooped from its very weight. He knew he could wear them down, as he had before, yet he longed for the night, the kindly night. Did he know why? Maybe not to give it clear expression, but the night meant frost, and the frost meant crust, and this would bear the Fox for hours before the Hounds could run on it. The night indeed meant peace.

Now he was plunging around these hills; his wonderful speed was down to half, but the Hounds were wearing, too. The snow and freshets were too much for the hunters. There were only two remaining, the master of the Hounds, and a tall stripling, Abner Jukes, the only one who knew that the hunted one was the Goldur Silver Fox.

But every advantage was now with the pack; they were closing in. The Domino had no chance to double back. It was straight away; it was wisest to go straight away; so he loped, and loped, and loped, always slower and slower, with heaving flanks and shortening bounds and breath, but on and on. Past one farm-house he went, and another, then at the doorway of a third he saw the young Human Thing with the basket. What is it that prompts the wild thing in despair to seek the help of higher power? Whence comes the deep-laid impulse in extremity? The Goldur Fox obeyed the sudden thought, rushed feebly to the Garden Girl, and groveled at her feet. She seized and dragged him unresisting into the house, then slammed the door in the face of the pack of yelling demons. Around the house they surged and bayed. The huntsman came; the farmer came.

"He's ours; he belongs to our hounds. They have a right to him; they ran him in here," declared the huntsman.

"He is in my house, and he's mine now," said the farmer, not in the least realizing the quality of the clay-reddened, bedraggled fugitive.

But the farmer had been losing his hens, and he had another weakness; this was easily satisfied, for the robe seemed worn and worthless now, and the hunter was told to "go get his Fox."

"You sha'n't! you sha'n't! He's mine!" cried the girl. "He's my friend. I've known him for ever so long. You sha'n't kill him!"

The farmer weakened. "We'll give him fair play," said the huntsman. "We'll give him a better start than he had when he came." And the farmer hurried away that he might see no more. He could forget the hunted beast that sought sanctuary in his house, but he could not drown that ringing in his ears: "You sha'n't! you sha'n't! he's my friend! Oh, Daddy, they are going to kill him! Oh, Daddy! Daddy!" And the father's was not the only heart in which that childish wail was a scorpion lash that rankled for long.

THE RIVER AND THE NIGHT

But they bore him off, and a quarter of a mile of "law" they gave him. "Fair play," they called it—thirty strong Hounds against one worn-out Fox, and the valley rang with baying. Again he bounded over the deep, wet snow, and for a time he won, forging far ahead. Down the long vale of Benton's Creek and across the hillside, over the ridge and back by the Goldur foot-hills and by a farm-house, whence out there rushed to join the pack a long-belated Hound. The tall hunter welcomed him with a friendly call. What chance had Domino now, with this third fresh relay against him? One chance alone was left: the night was near; if only it would come with frost. But the evening breeze grew milder. All day the river had been running, with the warming winds. Now the Shawban was a mighty, growing flood of racing, broken ice, filling the broad valley from brim to brim; heaving and jarring, it went toward the west. The sun was setting on the water-gap away out there. Its splendor was on a noble scene; this surely was the splendid ending of a noble life. But neither Hounds nor hunters stayed to look; it was on and on. The Hounds were panting and lunging; their tongues hung long; their eyes were red. Far in the lead was the fresh Hound—unbidden, hateful brute—and farther still, the Silver Fox. That famous robe was dragged in mud; that splendid brush was weighted and sagged with slush; his foot-pads, worn to the quick, left bloody tracks. He was wearied as never before. He might have reached the pathway ledge, but that way was his home, that way for long a noble instinct said, "Go not." But now in direst straits he headed for it, the one way left. He rallied his remaining power, racing by the mighty Shawban. His former speed for a little space was resumed, and he would have won but that there forged ahead of all the big, belated Hound, and as he neared the quarry, bellowed forth an awful, unmistakable cry—the horrid, brassy note of Hekla. Who can measure the speed and start it took away from the hunted one? Only this was known: he was turned, cut off, forced back along the river-bank, down along the rushing water, now blazing in the low sun-glow. His hope was gone, but on he went, his dark form feebly rocking, knowing he must die, but fighting for his life. The tall young huntsman—the only one in sight—now coming on, took in the scene, knew he was at the death, and gazed at the moving blots on the brightness.

O River flashing the red and gold of the red and golden sky, and dappled with blocks of sailing ice! O River of the long chase that ten times before had saved him and dashed red death aside! This is the time of times! Now thirty deaths are on his track, and the track is of feebling bounds. O River of the aspen-dale, will you turn traitor in his dire extremity, thus pen him in, deliver him to his foes?

But the great River went on, mighty, inexorable. Oh, so cruel! And the night came not, but lingered. And even as the victim ran, the fierce, triumphant cry of all the hunt became a hellish clamor in his ears. He was worn out. The brush—the prize and flag—was no longer borne aloft, but dragged, wet and heavy, a menace to his speed; yet still he loped along the glowing strand. The Hounds, inspired by victory in sight, came on bellowing, bounding, blood-mad. To them the draggled, wounded creature, loping feebly on the shore, was not a hunted beast far overmatched, but a glorious triumph to be reached.

On he went, following, alas! a point into the stream—a trap, no less. His River had betrayed him, and the pack was closing in. Hekla, howling his deep-voiced hate, was first to block retreat, to corner him at last. It was an open view for all—the broad strand there, with the hunted one; the broad field, with the scattered, yelling pack; the wide River, with its blocks of ice, all rushing on, with death on every side. Here had a faint heart failed and lost; here the strong heart kept on. The surging, roaring pack in Hekla's wake had reached the neck of land, and now came nearer. The surging, roaring River sang as it flowed by the aspen bank. The white Hounds dappled the shore as the white ice dappled the flood; and white they moved together, like mighty teeth to crush the prey. Closer the ice-blocks came, so that now they mass for a moment, and touch the shore with jar and grating. The hunted turns as though at a sudden thought: better to choose the river death, to die in the River that long had been his friend, and feebly leaping on the ice, from cake to cake, he halted at the last before the plunge. But as he stood, the floe was broken up, was rushed away, with the dark water broadened between; and on that farthest block the dark Fox crouched, riding the white saddle of the black flood. The pack on the shore yelled out their fury, and Hekla, rushing, reached the point of the ice-jam, sprang to the edge, to see the victim sail away. On the ice he blared his disappointment and his hate, not heeding, not knowing; and the River, irresistible, inexorable, drew swiftly out and whirled away the ice-block whereon he stood. And so they rode together to their doom, the hunted Fox and the hunting Hound. Down they went in that sunset blaze, and on the bank went the pack and the stripling hunter, riding.

A countryman of the other hunt leveled his gun at the Fox; the hunter dashed the gun aside, and cursed the fool. Then there rose on his lips a long halloo, that died, and left the pack in doubt.

At the bend of the River was reached the race, as they call it—the long reach before the River takes the plunge of Harney's Fall; and there at gaze they stood, the lad and the Hounds, staring into the purple and red sunset and the red and purple River, with blocks of shining ice that bore two living forms away into the blaze. The mists increased with the River's turmoil, the sun-shafts danced more dazzlingly, the golden light turned the ice and the stream and the Silver Fox to gold, as the racing flood and the blazing sky enveloped them from view. The strong heart on the floe gave forth no cry, but the night wind brought the cowering howl of a Hound on whom was the fear of death.

"Good-by, old fellow," said the hunter,—"the stanchest Hound that ever lived!" His voice grew rough. "Good-by, Silver Fox! You have died victorious, as you lived. I wish I could save you both; but what a death you die! Good-by!" Abner saw no more, and the pack on the shore stood shivering and whining.

The shadows fell, the hunter's view was done, but other eyes there were to watch the scene. The current charged fiercely on the last point above the race, and here by reason of the swirl the near blocks took mid-stream, and the middle blocks the farther shore. So the white courser of the hunted one went for a moment grating on the rocks, and Domino saw his chance. He leaped with all his gathered strength; he cleared the dark and dangerous flood; he landed safe. The River of his youth was the River of his prime.

And away out on the middle floe there came the long-drawn wail of a Hound that knows he is lost. Even as the mists had shut off the view, so now the voice of many waters hushed the cry, and the river keeps its secret to this day.

FROM

THE MOUNTAIN LION

BY JEAN STAFFORD

Uncle Claude put his hand on Ralph's shoulder and said, "I'm mighty glad you've come to stay a while this time," and Ralph, while he did not move, felt himself grow cold with withdrawal and with something like distrust for the enthusiasm in his uncle's voice, so boy-like that it actually cracked. For right now he did not want any attention paid to him at all. But when Uncle Claude went on, he realized to his relief that it was not he that had so inspired the man, but the tale he now commenced to tell him.

"Don't you know how I've always said I wanted to get me a mountain lion?" he said. "Don't you know that? Well, I'm on the trail of one now."

He paused and smiled, waiting to be questioned, and Ralph cried, "Where?"

Uncle Claude had seen the lion in the foothills before you got to Garland Peak. He had seen her only once early in April and had gone back time after time to have another glimpse of her or of her mate. He had been so bent on having her hide that he had wasted a lot of hunting time just fooling around looking for her and he hadn't got a piece of game this year, though there had been plenty to be had and the boys had stocked up well. She was about as big as a good-sized dog, he said, and she looked for all the world like an overgrown house cat. He thought about her so much that he had given her a name; he called her Goldilocks because, running the way she had in the sunlight, she had been as blonde as a movie star. He had told the boys, including Homer, that he would fire any one of them that drew a bead on her because if anyone got her, it was going to be him. Old Magdalene had ragged him a God's plenty, saying that *she* was going to catch the lion with fresh kid meat. No one had quite understood why he was so all-fired crazy to get her and he could not quite make it out himself. "But you know, every now and again a man will get a bug like this and there's no more rest for him." Sometimes he would go up and spend the whole day, packing his lunch along with him, and by sundown he would be cursing her, talking to her image as if she were a person.

He had decided that he was going to let Ralph hunt her too. They were never to hunt alone and were, when they separated, to keep within hailing distance of one another. This singular honor made Ralph feel as if he were actually rising in the air and he warmly thanked Uncle Claude while, deceitfully and unsportingly, he resolved that it would be *he*, not the man, who got the lion. . . .

RALPH DREAMED of the mountain lion and thought, "Oh, if I don't get her, I will *die!*" He saw himself standing where they had stood before Christmas, taking perfect aim, shooting her through her proud head with its wary eyes, and then running across the mesa to stroke her soft saffron flanks and paws. Ralph had always loved cats, and when Budge had died this spring of old age, he had been wretched for days, mourning the lost purr and the quiet feet. He would not skin the mountain lion, he decided, if he got her, but would have her stuffed and keep her in his room all his life. If he had to go to college, he would take her along with him. He wished that Uncle Claude were not so keen as he, for he felt, somehow, that he had more right to Goldilocks: he wanted her because he loved her, but Uncle Claude wanted her only because she was something rare. Besides, Uncle Claude would be here forever and could get another, but this was Ralph's last chance. Sometimes, indeed, he forgot that he was not her only hunter, and at such times he seemed to sink into a golden bath of joy.

They saw the mountain lion on Easter Sunday. This time she was beside the stream, nearer the gulch than the place where she had vanished before, close to the beaver dam. They had only a momentary glimpse of her and then she leaped away and was out of sight before they could even raise their rifles. They ran to the place where she had been and found that she had left her food, too startled by their voices to carry it off. A half-eaten woodchuck lay beside a tree stump, its entrails chewed but its silly head intact and twisted to a sheepish angle. It had been mauled and slobbered on and its grizzled hair was clotted. There was blood on some of the chips of wood left by the beavers when they had gnawed down the tree.

Uncle Claude, frustrated, angry, moved around the stump,

examining everything as if he expected to find a clue which would lead him to her den. Sighing, he said, "Blast the yellow bitch."

And Ralph, feeling himself on the verge of tears, said desolately, "What'll we do now?"

"Go home, I reckon," said Uncle Claude, "but by damn, I'm going to get me my cat yet."

Ralph kept the edge out of his voice but his heart was rapid. He said, "You mean, I'm going to get *me my* cat."

Uncle Claude glanced sidelong at him but said nothing and they started down the creek bank. The creek was swollen from the thaws and there were places where the water sprayed like a geyser in the hollows between the rocks. Between two boulders at a widening, Ralph saw the points of a set of antlers sticking up out of the water and he waded in, not bothering to take off his shoes. But what he found was not just one set of antlers: he found the skulls of two deer with horns so tightly interlocked that he could not get them apart. They were wedged in between the rocks and he had trouble getting them loose. The water was cold and insistently flicked up his pants legs and once he lost his footing and slipped on a rock. When he came out with his trophy, he found Uncle Claude sitting on a patch of grass smoking, watching Ralph without the least interest. . . .

HE MOVED around the beaver dam, looking alertly through the trees. Just beyond this black silent pool there was a little glade he knew of with a flat rock in the center of it like a table. He thought he heard someone across the dam and stopped to listen, but he concluded that it had only been a bird rustling. It had occurred to him that it might be Uncle Claude, but he realized that he could not have got back from the stud farm so soon. Quiet as it was, there was, as always in the forest, a feeling of life near by and when, softly moving aside a branch of chokecherry, he saw Goldilocks in the glade beside the flat rock feeding on a jackrabbit, he was not surprised. He had been certain, this last moment, that he would find her there. She delicately moved the rabbit with her paw and then savagely ripped it with her teeth. He stood, holding his breath, utterly motionless for a minute, debating, but he could not hold out against the temptation: Uncle Claude would have to forgive him; if he didn't, Ralph would go away.

As he raised his rifle, he heard another sound but this time from the direction of the face of the mountain. Goldilocks heard it too and lifted her heavy head; before she could find him with her topaz eyes, he shot and immediately he was stone blind. His blindness lasted for an exploded moment and when he was able to see again, to see the tumbled yellow body on the bright grass, he realized that he had been not blind but deaf, for there had been another gun, another shot a split second after his.

Uncle Claude came charging through the brush, hollering like an Indian. "By God, we done it! By Jesus Christ, we both done it." And he ran to the lion, throwing his gun on the ground. She had fallen toward Ralph on her wounded side and no blood was visible. Uncle Claude turned her over to look for the wounds and Ralph stepped forward.

"She's so little," said Ralph softly, as if Goldilocks were not dead but only asleep. "Why, she isn't any bigger than a dog. She isn't as *big*."

But what mattered was whose bullet had killed her. They looked together eagerly, pushing back the hair with their hands. Ralph was surprised to find how short and harsh it was. There was only one bullet hole, and it was not in the place where Ralph had aimed. He was sick with failure, sick and furious with his uncle for coming so quietly and winning so easily.

Uncle Claude said, "No man alive can judge which one of us got her. I reckon we'll have to call it a corporation."

There was a sound in the chokecherry bushes beyond them, opposite where Ralph had stood to shoot. It was a sound that could come only from a human throat. It was a bubbling of blood. Uncle Claude and Ralph stood up and looked at one another in an agony of terror and for a moment they could not move but stood, hatless, the sun blazing down upon them and upon the lion at their feet.

"Somebody . . ."

Uncle Claude, bending almost in two at the waist, ran across the clearing and Ralph followed, his body a flame of pain. Molly lay beside a rotten log, a wound like a burst fruit in her forehead. Her glasses lay in fragments on her cheeks and the frame, torn from one ear, stuck up at a raffish angle. The elastic had come out of one leg of her gym bloomers and it hung down to her shin. The sound in her throat stopped. Uncle Claude knelt down beside her, but Ralph stood some paces away. He could as clearly see the life leave her as you could see fire leave burnt-out wood. It receded like a tide, lifted like a fog.

When Uncle Claude stood up, Ralph began to scream. He threw back his head and with his mouth as wide as it would open he let the sound flow out of him, burning up the mountains. Then he was too hoarse to scream any longer and he threw himself down on the ground and pounded the pine needles with his fists and with his feet, moaning, "I didn't see her! I didn't hear her! I didn't kill her!"

COON HUNT

BY ANNABEL THOMAS

Nobody saw Quenby get out. Clara Fortune went to feed her and she was gone from the house, that was all.

"Quenby. You, Quenby!"

But you can't call a cat like you do a dog, can you?

"Kitty, kitty, kitty."

Pedigreed and not allowed to roam. Came into the house at six weeks old and never set foot out of it until now, seven years later. Why would she want to and her cushion so cozy and her food set out?

"Look under the porch," Mama had said, "and in the bushes."

Mama's voice was always warm and coaxing like a brood hen's.

Not in the bushes. Not in the long grass around the cistern top. The last light burst through cloud low in the west, brightening the saltbox shape of the Fortune house.

A star showed through the top branch of the oak like a tear in an eyelid, and the sunset wind moaned amongst its shaggy leaves. Booth's woods lay below, dark as deep water.

Clara threw herself on her back beside the porch steps. The day lilies around her were closed to shapes like fingers. The rising moon was white. There were moths on the screen.

Behind her breastbone all this summer there'd been flutterings like wings. She thought her soul was trying to come out but Mama said it was only her blood pounding because she ran too hard.

"Quenby?"

She crawled through the hole in the lattice and under the house, a tight squeeze. Only a year ago she'd darted in and out like a fish. Now her shoulders and breasts caught though the rest of her was skinny enough still. A beanpole, a stilt, a stepladder of a girl. Over her head she could hear Mama's quick light steps.

Clara found, not Quenby, but a nest with five eggs still warm from the hen. She put the eggs inside her blouse and slid out on her back. Coming around the house corner, she saw the end of the oak branch over the porch roof whip and set the leaves a-quiver. She put the eggs in the porch box.

Up it for sure and can't get down.

Clara swung herself onto the lowest limb. She climbed, scraping her knees and elbows, until she was on a level with the second-floor window. There sat Papa on his and Mama's bed with his galluses turned down. Across the hall she could see, in her own room, the chair with the red cushion on which Quenby usually dozed, purring, every afternoon.

Clara climbed higher to where the tree, still full of sun, swung in the breeze like a tolling bell. From this high she could see the complete round of the yard, already in shadow. There were Mama's flowerbeds, bright from the coming cold, round and square, triangle and rectangle with wire fencing at the edges. There was the woodshed and her bicycle leaning against it and the pear tree where her old swing drifted to and fro.

A scratching on the bark.

"Quenby?"

Clara climbed higher until her fingers closed on a warm smoothness. No cat. What, then? Clara tilted her head, staring up. A face looked back at her through the leaves. She held the branches aside and found Floyd Kilkinney perched in a crotch like a possum.

He opened his fist and showed her three locust skins sitting on the palm. Looking close, Clara saw locust skins everywhere clutched to the bark, staring back at her with empty eye bubbles.

She climbed up to where Floyd sat. He smelled of the fields, of dew and sumac and sassafras. He had locust shells stuck to his clothes and in his hair.

He moved his leg until it touched hers all along the calf. His face was in shadow but she felt his breath quicken against her neck.

She said, "I thought you was Quenby."

"That Quenby's gone off with some tom," he said.

He leaned down of a sudden and pushed his mouth hard against hers so that her lips puffed and stung and a strong pulsing began in her throat.

He settled back triumphant.

"I told you I'd do that before this day was done," he said.

All at once he lifted his head.

"Hark!"

They held their breath. Far off across Booth's woods came

a thin piping. When Floyd said, "That's Uncle Garret's Liza up front," she knew it was hounds after a coon.

"Doesn't your uncle ever get lost hunting in Booth's woods?" she asked him. "Papa won't let me go in it because he says I'd never find my way out."

"Uncle Garret gets lost. So do I. That's half the fun."

Floyd dropped a locust skin into her lap. "There's one never made it," he said.

The shell felt heavy as a bullet. Sure enough there was the dead locust, greenish and dull-eyed, still inside. She shivered and let it fall, hearing it hit branches as it dropped. The sun was suddenly gone from the tree as if a lamp had been blown out.

Floyd wound his leg around hers and kissed her again. The kiss lasted so long they both gasped at the end of it.

"Let's get the hell out of this before we fall out," Floyd said.

They inched down the trunk, hung by their hands from the lowest branch and dropped into a pool of shadow.

Floyd flopped belly-down in the grass.

"Let's run off and get married," he said.

Clara sat beside him, Indian-style. Till the day he came to help her papa make Fortune hay, she'd thought boys were silly. But his eyes, black and wild as sin, picked her out and picked her out wherever she stood. Soon he was talking to her every chance he got, she watching his soft, curving mouth shape the words.

All that summer he hung around her and on into autumn like a hummer at a blossom. Winter he came and waited in first light to walk her to school and waited by the school door to walk her home when last light was coming on.

The next spring he was still around her. Then the summer day she surprised him drinking at the Fortune well, he looked at her with water running down his chin and said, solemn as a sage, "This fall, we'uns'll get married."

She didn't say no. He was her choice, same as she was his. But when fall came, she didn't feel ready so she said, "In six months." And when that was up, she said, "In six months more."

And now that was up and she said, "We ain't got a dollar betwixt us, Floyd. We'd starve to death inside a week."

"I got the promise of a job at the sawmill down to Beloit on the river," he told her. "After we save some money, we'll go on down to New Orleans. I always wanted to look on the Gulf."

"I ain't going."

"Yo're scared to leave home, is all. Age you are, my ma'd been a wife two years. Yo're scared to let go of yore mama and papa. Chicken liver!"

Clara buried her fingers in Floyd's hair and gave a pull. It was so crisp and springy it started her fingertips tingling. Locust shells fell from it right and left. It was too lively to hold them.

He gripped her wrists one in each hand and bent her backward. They swayed, then toppled flat on the ground, where he held her arms pinned wide, leaned his forehead against her neck and blew his breath down her blouse so that all of her skin prickled.

He was quick as a weasel and too strong for her. Sweat from his chin dropped into her eyes and her mouth. It had a tangy taste like ocean water.

Twisting sideways out of his grip, she grabbed up one of

the eggs from the porch box and pelted it against his chest. It broke, the yellow popping like a bubble and spattering him chin to knee.

"By god, you'll answer for that!" he said through his teeth.

Scooping up the other four eggs, he caught her in the back with one as she ran through the yard and on the shoulder with another as she went down the hill. At the edge of the woods, she stopped to look back and the third egg caught her on the thigh.

Still she'd outfox him. He'd never get her with the last one. She slipped in under the trees where it was dark as a cave. She walked until she stumbled over a rotten log by a run of water, then crouched behind it panting.

She didn't hear him coming but suddenly he swept back the bushes so the moon, gone yellow now, shone on her.

"You look good enough to fry for breakfast," he said. "Here, you can throw the last one so you won't hold me no grudge."

He held out the egg cupped on his palms, ready to snatch it away when she reached for it. Quicker than thought she clapped his two hands together. He stood staring at his dripping fingers until she moved off, then, with one lunge, caught her by the skirt.

Pulling free, she gave him a push that sent him reeling backwards into the creek. He came out of the water shaking himself like a wet dog.

Floyd reached for her, bent on giving her a ducking, but she made off into the woods. He came after her, running. They ran until suddenly dogs were barking all around them and there stood Floyd's Uncle Garret with several other men beside a small campfire.

The flames lit a great tree around which dogs were leaping and yelping. One large yellow bitch was baying with a deep bell tone. Clara followed the raised noses of the dogs with her glance until she saw masked, bright eyes and a furry body on a high limb.

"Hold her, Liza!" the men whooped. "Hold her, girl."

They heaped dry leaves and light limbs on the fire and stood about it, staring up. Clara, too, couldn't take her eyes off the coon. When the fire brightened she saw black hands gripping the bark, heaving sides and the pricking of small pointed ears.

Floyd stepped into the firelight, kicking off his shoes. He shed his shirt like an old skin and stood for a moment gazing at the coon.

Then he was across the clearing and up the tree, pulling himself hand over hand up the grapevines that matted the trunk until he gripped the bare, curving lower limbs with his knees. The firelight shone on his dark skin as the muscles moved beneath it. The dogs leaped higher, yelping louder. The coon, immobile as a statue, watched Floyd climb toward her. Her lip was lifted from her teeth and her nose wrinkled in a snarl. As he drew nearer, her body quivered, her hands gripped tight to the bark and she crouched lower, gathering her feet under her. A rank, pungent odor coming from the coon filled the air.

As Floyd climbed higher, the coon backed away from the trunk, edging further out onto the limb.

"Keep a tight hold. Don't you slip," Uncle Garret shouted to Floyd. "Whatever falls from that tree, these here dogs is going to tear to pieces, boy or coon, don't matter which."

Clara looked at the hounds. Their long teeth were like knife blades and their tongues licked in and out.

Floyd reached the limb where the coon perched and began to shake it, bracing himself against the trunk and using both hands.

How tight the furry thing clung to her place! She must be dizzy from whipping up and down. Still she hung on. There on the branch, the coon looked like a cat. Like Quenby. But a wild Quenby. A Quenby gone mad.

"Fall, you goddamned varmint, fall!" the men shouted.

Floyd rested against the trunk, breathing hard. Through the leaves, Clara saw the coon's shiny eyes looking down at the dogs.

Floyd shook the limb mightily. Clara's mouth gaped open. The coon sprang out as though she would soar away, then fell on the dogs, limbs spread.

The hounds, in their scramble to get at the coon, scattered the fire so that the clearing fell into sudden darkness.

Clara could hear the snapping of the dogs' teeth, their yelps and their growling, the screeches of the coon and hoarse hollering of the hunters above the din.

Wild and sightless, the men ran this way and that, bumping into now one another, now the trees or bushes, as they tried to keep from being bitten by the dogs or scratched and bitten by the coon.

The fight subsided. Silence fell on the woods. The men kicked the embers together and piled on dry leaves and branches until the fire blazed up once more.

The hounds, bleeding from torn ears and bitten muzzles, milled about whining while Floyd lifted up the dead coon, dripping blood and urine, from their midst and held her high above their heads. From her ripped and bloody face, the coon's half-closed eyes looked out with a dreamy stare.

Uncle Garret danced a jig and pounded Floyd on the back. All the men cheered and shouted and talked at once, relating the hunt to one another while they brought out fruit jars and passed them around. Floyd came up to Clara holding out a jar.

"Since you're a coon hunter now, you might as well finish up right with a drink of corn," he said.

He was laughing and panting, his shoulders heaving. Sweat glistened on his chest and in his hair.

Numb to the lips from the coon's drop, Clara took the jar in her hands and looked into it at the raw colorless liquid. All the men were smiling, watching her, the firelight flickering on their faces. She raised the jar and drank.

At once she began to gasp and to beat at her throat and her chest where she felt a thousand matches suddenly lit and flaming.

The men roared. Uncle Garret fell on the ground and rolled. Clara wheezed and sputtered. When at last her breath came easier, a glow began in her belly and spread to all her parts until her skin was ablaze and her insides filled with heat and she thought she had fallen into the fire and herself become the flames, leaping, devouring the leaves and branches, giving off an astounding brightness.

Afterwards, she slipped to her knees and began to retch. She heaved and heaved again while Floyd held her forehead and the trees marched around and around them like soldiers. She ended, tired out and sobbing, and, weak as a day-old kitten, fell asleep against Floyd's chest.

When she woke, the fire had burned to a red ash and the men and dogs were gone. Floyd sat beside a lantern watching her.

"God a'mighty!" he burst out. "I thought you was poisoned and yore death coming on you."

Then he threw back his head and laughed until tears stood in his eyes.

"If yo're going to hunt coon, you got to learn to hold yore corn better than that," he said.

Clara stood up, mortified to the roots of her soul.

"I'm going home," she said and moved quickly off into the woods.

The blackness was full of briars and branches and night animals that started up under her feet with a great noise and ran off. She tripped over roots and walked into bushes. Behind her came Floyd, swinging the lantern at his side, laughing to himself.

She began to walk faster, looking to come out on the road below the Fortune house. However, no way she turned seemed right. She went on and went on and still there was nothing but trees. In front, behind, to left, to right, only trees.

A few stars shone down through high branches. She stopped, started off to the right, then turned left. Floyd came behind her, laughing.

"Which way?" she asked him over her shoulder. "Why don't you tell me which way?"

She stopped so that he walked into her. Feeling his chest come against her, she pounded it with her fists until her face was hot and her breath came in gasps.

"Show me the right way to go," she said, almost crying. "Pretty soon you'll get lost yourself. Then we'll never get out. We'll die in Booth's woods."

He gripped her arms so she couldn't pound him and kissed her neck, then down onto her breasts. His mouth was everywhere, pressing against her from every direction, scattering her out into the dark.

She heard a screech owl cry close beside them, then again further off. The woods swelled full of murmurs and clicks, scrapes and calls, whistles and barks, rustles and sighs. Loudest of all were the tree frogs, buzzing like the locusts in the day, only more shrill and not so loud.

Floyd laid his head on her shoulder and she felt his face hot through her sleeve. They stood without moving while the moon climbed over their heads and filtered down amongst the leaves.

When she tried to pull away, he held her fast.

"Clarie, meet me by the highway bridge tomorrow night," he whispered, muffled, into her hair. "We'll hitch to Kentucky and find a J.P. Come when the moon clears Booth's woods. Clarie, will you come?"

And wouldn't turn loose of her wrists until she'd nodded her head.

When Clara stepped out of the woods, the first sight she saw was Fortune Hill. On its top, the saltbox house stood out black with sharp edges like a cardboard cutout.

Mama's voice, faint and thin, was calling her name from the yard. By the time she started up the path, the calling had stopped and she heard the kitchen door closing.

FROM
THE HEART OF
THE HUNTER

BY LAURENS VAN DER POST

We went on for a while now without seeing more game or, what was far more discouraging, the spoor of any. When the noise of our vehicles finally woke a little Steenbuck from his sleep and he rose out of the bed he makes more neatly and snugly perhaps than any other quadruped in Africa, I felt I had to shoot. Yet I hated doing it. For me the Steenbuck has always been one of the loveliest and most lovable of African buck. It and the Klipspringer are part of my own childhood world of magic, and this little Steenbuck was a superb example of his kind. He stood at the end of a bare patch of crimson sand about twenty yards away, beside the purple shade of the bush behind which he had made his bed, and there he eagerly fed the precise little flame of his vivid self to the rising conflagration of another desert day. He stood as still and fine drawn as an Etruscan statuette of himself. His delicate ears were pointed in my direction, his great purple eyes wide open, utterly without fear and shining only with the wonder of seeing so strange a sight at this remote back door of life.

Remembering the gaunt faces of the famished Bushmen, I shot quickly before he should get alarmed or the sight of his gentle being weaken me. I would not have thought it possible I could miss at so short a distance. Yet I did. My shot merely made the little buck shake his delicate head vigorously to rid his ears of the tingle of the shock of the explosion from my heavy gun. Otherwise he showed no trace of alarm. I took much more careful aim and shot a second time. Again I missed. Still the little buck was unafraid. He just turned his head slightly to sniff at the wind raised by the bullet when it passed close by his ears. So near was he to me that I saw his black patent-leather little nose pucker with the effort. I shot until the magazine of my gun was empty and still he stood there unhurt, observing my Land-Rover keenly as if trying to discover what the extraordinary commotion was about. I believe he would have stood there indefinitely, taking in the strangeness of the occasion, had I not entreated Vyan to shoot from his vehicle, much further away. Vyan succeeded merely in nicking slightly the saffron petal of one of the Steenbuck's ears. Only then did the Steenbuck whisk swiftly about, a look of reproach in his eyes. The sun flashing briefly on the tips of his black polished toes, he vanished with a nimble bound in the scrub.

I drove on very much aware that I had not lightened what promised just then to become the long task of getting enough food for the Bushmen and, now that the Steenbuck was safely gone, more put out than I cared to admit by such poor marksmanship. Yet I was even more disconcerted to find both Dabé and the new Bushman apparently highly delighted at the outcome of the affair. Had they been amused, I would not have been surprised. Indeed I expected my companions to pull my leg about the incident for days to come. Yet delight in someone so famished as our new companion so amazed me that I interrupted something he was saying, a wide smile on his fine-drawn face.

"What on earth has he said to please you so?" I asked the grinning Dabé.

"Oh! He is just saying what we all know to be so," Dabé answered in the indulgent manner of someone instructing an ignorant child, which he and the other Bushmen at the Sip Wells had always adopted when discussing their own private world with me. "The Steenbuck is protected with great magic and very difficult to kill."

"What sort of magic?" I asked, remembering my association of the buck with my childhood world of magic. "His own magic or the magic of other people?"

"Oh. Just magic!" Dabé said in a superior voice, leaving unsatisfied the curiosity which always nagged me more than ever when the curtain between the mind of the Bushman and our own lifted only to flop back just as I thought I was to be allowed to see behind it. Yet my imagination had seized on the encounter more firmly than I knew. I know of few things more awesome than finding that all one's most determined efforts to injure another living creature have been unaccountably frustrated. Throughout the long hot day, at all sorts of odd moments, my mind returned to the vision of that gentle little buck standing untroubled amid blast after blast from my gun. . . .

THE RATEL

This little Bushman smoked our ordinary cigarettes indeed as if they were hashish of the purest kind. His first cigarette he drew in with one long pull, not ceasing until the fire reached his lips. All that time no smoke emerged from his mouth. I watched in amazement, thinking when he spat out the tiny butt that the smoke would follow. None came. The smoke had vanished somewhere deep inside him, and only when he spoke again some minutes later did it reappear in tiny curls of faded blue around his ears.

At the end of his third cigarette, he appeared to become quite intoxicated with tobacco. He suddenly stood up, stepped some few yards away from the thorn bush into the open, raised his hands above his head and turned his eyes inward so that the pupils vanished and only the whites showed under the half-closed lids. He began to sway rhythmically from the knees, and we saw the muscles in his stomach contract and gather into a round ball. This ball suddenly began to bound up and down, in and out, and from side to side of his stomach. I got the impression that his mind was no longer in his head and that he had rediscovered an older kind of consciousness in his solar plexus, which kept these inwardly turned eyes of his continually on the ball of muscle. For the movement of the ball was carefully controlled. In effect, his stomach was dancing a dance with a definite pattern. When he stopped, as abruptly as he had begun, his eyes opened as if they were emerging from a profound trance. He took a deep breath. For the first time I saw a sheen of sweat on his skin. Then he flopped down on the sand, the beginning of a smile of contentment curving his crushed lips.

Dabé, wildly excited by what he had seen, leaped into the air and shouted approvingly: "Oh, you Bushman! You child of a Bushman, you!"

"You may never have heard a Bushman say 'thank you,' " Ben remarked afterwards on the way back to the vehicles, "but you have seen one saying it with his stomach today in the biggest way a Bushman can."

But what was even more interesting to me was the cathartic effect of that abdominal dance on Dabé. It seemed to purge him of the last traces of the morning's bitter introspection. He began to observe the landscape intently again and to keep up a flow of lively comment on the scene. Thanks to the change in him, I saw something a few miles farther on which I did not realize existed in the Kalahari and would otherwise have missed. The Bushman's characteristic whispered whistle of amazement on his lips first drew my attention to it and made me stop the Land-Rover.

The fringe of thorn and stubble half-left in front of us was being violently agitated and then an animal burst out of it like a halfback breaking from the loose in pursuit of the ball. It had a shining coal-black face, pointed nose, and eyes like midnight sequins. Its shoulders were broad; its body long, with a skin so loose that it shook like a jelly and yet was thick and black as armour plating. Its back was covered with rusty hair, its legs short and shaped like a bow. The air of determination about it was extreme almost to the point of caricature. Seeing it streaking in the direction of the thunder I was so amazed that I jumped out of the Land-Rover to have a better look and make sure. The sound Dabé and I made tumbling out of the vehicle caused the animal to stop some fifty yards away and turn round. It glared at us utterly without fear, as if daring us to come near; but since we stood still it merely warned us with a sound between a whistle and a hiss to mind our own business. Then it whisked about and trundled on, the dust spurting at its claws. Even so I was not certain. The animal I thought it was normally wore a neat coat of grey hair with white stripes over a formal black waistcoat and trousers, not the rust-coloured sort of football jersey of the little busy-body hastening towards the rain. Yet I have seen lions in the Kalahari with flaming red hair, so why not he?

"But, Dabé!" I exclaimed feebly. "That was a ratel!"*

"Yes, Moren. He was a ratel." He was grinning at me and then we both laughed out loud. Yet normally I respect the ratel too much to laugh at it. I know of no creature in the world so without fear, so dedicated to its own way of life and with so much of the magic of the beginning clinging to its spirit. I was laughing today because, in that vast, desolate scene, the ratel looked so absurdly self-important. Dabé, I was to discover, was not laughing at it but with it, because of some remarkable associations of his own.

"Phew! Moren." He whistled again and said with a curious envy: "That one knows what is good for him. That one can take care of himself better than any other animal in the world."

* Honeybadger.

"But, Dabé, if he is so good at taking care of himself," I replied, dropping into the personal idiom he always used when speaking of animals, "surely he would have chosen a better place than this. What can he find to live on here?"

"Grubs and beetles like that eye-pisser there," Dabé said, pointing at an insect with long Chippendale legs and a white edge round its flat back, while uttering its homely Bushman name. The beetle, which defends itself by squirting acid into the eyes of its enemies, had appeared close by Dabé's feet. When he moved a toe it lifted a leg, tilted sideways and ejected at him a squirt of liquid fiery in the sun. Considering the size of the insect, the force and length of the jet were prodigious; but Dabé did not allow this achievement to interrupt him. He went on calmly: "Beetles, centipedes, scorpions, ants and snakes. Oh, he likes snakes, that one! There is no greater killer of snakes than he."

The skin of the ratel was so thick, he explained, that the fangs of no snake, not even the mamba, could penetrate it. When the ratel saw a snake, he would immediately go after it and not stop until he had killed it. He would even follow snakes into their holes and fight it out there with all the odds against him. He gave me such a vivid picture of the ratel eating snakes that I saw it gobbling up tangles of serpents like spaghetti. The ratel did not know what it was to surrender or to give up, Dabé told me. All the animals knew that, and small as he was, they preferred to leave him alone. Dabé had heard that in the days of the early people a hungry lion once attacked a ratel, and the ratel fought back so effectively that, although he was killed in the end, the lion was left too mangled to eat it. Since then even the lion let him be. But he had one great friend. Dabé paused dramatically until I asked who the friend was, then answered me with a question. Did I know a little bird that came fluttering out of the bush to perch on a branch where one could both see and hear it clearly, crying, "Quick! Quick! Quick! Honey! Quick!"?

That bird was the ratel's great friend: they were so close, you might say they slept under the same skin. Dabé held his forefingers straight, side by side and tight against each other, to illustrate the closeness of the relationship. Now the ratel we had just seen was in such a hurry because he was on his way to join his friend. He knew that where the rain was falling, there his friend would come to keep a pair of bright eyes on the bees making honey out of the flowers which rose, as I had seen at the Sip Wells, overnight out of the desert. When the amber combs were full in the house of the bees, the bird would come calling for the ratel. Whatever he was doing, the ratel would drop it and follow, holding his tail slightly arched just above his back and looking up only to keep an eye on his friend. Every fifty paces or so the bird would alight on a bush, look back to make sure his friend was following, and in case he was lost repeat his call. The ratel would answer in his own tongue with a soft whistling sound to reassure him: "Look! Look! Look! Oh! Person with wings, Look! Here I come!" Dabé imitated the sound so well that I almost thought the ratel we had seen had doubled back and was near.

Of all the sounds in the world, Dabé said that was the best to hear: friend calling to friend. When the sounds ceased, one knew the ratel was taking out the honey; but if a man could get near, he would hear the excited little bird bubbling with small noises like water coming out of a fountain. For in all the world no living things loved honey as those two did. They would eat it up side by side like the friends they were, each one choosing what he liked best.

Of course, the little bird helped men sometimes in the same way, but only when he could not find the ratel. He preferred the ratel to men. I asked why. Dabé looked infinitely wise and a little sad, remarking, "Auck! Moren! You know what men are these days: they always want too much." It had not always been so. In the day of the people of the early race the bird had preferred men to the ratel; but the bird had learnt since that men more and more took the best and most for themselves and left the least and the worst. Not so the ratel: he gives his friend what he gives himself, and as a result they are closer than ever.

Men had come to realize that the honey-diviner, as I called it, preferred the ratel to them. So they would walk about in the bird's favourite places, imitating the call of the ratel. The bird would come eagerly to them and guide them to honey; but when he saw how he had been deceived, he would tell the ratel next time they met. For this reason such men had to be very careful to cover their faces from the bird and leave no spoor leading to their shelters: otherwise the ratel would follow them and when they were asleep in the night bite off their testicles.

"And, Moren!" Dabé added. "That one when he bites does not let go until he's bitten through. You can beat him on the head, stick spears into him, but he does not let go until he has finished what he came to do. I have heard my father speak many times of men who were punished in this way by the ratel."

I thanked Dabé for telling me and remarked what a truly wonderful animal the ratel must be.

"But, Moren!" Dabé protested, with the look of the bene-factor who has preserved his greatest gift for the end. "I have not told you the cleverest thing about him yet. Have you thought how he gets the honey away from the bees?"

Indeed, I had not, I realized, feeling very much the amateur beside the professional.

"Well then," Dabé said gravely, "you must know it cannot be easy. The ratel's body is all right inside that thick skin of his: but what about his face and eyes and fine nose and that tender spot underneath his tail? You must know what bees can do to such places. So when the ratel has spotted the entrance to the house of the bees, he is very careful to ap-proach it backwards, with his tail tucked in tight between his legs. When he feels himself to be close, he will flick up his tail quickly, jam his behind fast into the entrance and before the bees inside can even wonder why it is suddenly night, he will let off one terrible smell after the other straight into the house. Moren! You cannot know how bad that smell is until you have smelt it! The bees cannot stand it. They fall down, all those who are inside, like dead ones, and the others smell-ing it from afar keep well away. Then the ratel turns about and quickly takes out the honey for himself and his friend."

I looked into Dabé's experienced old eyes; they were bright and innocent with the wonder of what he had just told me. He shook his head as a man does over things too great for words, smiled at me, and I smiled back. But the more I thought of it afterwards, the more wonderful it became. No animal is more of the earth than the ratel. It is in a profound sense the earth made flesh. No bird is more of the air than the honey-diviner. It is like a sliver of sunlit sky made alive. The two of them represent great opposites of life: one a kind of

Caliban, the other a sort of Ariel. For me it was right that in such a reconciliation of opposites, which their partnership created, their reward should be honey; for in the first language of things, honey is the supreme symbol of wisdom, since wisdom is the sweetness of the strength that comes to the spirit dedicated to the union of warring elements of life. Dabé's story held the truth of a parable that has passed the test of time. The account of what happened to the men who deceived the ratel and his friend seemed to me an accurate description of what happens to the human spirit which uses one opposite to deny the other: like the men tracked down by the ratel, it is deprived of its power of increase.

FROM
TARKA THE OTTER

BY HENRY WILLIAMSON

The little thin cub, on its couch among the reeds frozen and bent like the legs of dead spiders, greeted Greymuzzle with husky mewing whenever it heard her coming, and would not be comforted by tongue caresses. Frost had stricken its eyes. Greymuzzle prowled all day and all night when she was not warming and suckling her cub; and although she was so hungry, she still played with Tarka, sliding headfirst down a snowy hillock. They had to travel to the estuary for food, for every incoming tide piled up its floating floes at the pill-mouth, with grinding shrieks and shuddering booms that sounded far over the Burrows. At low tide the frost welded them in a high and solid barrier.

Both otters had blistered their tongues by licking ice, and to ease their thirst, they rasped them against snow on the sea-wall in the middle of the day. Greymuzzle went into the village one night searching the gardens for food. She found the duck-house under the chestnut tree in the farmyard above the bridge, and although she sought an entrance for more than an hour, she found none. The smell of the ducks was painful.

A fox slunk near her, passing with drooping brush and ears laid back, pad, pad, pad, in the snow.

Unable to get the ducks, she walked down the frozen pill to the estuary, meeting Tarka at the pill-mouth, near the salmon-fishers' hut built on the shillet slope of the sea-wall. The fox followed her, hoping to get another meal of salmon. He followed her until the dawn, and was near her at sunrise, when she returned to the couch in the reeds of the duckpond. She winded him and ran him, and although he was chased by the marshman's dog when she had left off pursuit, the fox returned, knowing that she had young somewhere in the reeds. His name was Fang-over-lip, and he had wandered far in his hunger.

While the pallor of day was fading off the snow a skein of great white birds, flying with arched wings and long stretched necks, appeared with a measured beat of pinions from the north and west. *Hompa, hompa, hompa,* high in the cold air. Greymuzzle and Tarka were eating seaweed and shellfish on the Shrarshook, but when the swans splashed into the estuary, they slipped into the tideway and drifted with the flow to where the wild swans were floating. Fang-over-lip licked out some of the mussel shells they had dived for, and cracked up a crab's claws, before following along the beach.

The beams of the lighthouse spread like the wings of a starfly above the level and sombre sands. Across the dark ridge of the Shrarshook a crooked line of lamps winked below the hill. In one of the taverns a sailor was singing a shanty, the tune of which came distinctly over the Pool. The swans moved up with the tide, the otters after them. They were thin and weak; for mussels, winkles, and sometimes a sour green crab were poor nourishment for an otter who, in careless times, had eaten a three-pound sea-trout at a sitting and been hungry two hours afterwards.

The tide beyond the tail of the Shrarshook was divided by a string of froth made by the leap and chop of waters beginning to move north and south, along the arms of the sea stretching to the Two Rivers. The swans turned north, borne by the tide racing past Crow Island. They paddled out of the main flow, and turning head to tide, began to feed in the shallow over a sandbank. The otters drifted nearer, only their wide nostrils above water. When they were ten yards away from the nearest swan the nostrils sank, and chains of bubbles rose unseen above them. A swan saw a dark form under the water, but before it could lift out its head, Tarka had bitten onto its neck. Heavily its wings beat the water. Every curlew on the sandbank cried in a long uprising whistle, *cu-u-ur-leek, cur-r-r-leek!*, and the alarm flew up and down the estuary as fast as sound travelled. The treble whistle of the redshank was piped from shore to shore, the ring-plover sped over the water, turning and wheeling as one bird. Old Nog cried *Kra-r-rk!* Wind from the swan's wings scalloped the water and scattered the spray, and one struck Tarka a blow that made him float slowly away. But Greymuzzle hung to the swan's foot, even when her rudder was nearly out of the water as she was dragged along. The swan trumpeted afar its anger and fear. Bubu the Terrible flew towards the sound.

Before the Arctic Owl arrived Tarka was undazed and swimming to help his mate. Seeing and hearing the struggle, Bubu stretched his toes, opened his beak, and gave a loud and terrifying hoot; but when he reached the conflict, fanning above like a shade of chaos, there was nothing to see save only feathers and bubbles. Silent as snow and fog, staring like the Northern Lights, taloned like black frost, the Arctic Owl flew over the Shrarshook and dropped upon Fang-over-lip, but the snarl and the snap of teeth drove him up again.

Across the pull of the tide, among the grating icefloes, the otters took the swan, whose flappings were getting feeble as the death-fear grew less. Tarka had bitten the artery in the neck. When the otters rested, the bird lay quiet on the water. It heard the wings of its brethren beating out the flying song of swans, *hompa, hompa, hompa,* high and remote in the night. It flapped thrice and died.

Tarka and Greymuzzle swam with the swan to the shore, where they bit into the throat and closed their eyes as they drank its hot blood. Soon mouthfuls of feathers were being torn away, but before they could eat its flesh Fang-over-lip crept upon them. He, too, was famished, having eaten only a mouse that night—and that small biter of willow bark was but fur and bone. With the boldness of starvation the fox rushed upon them. The snarling brought a boar badger, who had been digging for the roots of sea-beet in the crevices of the stones of the sea-wall. The boar lumbered down the slope, over the seaweed, and across the shingle to where Fang-over-lip, with fluffed-out brush and humped back, was threatening the otters. The badger, who was called Bloody Bill Brock by certain badger-digging publicans, had never before been so hungry. For two days the walls of his belly had been flat. He had no fear of any animal. The otters bit his hide, but could not hurt him, as under the long grey tapered hairs his skin was exceptionally thick. Pushing them away and grunting, he seized the swan in his jaws and dragged it away. He dropped it again to bite Greymuzzle; and then he stood absolutely still, except for his nose. Fang-over-lip did not move, nor did Greymuzzle, nor Tarka. Their heads were turned towards the cottage looming white on the sea-wall. A door had opened and closed.

The marshman had with him two bob-tailed cattle dogs, which rushed on the shingle. They found a circle of feathers. Downwind the wave-worn shells tinkled as though a wind had risen off the sea and was running over the beach towards the tarred wooden hospital ship. This was the sound of the fox's departure. Bloody Bill Brock was slower and clumsier, and his black bear-claws slipped on the boulders of the sea-wall's apron. Tarka and Greymuzzle were lying in three feet of water, with only their ears and nostrils showing. They heard the pursuit of the badger, and some moments later the hoarse voice of a man. One dog yelped, two dogs yelped, and both returned to their master on three legs, while the thick-skinned badger continued his way, with the swan, on four sound legs.

Some hours later all of the swan, except the larger bones, feet, wings, and bill, was inside Bloody Bill Brock, who was snoring inside a sandy rabbit-bury, where he slept for three days and nights.

Greymuzzle returned to the duckpond with only seaweed and shellfish to nourish herself and her cub. Unsteadily it dragged its little body towards her, and opened its mouth to greet her. No sound came from its mouth. Its legs trembled and could not carry its head, which hung over the couch of weeds. Its paws were frost-bitten, its eye-sockets empty. Greymuzzle stared at it, before lying down and giving the shelter of her body. She spoke to it and took it in her paws and licked its face, which was her only way of telling her love.

The cub tottered away, and sought the milk which it could not find. Afterwards it slept, until she left again to seek food in the wide daylight, following the slot of deer across the snow. The hind, which had come down from the high ground with a herd of red deer, with her calf that had been with her since its birth the previous May, caught the scent of the otter and ran away, the calf beside her. The otter followed, but turned away when she saw a small bird crouching on the snow, unable to fly further. She ate the fire-crested wren—a thimbleful of skin, bone, and feather. After a vain prowl round the garden of the marshman, she returned to the duck-pond, crossing the pill three hundred yards below the place where men were breaking up, for firewood, the bulk of an old dismasted ketch. In the field she picked up the skull of a sheep and carried it a few yards before dropping it. She had picked it up and dropped it many times already.

The ice-talons set harder in the land. No twitter of finch or linnet was heard on the Burrows, for those which remained were dead. Vainly the linnets had sought the seeds locked in the plants of the glasswort. Even crows died of starvation. The only noises in the frore air were of saws and axes and hammers, men's voices, the glassy sweep of wind in the black-ened thistles, the cries of lambs and ewes, raven's croaking, and the dull mumble of breakers on the bar.

Every day on the Burrows was a period of silence under a vapour-ringed sun that slid into night glowing and quivering with the zones and pillars of the Northern Lights. More wild red deer from Exmoor strayed to the Great Field, which even the rats had quitted. The deer walked into the gardens of the village, some to be shot stealthily, others to sleep into death. The shepherd of the marsh-grazing stamped at night round his fire, clad in the skins of sheep, and swinging his arms. Beyond the straw-and-sack-stuffed hurdles, foxes, badgers, and stoats slunk and prowled and fought for each other's bodies. Over the lambs in the fold flew Kronk the raven, black and croaking in the moonlight. *Ck!* cried Old Nog, tottering to the Shrarshook from the sandhills, where he hid shivering during the time of high-tides. The wind whined in the skeleton of his mate broken at the knees, near the skull of Marland Jimmy gaping at the crown, eyeless and showing its teeth in ice.

When two foxes and a badger had been shot, Greymuzzle went no more where ewes pared hollow the frozen turnips and suckled peacefully their tail-wriggling lambs. One night, raving with hunger, she returned to the wooden duckshed in the farmyard by the railway station. High over the shed rose the chestnut tree, black and bare and suffering, with one of its boughs splitten by frost. Other creatures had been to the duckhouse before her.

Fang-over-lip had started to dig a hole under the rotten floorboards, but returning the night after, he had smelt that during the day the hole had been deepened and a gin tilled there to catch him by the paw. When he had gone Bloody Bill Brock had grunted to the duckshed and, putting head between paws, had rolled on the metal tongue holding the jaws apart. The gin had clacked harmlessly against his grey hairs. The badger had scratched farther down and up again, reaching the floorboards by daylight; and departed, to return in the next darkness and to see a gin lying there with jaws as wide as his back—a gin unhidden and daring him, as it were, to roll across it. The gin's rusty jaws were open in an iron leer, its tongue sweated the scent of man's hand. Bloody

Bill Brock, who had sprung many gins in his life, grunted and went away.

There were no stars that night, for clouds loured in the sky. As Greymuzzle walked on the ice upstream, snow began to fall in flakes like the breast-feathers of swans. From the estuary the scrambling cries of thousands of gulls, which had returned with the south-west wind, came indistinctly through the thick and misty air. The South was invading the North, and a gentle wind was its herald. The dreadful hoot of Bubu was heard no more, for the Arctic Owl had already left the Burrows.

Greymuzzle walked under the bridge, and smelling the ducks, climbed up the bank. As she was walking past the beehives, she heard a sound that made her stop and gasp— the *ic-clack!* of a sprung gin. Tarka was rolling and twisting and jerking the heavy gin and chain off the ground. It held him. He lay still, his heart throbbing, blowing and tissing and slavering. The sight closed Greymuzzle's nostrils, so that she breathed through her open mouth. She called to him. The gin clanked, the chain clinked. She ran round him until Tarka's leaps, that wrenched the sinews of his leg, ceased in weakness, and he sank across the long rusty spring, blowing bubbles of blood out of his nostrils. A duck quacked loudly, and when its strident alarm was finished, the air held only the slight sounds of snowflakes sinking on the roof of the shed. They floated to rest on Tarka's fur, gently, and shrunk into drops of water. The chestnut tree suddenly groaned, and the corpse of a sparrow frozen for weeks to one of its twigs fell to the earth. It dropped beside Greymuzzle, and was flicked against the duckshed by a swish of her rudder as she stood over Tarka, gnawing in a fury the iron jaws of the gin.

Far away in the estuary gulls were running on the sand-banks through the yellow froth of wavelet-lap. Their jubilant and sustained cries told the winter's end. Under the tree Grey-muzzle rasped the bone of the trapped paw with the sharp stumps of her broken teeth. A rat passed near, brought by the smell of blood; it fled when it saw whose blood was wasting. Greymuzzle's face was torn, but Tarka did not know that he had bitten her.

She bit through the sinews, which were strong and thick, and Tarka was free. He rushed to the river. Greymuzzle re-mained, remembering her cub.

When the ducks heard the gnawing of wood, they began to run round inside the shed, quacking continuously. In the farmyard a dog in its kennel was barking loudly. There was an answering shout in the house that set the animal jumping against its chain. Both Greymuzzle and Tarka knew the se-quence of barking dog and the shout of a man in a house! Greymuzzle stayed until the farm door opened and then she ran away, splinters of wood in her bleeding mouth.

When the farmer came to the shed with his gun and lantern, he found his gin sprung and three toes of a paw lying in a red spatter about it. Seeing dots of blood leading away over the snow, he hurried to the cottage of one of his labourers and knocked on the door. He shouted, "I've got'n," as his father had shouted in the church door during a sermon half a century before, calling the men to leave and pursue the tracks of a fox through the snow. The labourer and his two sons put on their boots warming on the slate hearth, and went out to the farmer. Armed with a dung-fork, the handle of a pickaxe, a ferreting crowbar, and the gun, they set out on the trail of the wounded otter. The lantern showed the red dots leading over the railway crossing, and on the snow by the station yard. "Come on, you!" cried the farmer to three men going home after the closing of the inn. It was ten o'clock. One had a staff, and the others kicked up what stones they could see.

The collie dog found the otters for them, in a shed where Tarka had crawled for a refuge. Tarka stood back in a corner on a heap of artificial manure sacks, while Greymuzzle ran at the dog, tissing, and snapping her broken teeth. The lantern light made of her eyes two tawny orbs of menace. Tarka found a hole in the wall, while Greymuzzle fought the collie. Weakened by starvation she was not able to fight for long, and as the farmer said afterwards, it was not even necessary to waste a cartridge, when a dung-fork could pin her down and a ferreting bar break her head.

They carried the body back to the farm, where the farmer drew a pint of ale for each of his helpers from the XXXX barrel in the cellar. While they were drinking "Best respects, Varmer," the collie dog began to bark, and as it would not stop after several cries of "Shut that rattle, you," the farmer went out and gave it a kick in the ribs. The collie yelped and went to kennel, but hardly had the farmer gone into his kitchen again when it set up a furious barking. It was banged on the head with the stag's horn handle of a hunting whip, but even this did not check its desire to tell its master that an enemy was in the yard. It kept up an intermittent barking until the dawn, when it was flogged with its head wedged in the door. The farmer was a poor man and not very strong, and a sleepless night made him irritable. When he felt better he gave the dog the skinned carcass of the otter, and praised its courage and virtue in the Railway Inn, telling how it had warned him and how it had tracked the "girt mousey-coloured fitches" to the shed, where one escaped through a hole behind the sacks. He forbore to say how noisy his dog had been afterwards, deeming this a point not in its favour, for how was he, his natural senses dulled by civilisation, to have known that an otter had remained all night in the farm-yard, waiting for the mate that never came.

TARKA WAS GONE in the mist and rain of the day, to hide among the reeds of the marsh pond—the sere and icicled reeds, which now could sink to their ancestral ooze and sleep, perchance to dream—of sun-stored summers raising the green stems, of windshaken anthers dropping gold pollen over June's young maces, of seeds shaped and clasped and taught by the brown autumn mother. The south wind was breaking from the great roots the talons of the Icicle Spirit, and freeing ten thousand flying seeds in each brown head.

Water covered the pond ice, deep enough to sail a feather, and at night every hoof-hole held its star.

After seven sunrisings the mosses were green on the hillocks, lapwings tumbled and dived and cried their sweet mating cries, the first flower bloomed in the Burrows—the lowly vernal witlow grass, with its tiny white petals on a single leafless stalk. Under the noon sun sheep grazing in the marsh had silver outlines. Linnets sat on the lighthouse telegraph wire, wing to wing, and talking to the sky. Out of the auburn breasts fell ravishing notes, like glowing strokes of colour in the warm south wind.

And when the shining twitter ceased, I walked to the pond, and again I sought among the reeds, in vain; and to the pill

I went, over the guts in the salt grey turf, to the trickling mud where the linnets were fluttering at the seeds of the glass-wort. There I spurred an otter, but the tracks were old with tides, and worm castings sat in many. Every fourth seal was marred, with two toes set deeper in the mud.

They led down to the lap of the low water, where the sea washed them away.